THE RAT CATCHERS'
OLYMPICS

"HILARIOUS."
–THE NEW YORK TIMES
BOOK REVIEW

COLIN COTTERILL

The Rat Catchers' Olympics

BOOKS BY COLIN COTTERILL

The Rat Catchers' Olympics

COLIN COTTERILL

Copyright © 2017 by Colin Cotterill

Published by
Soho Press, Inc.
853 Broadway
New York, NY 10003

Library of Congress Cataloging-in-Publication Data
Cotterill, Colin, author
The rat catchers' olympics/Colin Cotterill.

ISBN 978-1-61695-949-4
eISBN 978-1-61695-826-8

1. Paiboun, Siri, Doctor (Fictitious character)—Fiction.
2. Coroners—Fiction. 3. Laos—Fiction.
4. Olympic Games (22nd : 1980: Moscow, Russia)—Fiction.
5. Murder–Investigation—Fiction. I. Title

PR6053.O778 R38 2017 823'.914–dc23 2016057429

Printed in the United States of America

10 9 8 7 6 5 4 3 2 1

This book is in memory of Grant Evans, who wasn't that fond of my books but whose taste was otherwise impeccable, whose knowledge was boundless and whose nature was gracious.

With my warmest thanks to Micky M, Martin W, Martin S.F. Ulli, Magnus, Regina, Michael B, Daniel and Judy K, Sittixai, Simon C, K, Shelly, Randy, Peter J. Masha, Dr. Leila, David, Lizzie, Rachel, Paul, Dad, Bambina, Bob, Kate, Roman and Elmar.

Dtui was feeling for a pulse.
"He's alive," she said. "He's alive."

TABLE OF CONTENTS

CHAPTER ONE
March 1980 – The Bald Eagles Have Landed

There were occasional relaxed periods of what the Lao called *sabai*. The weather was comfortable, the markets had fresh food and the children played in the road with no danger of being hit by vehicles. Nothing moved fast enough to cause injuries. Everything seemed to be so peaceful and casual you'd forget there was another layer— the echelon of the impossible. You didn't experience it until you attempted to rock the boat. It might take you so long to obtain a *laissez passer* to visit an ailing aunt in another province that she'd have gone up in smoke long before you arrived. Your name on a housing list was more prone to retreat than to advance as the names of those of influence were slotted in above you. And a stay in a hospital was as likely to kill you as to cure you.

Then there was one more stratum that was unfathomable. It was so dark and sinister you'd never make any sense of it. There needed to be nothing more than the perception of antisocialist activity. It was a nether world where neighbors disappeared, where trusted members of the Party were ousted as traitors, where the paranoid ruled. Comrade Noo the Thai forest monk had been enticed into that twilight zone from which few returned. He'd vanished for two weeks. Not the supernatural vanishing that had recently hounded Dr. Siri Paiboun—more a bureaucratic disappearance, like a file or a record lost in the system. A misplaced person for whom nobody was accountable.

Most agreed that Thai Comrade Noo was primarily a conservationist, a man who would bury himself up to his neck to stop a bulldozer destroying national parkland. Others saw him as a journalist reporting on the abuse of monks in a socialist state. The Lao authorities might have seen him merely as an illegal immigrant or a troublemaker or a religious zealot. You'd never know because the administrative line was ignorance.

"No. Never heard of him."

And it made no difference what he'd actually done because he was perceived to be an enemy of the state so even the story of his life was irrelevant. The Party had its bloodhounds. It was their duty to drag in trophies to justify their existence. Noo had headed off on his bicycle one day only to be kidnapped by some military thugs. There was no announcement, no trial, no trace of him. They'd gobbled him up as they did anyone who dared defy the overlords. But mysteriously they'd spat him out. None of his friends and supporters who'd gathered around him in that small concrete room knew why he'd been released. It was unprecedented. He'd quite obviously been beaten and had horrific injuries from being thrown from a truck. But he was still unconscious so the details of his detention remained wrapped inside him. For three days he'd teetered on the edge, bones not setting, wounds not healing, deep in a coma. But if he were to die, Comrade Noo would not have been forgotten like the many before him. He was admired and loved and it could only have been the will of his supporters that kept him alive.

Nurse Dtui was there with him. She was the one who'd found his pulse that night he was thrown from a truck in front of Madam Daeng's noodle shop. Mr. Geung was there. His physical and mental strengths often overshadowed his Down syndrome limitations. He was the one who'd carried the broken body of the monk to the upstairs mattress. His partner, Tukta was there, she too a member of the secret club of those with Down syndrome. She was the one who'd ridden the noodle shop bicycle to Mahosot Hospital and returned with dressings and ointments and morphine although nobody knew how she had achieved this feat without money. She refused to say.

Nurse Dtui had done her best but she wasn't a doctor. There were forty qualified doctors at Mahosot, none of whom she trusted. The one she really needed was Dr. Siri himself, the country's last coroner.

"So, where is he?" asked Gongjai, the reformed prostitute.

"Still in Thailand, as far as we know," said old Inthanet, the puppet master.

"He'd know what to do if he was here," said Gongjai.

There followed a silence as dense as river clay.

"Dtui kn-kn-knows what to do," said Mr. Geung.

"I know," said Gongjai. "I'm sorry, I didn't mean . . ."

"It's all right," said Dtui. "I wish he was here, too."

They were assembled in the front bedroom of Siri's government-allocated house just a short walk from the

That Luang monument. It was a building that housed far too many characters to commit them all to memory. Even the doctor lost count and muddled the names. The inhabitants had been collected from the uncharitable streets and ideological gutters of the city. They were characters who didn't fit the system. There was Crazy Rajhid, the homeless Indian who'd spoken only three times in the past four years. There was Inthanet's portly fiancée, Jit, who had fled to the city to escape a farming cooperative that was starving her family. There were the young, the elderly, the brilliant and the insane. Joining them in the circle around the patient this evening were two monks who'd turned up one day without explaining how they'd heard of Comrade Noo's plight.

Nurse Dtui's little daughter, Malee, was asleep in a hand-made cradle. Her father, Phosy, often attended these candle-lit vigils, but tonight he was off investigating a case. The senior police inspector found himself working odd hours.

Also missing from the group was Siri's best friend, Comrade Civilai, the ex-politburo member. He'd taken it upon himself to drive his old Citroën to Wattay Airport to meet every flight from Bangkok on the off-chance Dr. Siri and his wife, Madam Daeng, might alight from one of the Lao Aviation DC3s. As a retired senior Party member, Civilai had been allowed to stand on the tarmac beside the ground controller, whose signals were generally ignored by the Russian pilots.

The March nights were balmy, still carrying the weight of the hot season days but fresh and breathable. On this particular evening Civilai sweated as he watched the 3:40 P.M. scheduled flight arrive from Don Muang. It was after eight. The porter wheeled the steps to the exit, climbed to the top and banged on the door. He then ran back down the steps and dragged the stair unit away from the fuselage so the stewardess could open the door. Civilai was ever bemused by the inefficiencies he saw around him every day.

A number of elderly, dark-suited men were first down. They were met by small delegations that whisked them off to waiting Zil limousines. They were followed by foreign-looking gentlemen in unfashionable clothes, men Civilai took to be Eastern European "experts." Technically, an expert was somebody who knew more than the Lao, which, Civilai conceded, included most of the civilized world. He watched the Soviets and East Germans and Poles, a smattering of Cubans and one or two Vietnamese advisers walk across the tarmac to the dilapidated terminal. They'd been shopping in Bangkok and proudly carried their duty-free goods for all to see. Even inside Laos these were good shopping days for the few people with money to spend. The Thai borders were currently open, the markets were full, consumer goods were available. But the locals knew this cross-border romance would not last for long so they had to stock up while they could.

Just as Civilai was about to head back into the terminal the last passengers stepped out of the aircraft. They were an odd-looking couple. They stood at the top of the steps and waved royally at nobody in particular. They blew kisses willy-nilly. They were dressed like golfers in loud slacks and even noisier polo shirts. But the oddest thing about them was the fact they were as hairless as boiled eggs. Dr. Siri's thick white mane and bushy eyebrows were gone. Madam Daeng was equally naked above the neck. Both seemed unconcerned about their looks. When they saw Civilai their smiles beamed.

Civilai approached them at a seventy-five-year-old trot and they descended with an equally mature enthusiasm. They hugged and kissed messily.

"*Bonsoir, mon copain,*" said Siri.

"I told him you'd be here to meet us," said Daeng.

"I never doubted it," said Siri.

"You both look even more bizarre than I remember you," said Civilai, breaking free from the embrace.

"And why not?" said Siri. "We have avoided a firing squad by a nipple and a half. We are back in our beloved Laos."

"And we bring souvenirs," said Daeng, handing him a bar of chocolate.

"How's Noo?" Siri asked.

"No better than I told you in our last phone call," said Civilai. "But still alive. I was worried when I didn't hear from you again."

"We got a little tied up," said Siri. "In fact the Thais placed a sort of discreet bounty on our heads. They didn't exactly put wanted posters up in post offices or in the newspapers but they did alert the scouts and the military checkpoints. Of course the land crossings were on alert."

"Flying was the safest way to get here," said Daeng.

"Does one no longer need passports for international air travel?" Civilai asked.

"That's a long story that needs a drink to be told properly," said Daeng.

"But it's true, we're lacking certain documents so it would be better if we didn't attempt to clear immigration," said Siri.

"Our passports are not exactly our own," said Daeng.

They were walking away from the terminal in the direction of the VIP gate. A security guard in a uniform that was too small for him called out, "Hey, Comrade. This way." He pointed toward the terminal. Civilai ignored him. Two porters were wheeling the baggage on a trolley whose wheels were diametrically opposed. It would be several days before the passengers could claim their bags.

"I hope you don't have any checked luggage," said Civilai.

The old couple patted their shoulder bags and smiled. At the VIP gate they didn't even bother to speak to the guard. Civilai glared disdainfully and the sentry opened the door a crack. Arrogance was a badge of authority in Laos.

In five minutes they were in the car and headed for That Luang. Civilai produced a bottle of Chardonnay and a corkscrew from the glove box.

"Well, it appears the borders are open again," said Daeng.

"We old politicians get first crack at the imports," said Civilai. "It was a present from the Thai coup leader's family cellars to our politburo. Wine isn't to the old boys' taste so they gave me a crate of the stuff. I'm afraid it isn't chilled."

They toasted their return.

"And I believe I've earned a story," said Civilai.

"Too right," said Siri. "And it all began, as you know, with us paddling across the river in a PVC rowing boat. So we didn't exactly clear Thai immigration on the way in. We did a little bit of business in Udon."

"Funny business," said Daeng.

"I'm telling the story," said Siri.

"Sorry, darling."

"Daeng had always wanted to visit Bangkok," Siri continued.

"It had been a dream of mine since I was a little girl," said Daeng. "But our budget was a little low."

"In fact we didn't have any money," said Siri.

"So my husband had the idea to impersonate the Supreme Patriarch of Laos and go to Bangkok on an official state visit."

Civilai inadvertently veered to the wrong side of the road in surprise. It didn't matter because his was the only vehicle at the time.

"You didn't!" he said.

"Yes, we did," said Daeng. "They were expecting the actual Supreme Patriarch and we sort of stepped in on his behalf. We knew he wouldn't be turning up. I was Siri's personal secretary-nun. Hence the haircut."

"They bought that?" said Civilai.

"It's amazing what you can get away with if you slot into people's expectations," said Siri.

"So I got my sightseeing tour," said Daeng. "And we were put up at the Dusit Thani and given the best treatment."

"And chocolate," said Siri.

Coming from anyone else, Civilai would have labeled such a claim ridiculous. But this was Siri and Daeng and they didn't follow any human rules.

"Wait," said Civilai, "this didn't have any bearing on Noo's unexpected release from custody by any chance?"

"Hard to say," said Daeng.

"We'd like to think so," said Siri. "We did ask a favor from the junta's own prime minister."

"You met the prime minister?" said Civilai, swerving again.

"Of course," said Siri. "I was the Supreme Patriarch. He wanted me to defect and make public my anti-socialist feelings. As you know, the Thai military are a little threatened by the thought of communism."

"You are insane, the pair of you," said Civilai, but he couldn't hold back his delight.

"*Merci*," said Siri.

"Didn't they even check your ID?"

"When Margaret Thatcher steps down from a jet do you see anyone rush up to check her passport?" said Siri.

"Surely someone would have noticed your face didn't match."

"Civilai, if you donned saffron robes and glasses they'd have given you the same reception. Most men over seventy look alike."

"You could have been killed if they caught you out."

"What a lovely way to go," said Daeng.

"We didn't get out a minute too soon," said Siri. "That phone call to you was our last official act. We were due to keep an appointment with the Thai Supreme Patriarch and he'd met our guy a few times. So we had to flee the scene. We borrowed clothes from a golfing Japanese couple in the suite below ours without their knowledge, evaded the security detail watching us and blended into Bangkok street life."

"We discovered Khao San," said Daeng. "Even the oddest-looking backpacker fits in there. We found a kindly but dishonest Chinese gentleman who was able to provide us Lao passports in twenty-four hours. He charged an absolute fortune."

"Which we didn't have," said Siri.

"So we broke into his office late that night and stole our

passports and enough money for the flight," said Daeng. "He wasn't likely to complain to the police."

"And here we are," said Siri.

"Bravo," said Civilai.

Comrade Noo looked awful but Siri's prognosis was positive.

"Everything seems to be in working order," he said. "I couldn't have done anything Dtui didn't."

The household clapped.

"So why doesn't he wake up?" asked young Mee.

The girl lived there with her mother and younger brother and several other squatters. It was hard to keep count. Siri and Daeng had turned their government allotted residence into something of a hostel for the homeless and helpless. It was a functioning commune embedded deep in a non-functioning communist state. Siri and Daeng themselves lived above their noodle shop.

"It's called a trauma," said Siri. "Sometimes, something so horrible happens that your mind can't take it anymore. It shuts up shop and puts a 'closed' sign in the window. Comrade Noo is in there and his parts are recovering very slowly but his mind isn't ready to come out. I can't imagine what they did to him but he needs time every bit as much as he needs medicine."

Over some eleven bottles of Lao rice whisky and endless plates of pork *lahp* and spicy salad, the residents listened to Siri and Daeng's amazing adventures in Thailand. All the couple left out were tales of possession and séances and running battles with malevolent spirits, even though they were true. Just as there were bureaucratic layers of impossibility, so there were supernatural dimensions that rational educated people in the West would never believe to exist.

The average Lao, brought up in a small community, had no doubts that there were spirits. They sought advice from them. They asked for forgiveness. Even the business people in the capital erected spirit houses to placate the ghosts. Many claimed to have seen the phantoms but few would have had the type of relationship Dr. Siri had developed. Despite his scientific training, Siri had been forced to concede that there were spirits. He would have preferred it to be otherwise but he was undeniably possessed by a thousand-year-old shaman by the name of Yeh Ming. The old Hmong had never made direct contact with Siri but had been a magnet for a menagerie of ghosts that had passed in and out of the doctor's life. This science-versus-supernatural dichotomy had fascinated and confounded him in equal measure.

Only recently had Siri learned the fundamentals of communication with the dead. Portents had shown that he would someday gain control over his innate abilities. But he was seventy-five—a few months off seventy-six—living in a population that barely made it past fifty. He was starting to wonder whether being dead would be such a bad thing. It would certainly simplify matters. What better way to communicate with spirits than to become one?

In the meantime, his only functioning spirit guide was a boisterous transvestite fortune-teller by the name of Bpoo. They didn't get along. She was sarcastic and rude and even though she saw the future she kept it to herself. She was forever criticizing the doctor for his slow progress as a medium.

Of late, Siri's social circle had changed somewhat. He

spent more time with shamans and healers. During an audience with a witch in the north, for example, he'd made a dubious deal that affected both himself and Daeng. The woman produced elixirs that substituted one condition for another; the witch had replaced Madam Daeng's chronic rheumatism with a tail. This was an exchange Daeng was delighted with; Siri had no complaints. In fact he found her new appendage somewhat erotic.

The witch's solution to Siri's problem, however—that of his inability to talk to spirits—was a little more complicated. And as a result of her elixir he had started to disappear from time to time. He found himself in places created in his own mind. Daeng would turn over in bed to find a warm but empty place beside her. Yet lately, when he was no longer in the same dimension as his wife, he had discovered portals to the other side. He learned that those who resided there believed that the other side was where Siri had come from. All very confusing even to the doctor and not at all helpful when it came to his hobby. Dr. Siri was in fact a most competent amateur detective and as such one should imagine that seeing spirit signs everywhere would be an invaluable asset. Yet only once had he been able to interpret their significance before the case's resolution. Invariably he was left to his own devices to solve mysteries in the old fashioned traditions of his hero, Inspector Maigret.

CHAPTER TWO
The Words of a Stupid Husband

The old man studied the face of the young fellow sitting opposite. They were in one of those Chinese rooms cluttered with opulent furniture designed to make a visitor feel out of place and inferior. The chairs in which they sat were teak thrones with mother of pearl inlays that cut into the young man's backside every time he shifted his weight. The only sound was the hum of a hornet trying to find its way back out through the open window.

"I don't just want him dead," said the old man.

"No?" said the youngster.

"No. I want him so dead there's nothing to bury."

"That's not a problem."

"I'm told you have skills," said the old man. He leaned forward for his glass of cranberry tea. The young man nodded.

"As long as you can get me there," he said, "I'll do what needs to be done."

"Of course I can get you there. I just want to be certain the expense will be worth it."

"I don't fail. And as you know I have my own reasons for

doing this. It will be a shock for him to see me, assuming he remembers me. And a nasty end is the least I can offer."

The old man smiled and sipped his tea.

Siri and Civilai were sitting on their log on the bank of the Mekhong eating baguettes that Civilai had baked himself. Since his retirement he'd thrown his wife and their cook out of the kitchen and established a culinary occupation there. Thanks to the current détente with Thailand he'd been able to stock up with ingredients. Today's baguettes contained processed ham with mustard to be washed down with one more bottle of Chardonnay.

Ugly the dog growled in his sleep at Siri's feet.

"So, tell me," said Civilai. "How on earth did your dog make it back from Thailand? I can't see him chasing the plane from Bangkok."

"Although I'm sure he could," said Siri. "But no. We'd left him in Udon with a friend. Once we were sure we wouldn't be flogged in the dungeons below Chitlada Palace we phoned him—the friend, not the dog. He drove Ugly to the river and launched him back home. He was waiting for us at the noodle shop when we got there."

"You know most people would just get another dog," said Civilai. "There are plenty of unpleasant looking strays to choose from."

"None like Ugly."

Siri patted the dog's head and his tail stub thumped against the clay. The old friends ate and drank and looked across at Thailand. The river was running so low grasses had taken over the river bed and there was just a shred of water visible near the far bank. It all gave the false impression you could walk to Thailand. Unlike many great rivers, the mighty Mekhong had its humble moments.

"So, what's next?" said Civilai. "I imagine once you've successfully scammed the junta führer of Thailand there's nothing more to aspire to."

"On the contrary," said Siri. "Daeng and I are thinking about gate-crashing the next Party Convention and nominating each other for seats on the politburo. The elderly can get away with anything. We're an untapped market. What about you?"

"What about me?"

"What menial duties has the committee lined up for you for the next few months?"

Siri noticed a brief uncomfortable sideways glance before Civilai answered. It usually signaled that he was about to be lied to.

"Oh, nothing special," said Civilai.

"What about unspecial?"

"Well, I don't know. I might have to go to Moscow in a couple of months."

"Trade delegation again?"

"Not exactly."

"What then?"

Silence.

"Civilai?"

"I might . . . you know. The Olympics."

Siri got to his feet and adopted his most disdainful stare.

"Olympics?" he said.

"Maybe."

"You're going to Moscow for the Olympics and you thought it unnecessary to tell me?"

"What's this? I'm telling you now. We've been so

occupied listening to your Thai stories I haven't had a chance to mention it."

"You don't think it could be of interest to me, Civilai? Little Laos gets invited to the Olympic Games for the first time in its history, a chance to mingle with the world's greatest athletes. You don't think your attendance at such an event might warrant a brief newsflash?"

"I didn't really want to bring it up."

"Why not?"

"I knew how you'd react."

"And how have I reacted?" Siri put his hands on his hips and puffed out his chest.

"You've automatically decided you'll be coming with me."

"And what, may I ask, is so wrong with that? I'm a qualified physician. Every sports team needs medical personnel. I was a highly placed university wrestler and boxer in my day. I have certificates. I'm fluent in French and Vietnamese."

"The Games are in the Soviet Union," Civilai reminded him.

"I'm aware of that. They'll have interpreters, won't they? I can't believe you didn't recommend for me to go with you."

Civilai looked away and blushed.

"Wait," said Siri. "You did recommend me, didn't you?"

"Siri, I . . ."

"What did they say?"

"I don't—"

"What did they say?"

"They said they'd sooner bring in a monkey than have you represent Laos at an international event. They think you're a liability. That you'll embarrass the Party."

Siri wobbled a little and sat back down on the log. "So who's going as the team doctor?" he asked.

"Not decided yet. They have a list. All the overseas qualified doctors at Mahosot with Party membership. Eight of them."

"Am I not even on the list?"

"You're eighth."

"Behind Supasit the optician?"

"Sorry. I've requested to have Dtui in the team. She's a nurse and she speaks Russian. And I've insisted there be at least two women in the party."

"You've insisted? So, what exactly is your role in all this?"

"Siri, I . . ."

"I'm waiting."

"Head of Mission."

"You're running the show and you can't even get me included?"

"It's political. I don't really have much power."

"Yet there you are requesting team members. And you're not even a sportsman."

"It's a diplomatic rather than a competitive mission, Siri. We don't have any athletes who stand a chance of competing at that level. It's a public relations campaign. The first time the Olympics will be held in a communist country. The Soviets have invited all their socialist allies to make an appearance. They're paying for the trip, equipment, uniforms. All we're lacking is ability."

"When does it start?"

"We go in June."

"Isn't it a bit late to start putting a squad together?"

"They've been running competitions in schools and colleges since January. We have visiting Soviet coaches here as advisers."

"Oh, well, that's all right then. We'll win medals for sure."

"I knew you'd be upset."

"Upset? I won't be upset until the Aeroflot flight leaves Wattay without me."

"Siri, this is one you can't win. You've antagonized everyone on the politburo. None of them likes you and if they find out what you got up to in Thailand . . ."

"Yes? What will they do? Throw me out of a fast-moving truck?" He stood and put his half-eaten baguette on the log.

"Siri, don't do anything stupid."

"Stupid is my middle name," said Siri. "And to be honest I'm a little disappointed you didn't put up more of a fight on my behalf, Comrade VIP Head of Mission."

"Siri."

But Siri was in a huff. He headed off along Mahosot Avenue with Ugly at his side.

"And there's too much yeast in the baguettes," he shouted.

"Siri!" Civilai called after him.

"Don't talk to me."

"Your sandals."

"What about them?"

"They're here."

A month had passed since Siri learned of his exclusion from the Moscow Olympics. Comrade Noo was hanging on but an intravenous drip was a poor substitute for actual food. His wounds refused to heal and his body lost mass every day. The doctor could find no physical reasons for the monk's decline. It was as if he'd abandoned hope. Siri had seen it before on the battlefield. In very young boys who never asked to be fighting in a war that made no sense to them, scared and desperate for a way out. Their prayers would be answered by a hand-grenade or a mortar. They'd arrive at the mobile surgery with horrific wounds. Horrific but not terminal. The surgeons would do their work and know that in a month the soldiers would be on their feet.

But they'd died. And they died because they'd decided to. Because being dead was better than having bullets part their hair. Better than watching their bunkmates turned to raw meat. The will to die could be much stronger than the will to live. For whatever reason, forest monk Noo had no fight in him.

"What do I do?" Siri asked.

Auntie Bpoo was always there in his mind pretending she wasn't. It had been a while since their last conversation. He tried to get through to her every day, like a novice desperate to keep the faith, asking for a sign, but he'd reached a stage where he was just talking to himself.

"I suppose his not being dead makes him the responsibility of a different department," said Siri. "Live people are none of your business. I need to speak to someone in the limbo office. Must be someone there who can tell me what the hell I should do for him."

He turned to see Mee in the doorway. They nodded at each other.

"Been standing there long?" he asked.

"Yes," said the child.

"It'll happen to you," he said.

"What?"

"You'll reach an age when talking to yourself makes more sense than talking to someone else."

"You have a note," she said, holding up an envelope.

"Where from?"

"Ministry of Health."

Cracks were beginning to appear in the system. Party media outed corrupt officials and there were inquiries about abuse of power up to the ministerial level. Instead of being sent to the overcrowded reeducation camps in the north, midlevel cadres were forced to attend seminars at the Vientiane School for Political Theory, whose curriculum had been designed by the Vietnamese. Major purges were in the pipeline but none of this meant a thing to the rural majority. They'd seen it all before and to be honest they didn't expect much better from the boys in Vientiane.

Like most ministries in Laos, the Ministry of Health looked more like a Caribbean hotel than a place where top-level decisions might be made. It was white and open-plan with external staircases you could walk up without getting permission from a guard or a gruff receptionist. In fact Siri was hard pressed to find anyone at all. He walked into an unmarked office on the second floor. There at a wooden desk sat a woman whose hair was pulled back into a bun so tight her eyes were where her ears should have been.

"The vice minister wants to see me," he said. "Can you tell me where his office is?"

"Not really," she said.

"Why?"

"Well, he doesn't actually have one," she said. "Two Vietnamese advisers have taken it over for the month. The vice-minister is sort of . . . floating. Oh, wait. There he goes now."

Siri caught the shadow of a man passing in front of the

little office. He ran outside and called the man's name. The vice minister was young and untidy with the build of a soccer player.

"Ah, Siri," he said.

"Have we met?" Siri asked.

"I was your student on the emergency field surgery course."

"Right," said Siri. It was the only course the Party had successfully coerced the doctor to teach. He hadn't enjoyed it.

"Yes."

"And now you're . . ."

"Vice Minister of Health."

"Ah, the land of opportunity," said Siri. "Just think what you might become when you turn twenty-five."

"I'm forty-seven," said the vice minister, more eager to correct the math than to tackle the sarcasm. "Come with me."

They found an unoccupied office with only one chair. The vice minister beat Siri to it. Under his arm he had a file which he placed on the desk in front of him. He flipped open the front cover.

"Do you know what this is?" he asked.

Siri took particular pains to study the top sheet. "I believe I do," he said.

"What do you know about it?"

"I read it," said Siri. "Powerful stuff. It was pinned to the notice board at Mahosot."

"And downstairs here at the ministry."

"Well, I commend the ministry for its vigilance in making us aware of the dangers of going to the Soviet Union. An outbreak of pulmonary anthrax, no less. Frightening."

"But that's just it, Siri. We had nothing to do with this."

"Isn't that a government stamp at the bottom and the minister's signature?"

"From a distance it would appear so," said the man. "But if you look closely you'll see that the stamp has been rendered in red crayon."

"My word."

"And the minister's signature has been forged."

"How could you tell that?"

"Because it's dated April eleventh and the minister, ehr, ceased his duties on the third."

"Really? Where's he gone?"

"He's . . . you know, that's not really your business. Suffice it to say he's moved on to another role."

Siri had a mental image of the Minister of Health in a straw hat digging up cassava in some distant province.

"But why would anyone go to the trouble of forging a health warning?" Siri asked.

"That's what I've been instructed to ask you."

"Me? Goodness. I wouldn't have any idea. But this notice put the fear of Satan into me, boy. I can tell you that. There was no way on earth I'd be going to Moscow after reading it. Do you know the symptoms of pulmonary anthrax? It's awful. You get horrific blisters and sores. Your neck swells up till it's agony to swallow. Your diarrhea's soaked in blood and your vomit's green. Eventually you get deep skin abscesses that eat through to your organs. Only ten percent of victims survive."

"The poster did mention some of that," said the vice minister, "but in fact it isn't true."

"The symptoms?"

"The eventuality. There had been a small outbreak a year ago in a distant province when a biological weapons factory exploded but it never became a threat to the Moscow region."

"Who told you that?"

"The Soviet ambassador."

"Well, he would, wouldn't he? His job is to wear shiny suits and placate people. They'd keep something like this under wraps. No, son. Somebody knows the truth and as a public service, he . . . or she has warned us. And I salute him . . . or her."

"You wouldn't consider going?"

"To Moscow? Are you mad?" Siri turned and headed to the open door. He stopped just beyond the doorway. "Why do you ask?" he said.

"All the other candidates have withdrawn their applications."

"Even Supasit, the optician?"

"Yes."

"I don't blame them. If I'd been given an application form, which I wasn't, I'd have ripped it up immediately."

The vice minister laughed. He stood and walked past Siri to sit on the concrete bench out front.

"Siri," he said, "I'll be perfectly honest. The minister wasn't that fond of you but he's no longer in a position to make decisions on the Moscow trip. They've thrown it all in my lap. There are some on the committee who believe you were responsible for posting the warning and I tend to agree with them."

Siri strode off in a huff, but not terribly quickly.

"Wait!" called the vice minister.

"Why? So I can be further insulted?"

"Unlike them," said the vice minister, "I don't consider what you did to be such a terrible thing."

Siri stopped and turned around. "You don't?" he said.

"Siri, I respected you as a teacher. I admire your nationalism and the many acts you've selflessly performed for our country. In a way I believe I would respect you even more if you did indeed post the warning at Mahosot to eliminate the opposition. It tells me how committed you are to represent Laos. The committee said you were the absolute last choice; that they'd only consider you if there were no other candidates. Well, today I heard from the optician and he prefers not to travel. The Soviets will only accept a team medical officer who has been trained by a recognized institution overseas. That makes you the last surviving contender. I know I'll be given a grilling by the committee but I'd sooner have the best candidate than the safest. So, what do you say?"

Siri gazed beyond the open air balcony to the dusty city, to the silver-grey threads of the Mekhong and Thailand sitting smugly on the far bank. He stretched his back, walked to the vice minister and shook his hand.

"Of course I'll have to take my wife," he said.

"It looks like we're going to Moscow, old girl," said Siri nonchalantly. He and Daeng were helping Mr. Geung clean up after the morning noodle rush.

"Oh, yes?" said Daeng.

"Well, don't go turning cartwheels."

"What?"

"I thought you'd be excited. I went to great lengths to make it possible."

"I know you did. But it's just so soon after our narrow escape from Bangkok."

"That's not really the problem, is it?"

Daeng sat on one of the stools and whipped the wipe cloth across the table as if she were swatting a fly. "No."

"Then what?"

"It's the way I look," she said.

He sat opposite her.

"You look marvelous," he said. "You always have."

"Siri, the Games are in July. The Lao team and officials will be flying out in June. That's just under two months away. I won't even have head stubble by then. The older you get the slower the growth. I can pencil on eyebrows but not a head of hair. And then there's the tail."

"What about it?"

"Do you know how hard it is to find fashionable clothes that disguise a woman's tail?"

"Daeng, you're starting to sound like a politburo bride."

"I know. I'm sorry. But it's Europe, Siri. Glamorous women. The opera. Tea shops and discussions on women's equality. I don't want to let you down."

"Daeng, if you stood in front of an Antonov Twenty-two and were cut into slices by the propeller and there was nothing left of you but a toe, I would be just as proud to walk around Moscow with your toe and take it to the Bolshoi. I'd mingle at cocktail parties with your toe. Nothing about you could disappoint me."

She whipped her wipe cloth again.

"And that was supposed to make me feel better, Dr. Siri?"

"Vanity deserves ridicule."

She glared at him for as long as she was able but his boyish grin defeated her once more. She laughed and threw her damp cloth in his direction. He ducked. Although he had no tact to speak of, his reflexes had not deserted him.

◙ ◙ ◙

"I'm not angry," said Inspector Phosy angrily.

"It's a great opportunity," said Nurse Dtui.

"I know it is," said Phosy. "And if you were a young unmarried woman without a child there would be every advantage in pursuing it. But you have a family."

"I have a daughter . . ."

"We."

"We have a daughter and we live in a socialist system that provides excellent child care. Communism has crèches exactly so that the parents, father and mother, can go out to work."

"Not to the extent that the child might forget who her mother is," said Phosy.

They were in the compact dormitory room allocated to them by the police department. They shared a bathroom with eight other families in a dark, single-story building. They were kept awake night after night by the crying of babies. If nothing else, the police were fertile. The walls were thin so they were communicating at the loudest level of whisper possible.

"Don't make this about Malee," said Dtui. "She's two. I'm not breastfeeding her. Being without a mother for a month isn't going to traumatize her. If you don't want her here with you—"

"Of course I want her here."

"We have any number of friends who'd be glad to take her in while I'm gone."

"I'm not going to farm our daughter out to strangers."

"Good. Then you'll get to know how it feels here. All those nights Malee and I spent in this grubby little dorm while her father is in some far-off province. No word of when he'll come back or if he's alive or dead. Perhaps you'll understand what it's like."

"So this is revenge?"

"Don't be silly. This is a career opportunity."

"Being a mother isn't enough of a career?"

She clenched her fists. "If you'd wanted a career mother for your child you should have married a farmer. There are thousands of pretty, slim, uneducated women who fantasize about churning out babies for a man in uniform."

He turned on his chair and shuffled through the papers on the table.

"And perhaps she'd appreciate me," he said.

"Then why did you choose me?"

"Because you were pregnant with my baby."

Dtui smiled as only a wounded Lao woman can. She gently scooped her daughter from the mattress, put the child's head on her shoulder and walked out of the room.

"That's right," said Phosy. "The silent treatment. Works every time."

But Dtui was humming a nursery rhyme in her daughter's ear and had no mind to listen to the words of a stupid husband.

CHAPTER THREE
What Exactly Is an Olympic?

Laos was quickly becoming an experiment that failed. The country had just reached the end of its national three-year development plan conceived (but implemented at a snail's pace) when the Pathet Lao took over in '75. There was still nothing to show for it. In his State of the Nation address the prime minister admitted his own past policies had been "inappropriate, stupid and suicidal." Yet another devaluation of the kip had seen prices soar. Vietnam was pumping in foreign aid to support basic services. To offset the four-hundred-percent rise in costs, the government gave its officials a seventeen-percent pay increase, which resulted in a new surge of escapees crossing the river. Things had to change. Those families who had been chastised by cadres for not joining cooperatives were now being applauded for their resilience. The private farmers had out-produced the collectives. The government began to woo the small private sector with an eye to joint ventures and the repression of private traders was discouraged. As Civilai said, "Hold on to your hats. Here comes Das Kapitalism."

As the Party was doing a poor job of plastering over the

cracks, the central committee agreed something had to be done to divert the attention of the dissatisfied populace. And that distraction came in the form of the Olympic Games.

The Lao Olympic team was made up of shooters, boxers and runners, twenty in all. Siri and Civilai had already paid a visit to the boxing camp but had been denied access to the shooters, all of whom were members of the Lao People's Army. On this day, the track and field athletes were behind the lycee at kilometer six for the first joint training session. The track team comprised four men and four women, most of whom were sprinters. But there was one race walker named Khamon who claimed to be able to walk twenty kilometers at speed.

This particularly fascinated Siri and Civilai, who had been unable to take the concept of race walking seriously. As most Olympic competitions had originated from combat, throwing heavy or sharp objects, jumping over fences, wading through ditches, fighting, shooting, boating, and, particularly, running fast all seemed perfectly suited to battle. But Siri argued that walking at speed was neither here nor there. If you were charging a bank of archers you'd want to get there as quickly as possible so as not to provide a target for a second volley. If, on the other hand, you had realized your inadequacies and were about to retreat, "Get the blazes out of there as fast as possible" should have been in every soldier's survival manual. So where did race walking come in? It looked particularly silly and no race walking champion's portrait ever graced the walls of teenaged girls' bedrooms. So it fascinated Siri that a young Lao man like Khamon would bother to teach himself the art.

They cornered him at the first group training session and asked him straight out.

"Why?"

Like all the Lao athletes, he was polite and enthusiastic. He had a sort of international face that didn't immediately mark him down as a Lao. He was tall, skinny as a Champa branch and had unusually large feet. Perhaps that was why he'd chosen to walk.

"I was born into it," said Khamon. "My father was a fanatical walker. He'd race walk every morning. If he'd stayed in France he'd probably have been a champion."

"What do you mean, stayed in France?" said Civilai.

"My father was French."

"Which explains your looks," said Siri.

"Not really. I was a disappointment to my mother," said Khamon. "She courted and wed a foreigner because she really wanted to harvest those European seeds. She had dreams of producing tall blond offspring but her dominant genes left me dark haired and pug nosed."

"How did you get recruited for this?" Civilai asked.

"Trials," he said. "They came to the provinces and invited runners to the schools to show what they could do. They timed everyone and whittled the list down to the fastest. Of course, nobody got close to the Olympic qualifying times but it was a lot of fun. I told them I'd like to apply for the walk. It wasn't even on their list. They said I'd have to find someone to race against. Of course there wasn't much of a queue. So I ended up walking alone, bare foot on clay. I imagined my dad was there beside me. Even after he left us I didn't stop walking, just for the health benefits, really. I walked round and round the track at the trial and the Olympic people drank tea and played checkers and I finished and they looked at the clock and referred to the log book and I'd set an Indochina record.

"They assumed they'd made a mistake, miscounted the laps or something. So they asked me to do it again the next day. And I did. But this time they concentrated and they had other people counting the laps and I was a minute faster than the day before. They still didn't believe it. They even took out a tape and measured the track to make sure it wasn't too short."

"And it wasn't?" said Siri.

"It was ten meters too long. I'd never bothered to time myself before but according to the stopwatch my performance would have been good enough for a second place at the previous Southeast Asian Games. So, here I am."

Like Khamon, the other contestants had won their places on the team as a result of time trials but none seemed to grasp the significance of the competition they were about to take part in. At the orientation session one of the runners, a muscular boy with a tiger tattoo on his shoulder, asked Civilai,

"Uncle, what exactly is an Olympic?"

Many of the athletes had grown up in the countryside with no media, no news of the world beyond their villages. Some had done well in the temple school and been nominated by the local cadre to attend a high school in the town. But even there the picture they saw of the planet was filtered through a red socialist lens. Their government didn't want them to be too curious for fear they'd be dissatisfied with what little was on offer. Then, suddenly, here was a passport, not only to head out into the world but also to represent a country they didn't really know much about. Of course it was overwhelming. There were many questions.

The Ministry of Sport had insisted the first evening assembly be staged around a large table arranged with a yellow tablecloth, an elaborate centerpiece of imitation flowers, one warm bottle of orange Fanta and a plastic mug per person. It was set up on the basketball court in the gymnasium. The eight athletes had been seated along one side with nametags, and the administrators sat opposite. From left to right there was Comrade Civilai (General Manager—Head of Mission), Siri (Team Physician), Daeng (House Auntie) Nurse Dtui (medic and translator), Mr. Ivanov (Soviet athletics coach), and General Suvan, the senior and ever-senile Party member who was co-opted onto most of the diplomatic missions because he was non-confrontational and had a lot of medals. The politburo had insisted on one active Party member's taking part—although there was nothing particularly active about the general. Behind them against the wall were two observers from the Ministry. General Suvan's welcome speech of the evening lasted twenty-four minutes. He concluded with the line, "As I have described in great detail your purpose in Moscow I doubt you'll have any questions but now would be the time to ask if you did."

The most curious and vocal of the runners was Chom, the two-hundred-meter runner. He was around twenty-eight but looked much older. His skin was pockmarked from some childhood disease and his hair was as scruffy as a lark's nest dipped in charcoal. Despite his looks he was Mr. Popularity and his most endearing quality was his honesty.

"If I understand this right, comrades," he said, "we're being sent to the USSR, where the best athletes in the world live, to join sportsmen and -women from the entire world—people who spent their lives training and getting fit. And they'll be beside us on the track looking down at the little Lao runners in our cheap cotton shorts and plimsolls. And they'll be at the finishing line before we even start running and the only thing the world will remember is what losers the Lao are. Am I right?"

Their own small world went quiet. It was a question that had come too early. Siri and Civilai hadn't planned to get on to international perception until just before they left, if at all. But it was Madame Daeng who took up the point.

"Firstly," she said, "cotton shorts would be quite healthy, allow the skin to breath, and I think the other athletes would be envious if we wore them. But, in fact you'll all be kitted out in nylon in the official Lao colors and you'll all look splendid if a little itchy. Tomorrow you'll be getting your first taste of Soviet spikes. I tried on a pair last night before going to bed. Dr. Siri couldn't catch me. Could you, dear?"

Siri shrugged and blushed. The comment was met with surprised but honest laughter from all but the ministry reps, who contributed an official scowl. Regardless, the ice was broken.

"But the way you look won't have any bearing on how the other athletes see you," she added.

"No," said Civilai, "the world isn't remotely interested in losers. Not one camera will be trained on you stumbling from the starting blocks and hobbling along your lanes. In fact, even the second- and third-placed athletes will be forgotten within seconds."

"Then why are we going?" asked Chom.

Civilai looked at him and smiled. "Comrade Chom," he said, "what do you do for a living?"

In fact he'd already been through the application forms and knew very well what Comrade Chom did.

"I'm a vermin eradication officer," said Chom with some pride. "I'm employed by the Savanaketh municipal council."

"And are you good at your job?" Civilai asked.

"I'm the best there is," said Chom. "I come from four generations of rat catchers. Naturally we don't limit ourselves to rodents. We are equally proficient in the eradication of snakes and cockroaches and termites."

"Of course," said Civilai. "And how do you rate your success internationally?"

"What?"

"I mean, how often do you turn on the radio to see how you compare with rat catchers in say . . . Canada?"

"I haven't got a radio," said Chom.

Civilai grimaced. "But if you did, would it matter whether you caught two fewer rats last year than your Canadian counterpart?"

Chom gave it some thought. "Can't say I know anything about Canada," he said.

"Then, suppose there was a rat catchers' Olympics," said Civilai. "You would be competing with vermin eradication officers from a hundred other countries. You'd be compared to, say, the Mexican rat catcher who every day encounters rats the size of small pigs. He uses a lasso to bring them under control. And to the Icelandic rat catcher whose vermin are no bigger than spiders. He catches them with large sheets of paper covered in glue. How could anyone judge a winner between them? How can you compare yourself to them? You all come from unique backgrounds. We'd just have to appreciate your individual skills, your humility, your humor, your professionalism. Nobody would think less of you because you're different. They judge you as a human being, not as a champion. It's not whether you win or lose that's important, it's how you play the game." He looked at the observers from the ministry. "Marx said that."

When the Fanta was gone and the reception was over, the ministry people shook Civilai's hand and went home to contemplate his rat catcher theory. The athletes and team leaders had been allotted accommodation in the American compound, which now housed mostly Party members and their aides. A small block behind the old stables had been put aside for the Olympic heroes. Ivanov walked General Suvan back to his room but Siri, Dtui, Daeng and Civilai remained behind in the high school gymnasium to go over administrative issues. This activity was sometimes known as *drinking a lot*. Madam Daeng had a friend at the morning market who was currently importing a most delicious Thai rice whisky.

"That, brother, was probably the most pathetic team building speech I've ever heard," said Siri.

"I thought it was inspiring," said Dtui.

"I promise you the team members are all in their beds formulating a new philosophy of what is 'victory,'" said Civilai.

"I promise you they're all in their beds feeling queasy from the warm Fanta and images of rats the size of pigs," said Siri.

"Enough, boys," said Daeng. "Let's raise our glasses to a worthy cause."

"To incomprehensibility," said Siri.

"To the Olympics," said Dtui.

"To the Olympics," they all repeated.

They drank and savored and sat back in their chairs.

"Shouldn't the whole squad have been together for this first night?" said Dtui.

"That isn't such an easy thing to accomplish," said Civilai. "The boxers are up in Vang Vieng running up mountains and I'm not even sure the army has finalized its list of shooters yet. Each battalion has nominated its champion and they have to get that number down to seven without offending the commanders. I get the feeling their team won't get together until we're on the flight to Moscow."

"So that's it?" said Daeng. "Shooters, boxers and runners?"

"And a walker," said Siri.

"What about football?" said Dtui.

"The qualifying rounds were a year ago," said Civilai. "You can't just slot in a team at this late stage."

"Swimming?" said Dtui.

Siri laughed. "Anyone with swimming ability would be on the other side of the river by now," he said. "No, what you see is what you get. Twenty men and women with no hope of winning. They'll travel to Moscow, do their best and return with open hearts and minds and a more positive view of the world."

"It's a pity we can't dress the central committee in nylon tracksuits and take them with us," said Civilai.

"I wouldn't go if that happened," came a voice.

They turned to see Chom the rat catcher in the far doorway with a bottle of clear liquid in his hand.

"I sincerely hope that's coconut water you have there," said Civilai.

"The best rice whisky Savanaketh has to offer," said the runner.

"You're in training," said Siri as he reached out for the bottle.

"To lose," said Chom. "This helps."

Two of the teenaged girl sprinters had followed him into the gym. Their offering was a bottle containing some light brown liquid with lumps in it.

"Millet beer," said Nat, the elder of the sisters.

"Puts hair on your chest," said her sister, Nah. The girls were, in fact, not related but the Lao concept of sisterhood did not preclude having different parents. The two had spent the day hand in hand and still they refused to break the link.

Within ten minutes the entire track team had arrived with their offerings. They ignored the chairs and the table and sat on the ground sampling one another's hooch. It was like a French wine tasting except the alcohol level was higher than the Eiffel tower. After two tumblers the athletes and their minders were closer than kin.

At one stage Siri raised his glass and proposed a toast of his own. "Ladies and gentlemen," he said, "Remember, the road to success is paved with potholes and buffalo dung and broken beer bottles and unexploded ordnance. Sometimes it makes more sense to sit under a tree and have a drink."

The athletes cheered but they were in the mood to cheer anything.

"Marx said that," Siri added.

"He did not," said Civilai.

"Well, he seems to have said everything else," said Siri.

CHAPTER FOUR
To Russia with *Lahp*

There was a brass band playing at Wattay airport and half the population of Vientiane had turned up to see off the Olympians. An official photographer snapped the sportsmen and -women individually with the Aeroflot jet in the background, then in their specialty groups standing on wonky chairs with the officials in front of them.

Apart from Gongjai's sister, Tong, who'd stayed behind to monitor the slow decline of Comrade Noo, Siri's household was there in their Sunday best, except it was Thursday. Even Crazy Rajhid had hitched a ride on the house motor scooter. He was wearing shorts and had found a burst bicycle inner tube which he wore as a tie. He hadn't found a shirt so he was bare-chested. Blind Pao and his granddaughter Lia waved a hammer and sickle pennant. Inthanet and his fiancée were dressed in red, white and blue to match the national flag. Inspector Phosy, who was not one for public displays of affection, didn't even attempt to hold Nurse Dtui's hand while she cuddled their daughter. Their relationship had been strained these past few weeks but Phosy had yet to apologize for his sulking or to accept his wife's right to head off overseas by herself. Mrs. Fah had her children salute for the cameras and Gongjai brought a bunch of flowers for Madam Daeng. Ugly the dog lay depressed at their feet as if he knew what little chance there was of getting on board a Soviet aircraft.

The prime minister was there briefly. He shook hands with each of the competitors and administrators and made several comments that were inaudible against the roar of the jets. He wouldn't be staying long enough to hear that the band only had a repertoire of three patriotic tunes played on a loop.

During their training, the Lao team had received some splendid news. In protesting the Soviet invasion of Afghanistan, the Americans had voted to boycott the Games. In turn they'd bullied sixty-five other countries to stay home. Others, like Great Britain, were leaving the decision to participate or not to its athletes. The news delighted the socialist bloc and especially the Lao, who would now be able to boast of finishing seventh in their event rather than twelfth as there would be fewer competitors.

The final photograph was of the entire squad seated on a hurriedly put-together bleacher. Civilai was between the prime minister and General Suvan in the front row. As they waited for the cameraman to find a focus, Civilai looked around at the familiar and unfamiliar faces of the athletes. He had spent much of his career traveling around the country and he had a remarkable memory for faces. In a country of four million people, on any given day there was a strong likelihood of bumping into someone you knew or were related to. It was the first time the military shooters had been together as a group. They were still being introduced to one another. In the third row, Civilai recognized an officer called Lien he'd had dealings with in the past. At that time, Lien had been a captain but had since reached the rank of major. Civilai nodded at him and the major nodded back. The soldier smiled as if remembering some past adventure they'd shared. It appeared that Lien was one of the shooting team, which pleased the old politburo man no end. They'd be together for over a month in the Soviet Union and would have time to relive those good old days. Civilai pointed to the plane and the major put up his thumb.

The taxiing area was crowded and even after the Olympians and the officials had boarded the plane the onlookers refused to budge. They waved at the now familiar faces whose photographs had graced the front page of *Pasason Lao* and mouthed, "Good luck." As Aeroflot did not equip its planes with horns, it was left to the Russian co-pilot to open his window and wave away the unruly throng so the plane could make its way to the end of the runway. The crowd continued to wave even as the aircraft left the ground and carried their hopes up into the sky and away to the great Soviet Union.

Even on a calm, cloudless day, flights out of Wattay could find a bank of turbulence. Most of the passengers had never flown on an airplane before so when the beast dropped forty meters with no warning, the scream could be heard back at the airport. White clouds of air conditioning gushed from overhead and to the uninitiated looked exactly like smoke. Nurse Dtui wrenched Siri's arm from its socket.

"Don't panic," he said.

"Don't panic?" she said. "This is exactly why I avoid airplanes. Challenging the fates. Putting myself in a tin box and throwing myself into the sky. Defying the gods to knock me down. It's unnatural."

Civilai leaned forward from the seat behind and said, "The odds of having a buffalo fall on you from a tree are greater than dying in a plane crash."

"That doesn't make me feel any better at all," said Dtui.

The aircraft dropped again and for the next five minutes it flipped and flopped like a sandal in a tumble drier. Even when the pilot said the turbulence was over and passengers could unfasten their seatbelts, nobody did. Except, that is, for Civilai. He rose from his seat and headed back through the cabin.

"Bladder," said Siri to his wife. "Thank goodness airplanes have toilets."

But Civilai seemed in no hurry to relieve himself. He walked slowly along the aisle looking left and right, nodding and making comments. When he reached the last row of seats he confirmed that the lavatory was not in use but didn't avail himself of its amenities. Siri and Daeng had no idea what he was looking for. They watched him pass them again, this time heading for the front of the plane. There he leaned over the senior military officer, a handsome middle-aged man in a brand new uniform, and engaged him in a brief conversation. The officer stood, counted the military contingent, consulted a list and saluted Civilai before retaining his seat. By the time he was back in his own seat Civilai seemed thoroughly confused.

"Met everybody?" asked Daeng.

"It's the damnedest thing," said Civilai.

"What's the problem?" asked Siri.

Civilai knelt on his seat and leaned over Siri's seat back.

"Back at the airport when we were having the team photograph taken with the prime minister, I saw an old friend," he said. "From his uniform I could see he's a major now, but he was a captain when I first met him. He was sitting behind us with the shooters. He recognized me and we smiled and I gestured we should get together on the flight and he agreed. But he's not here."

"So you didn't actually talk to him?" said Siri.

"It was chaotic," said Civilai.

"So he might have been just a trainer or a VIP there for the photo shoot," said Dtui.

"No, I mean . . . yes," said Civilai. "I mean, it's possible, but he was dressed exactly like everyone else in the shooting team down to the red Olympic armband. And he was in the team photo. And he was keen to talk on the plane."

"Or that's what you understood and he just went along with it," said Siri.

"I know when a man is enthusiastic," said Civilai. "You see it so rarely in our country."

"Perhaps he wanted to talk to you before you got on the flight," Daeng suggested.

"Look, that's not impossible either," said Civilai. "But to tell the truth it didn't surprise me at all that he'd be on the team. He was always brilliant at the range. He was already instructing when he was in his twenties."

"Then that's it," said Siri. "He's a non-traveling instructor. Came to say goodbye to his boys. What did the uniform at the front have to say about it?"

"He asked me what the major's surname was but I couldn't remember it. We called him Lien, but there was no Lien on the team list. Nor was there a name that contained the word Lien. No Lienkum. No Bounlien."

"Then that's the end of it," said Daeng. "Senility. Memory loss and the misinterpretation of standard signals."

"I was just so certain he . . ."

"He's not on the flight, uncle," said Nurse Dtui.

"No," Civilai agreed. "He's not on the flight."

◙ ◙ ◙

The so-called "virgin countries," those that had never been at the Olympics before—Angola, Botswana, Jordan, Laos, Mozambique, and the Seychelles—had been invited to come to the Soviet Union two weeks before the games proper began for what the organizers called "intensive coaching." But it was more of an acculturation program making sure they knew how to flush toilets and not eat with their fingers. No amount of sports coaching would bring the little teams up to international standards.

The Lao athletes disembarked at the brand new Sheremetyevo Airport, a glary white building that seemed to exist only for them. After one minor incident at Customs, where an athlete was not allowed to enter the country with a tub of homemade fish *lahp*, they were met by a reception committee of interesting characters. There were chubby women in ethnic costumes carrying leis. Large men in suits with hairstyles that looked like toupees. Military officers in flat hats so broad you could land a helicopter on them. And, most importantly, breaking free of the crowd came Comrade Baronov. The young man's hair was constantly flopping over his eyes and the act of clearing a path through the fringe gave the impression that he was waving at everyone. He was a notable member of the reception committee in the eyes of the Lao because he spoke their language. The Lao delegation stood in awe as he walked from handshake to handshake wishing each athlete good luck, asking them about the weather back home, and showing concern as to whether they'd eaten yet, all in beautiful standard Lao.

One might have felt a fog of pity for a young man who chose to spend his allotment of educational opportunity learning a language that would allow him no professional or financial advancement. A language that even forty percent of those living within the Lao borders had yet to master. But without doubt all the team members and administrators fell in love with this white-skinned, over-weight, unfashionably attired Soviet.

The shooters were gathered up and whisked away by the Red Army representatives and they wouldn't be seen again until the opening ceremony on July 19th. This was of concern to Civilai, not only because he'd been charged with creating a Lao team spirit but also because he was still disturbed by the disappearance of his friend. He scanned the faces again as they boarded a coach. Perhaps it was true that the major was merely a non-traveling trainer, but Civilai's instincts told him otherwise.

The others were ferried from the airport in three luxurious vans driven by men in pale blue uniforms. There were two unarmed Soviet guards on each vehicle. Siri couldn't help thinking that everything had been unwrapped for the first time, including the hospitality. Both Siri and Civilai had been to the Soviet Union before but neither had experienced a smidgen of warmth. Meanwhile, the Lao who had never been overseas gaped silently through the windows. It was the size of everything that struck them dumb. Coming from a country with only one building of over three stories, they felt as if they themselves had been shrunk. The route from the airport took them past grand, earth-colored blocks with spires, interrupted here and there by slab-like structures that didn't stop at the clouds. They'd never seen so much concrete in their lives. The streets were broad with neat, even footpaths and there was no litter, not one pile of molding food or roadwork debris. And all the vehicles were painted in primary colors like toys.

When the vans pulled up in front of the thirty-story skyscraper on the north bank of the Moskva River, the runners and pugilists assumed they were visiting a grand palace. They stepped down onto the driveway with their government-donated instamatic cameras and began snapping away. They barely noticed the train of bellboys in matching uniforms who marched to the rear of the vans and began to offload the team luggage. They even ignored the two middle-aged managers in oversize silver-grey suits who stood on the front steps beckoning for them to come inside.

"You'll have plenty of time for photos," said Siri. "Save your film."

"Why, granddad?" asked Maen. He was the best looking and most conceited of the boxers. In their brief spell together in the van he'd already attempted to woo one of the sprinter sisters, Nah. The male runners had gathered around her like a pack protecting its youngest from a tiger. And Maen was certainly a tiger. On the flight he'd even been bold enough to remind Nurse Dtui she'd be away from her husband for a month and he'd be happy to keep her company on those chilly Moscow evenings. She'd reported the approach to Civilai but following her acrimonious departure from her sanctimonious husband she may have allowed herself to flirt a little. It was invigorating that a young man with a well-defined musculature might find her sexually attractive.

Siri objected to being called "granddad" by such an unpleasant young man.

"Because this is your hotel," he said. "You'll have over two weeks to take as many photos as you like to send to your network of women of dubious taste around the world."

Jaws dropped, mouths gaped all around.

"We're staying here?" said Khamon, the walker.

"According to the itinerary," said Siri.

Their eyes scanned the cliff face of windows all the way to the spire. This was the Ukraina Hotel on the west side, one of Stalin's many flights of architectural fancy. A thousand rooms with suites and apartments and domed ceilings and plush imported carpets. And this was where the sons and daughters of rice farmers would be spending their first fourteen days in Moscow.

"I hope our rooms are near the bottom," said Thip, the eldest and prettiest of the lady runners.

"Why, love?" asked Madam Daeng.

"Cause it'll be a bastard of a climb if we're at the top."

In just over two weeks, when the Games were due to begin, the Ukraina would be given over to the world's journalists, but for the time being the virgin countries had the place to themselves. Comrade Baronov had accompanied the team to the hotel, made sure they were settled in, and now stood like an out-of-order vending machine in the gaudy reception area. Given the boy's choice of studies, Civilai doubted he had friends. He decided to adopt him.

"Young man," he said.

Baronov squinted, smiled and said, "Yes, uncle?"

"Uncle? Shouldn't you be addressing me as comrade?"

"Goodness no," he said. "These are the eighties. Life has changed. And this is the Olympic rebirth. The dark days are over. No classist language. No racism. No xenophobia. We're all one big family and the Lao team are my brothers and sisters. You are my uncle."

As a man who spent much of his life listening to the bull dung of communist rhetoric, Civilai could only assume that these sentiments had been instilled in the minds of the official translators to last only for the duration of the Games.

"Then you may call me uncle," he said. "And am I to assume that you are at my team's disposal while we're here?"

"Anything legal," said Baronov. "Although there are one or two moderately less-than-legal things I've been instructed to turn a blind eye to."

"Such as what?"

"Marijuana. Ladies of the night. Gambling. Fighting in public without weapons. Theft of small hotel property."

"What about anti-Soviet sentiment?"

"Absolutely out of the question."

"I'll bear all that in mind. I'm assuming Baronov is your family name."

"Yes, uncle."

"What's your first name?"

"Vladimir Svyatoslav."

"No, that's far too complicated."

"I have a foreign name: Roger."

"Yet another good choice. Well, Roger, I'm in desperate need to contact my country to let them know we have arrived safely."

"I was anticipating such a request," said Roger. "You can phone directly from the hotel. All phone calls are complimentary."

"Ah, yes. It's just that my country does not have a vast network of international telephone lines. I was hoping you might have something more . . . archaic."

"We have a telex service," said Roger.

"Excellent."

The telex Civilai sent was to Inspector Phosy, care of the national police headquarters. It read,

> *Phosy,*
> *At Wattay I saw an old colleague, a major called Lien. That was his nickname but it's a derivative of his actual name. Boulien or Khamlien, something like that. He used to be based in Buagaew, Unit 6. I was certain he'd be coming to Moscow but he didn't get on the plane. Please follow up.*
>
> *Thanks. C.*

As the keyboard was set out in Roman characters and Civilai didn't know English, he wrote the telex in French and Phosy would have to get it translated. As Laos modeled its security and spy network on the Soviet system, Civilai assumed somebody would be monitoring communication into and out of the country. But all he was doing was trying to locate an old friend. No national secrets to be had there.

Madam Daeng had discovered the turban when she and Dtui were thumbing through 1950s copies of *Paris Match*

on the eve of their departure. The French hadn't contributed very much of value during their stay in Indochina
but they did leave behind some interesting magazines.
And it was in one of these that Daeng saw Marlene Dietrich
in a silk turban. It was the answer to her fashion dilemma.
She'd been right about her hair. It was taking its sweet time
to grow. She no longer looked like a billiard ball; she now
could be compared to a grassy clod of earth. But with a silk
turban, crayoned eyebrows and a light girdle to hide the tail,
she would no longer feel out of place. Dr. Siri, on the other
hand, preferred his women as nature intended them but he
wisely kept his comments to himself.

The doctor hadn't heard a word from his spirit guide,
the obnoxious Auntie Bpoo. He wondered whether the
occult might be like radio—getting weaker the further
from the source you journeyed. But he also hadn't had a
disappearing episode for a month, which was not a bad
thing. How would it look for the Lao team physician to
vanish during a reception? He continued to wear his stone
talisman on a string around his neck, although he'd taken
to leaving it on the bedside cabinet of a night. At home
the pendant kept him safe from malevolent spirits. But
this was Soviet Russia. How far could ghosts really travel?

It was probably as a result of this complacency that a
further breakthrough was made on his second night at
the Ukraina. Their room was like one of the roped-off
boudoirs he'd seen at Versailles. He'd visited the palace
as a student and wondered how comfortable Marie Antoi-
nette would have felt there constantly afraid of damaging
an antique or spilling red wine on a priceless counterpane.

The boxers and athletes had been placed in apartments
on the seventeenth floor. Fortunately there were elevators,

but the management had formally requested the Lao stop riding them for pleasure. One group had spent the first morning traveling from the ground floor to the roof and running to the windows at the end of the corridor to see how high they were while one of them held open the lift doors.

Siri and Daeng were in the VIP suites, which were like the private quarters of rich grandmothers: a bed so high there were lacquered steps on either side to mount her, a stuffed couch like a patchwork loaf, a television in a finely crafted cabinet, and curtains so heavy it took two to pull them apart of a morning. But the view across the river to the Garden Ring was glorious. And neither complained about the complimentary wines and liquors lined up in rows atop the cabinet like the Russian cavalry. And perhaps it was a slight overindulgence in the free booze that threw Dr. Siri into one of his dreaded dreams. It was about 1 A.M. and Daeng was awoken by her husband saying, "Fasten your seat belts," over and over again. She reached across to calm him but he wasn't there.

He was, in fact or in fiction, upside down in an Aeroflot Tupolev and he had no seatbelt. He knew at any second he could plummet to the overhead lights. He could hear screams over the intercom. Flames lashed the windows. The door to the cockpit opened (it was a finely carved temple door with garuda motifs) and Auntie Bpoo in an Aeroflot stewardess uniform stepped out. She was walking on the ceiling but as the aircraft was upside down it was the only place to walk. She looked even less like a woman than usual. Her hair was cropped and she'd started to grow a beard. A scar like a glued-on centipede ran down one cheek.

"At last," said Siri.

"Chicken or beef?" said Bpoo.

Their heads were at the same level but one of them was upside down.

"I've been trying to get through to you for months," said Siri. "What happened to our arrangement?"

"If you don't want chicken or beef I'll have to recite you a poem," she said.

"Beef," said Siri.

"Ingrate."

The cockpit door reopened and a small buffalo walked out. The fuselage rocked.

"That's not beef," said Siri.

"These are hard times," said Bpoo and held up a machete. "Brisket or rib?"

"I said, what about our arrangement?" Siri tried again. "You're supposed to be tutoring me."

"In what?"

"In communicating with the other side. You promised."

"And was there a time limit applied to this promise?"

"I've just turned seventy-six. We have a lot to fit in before I'm on the pyre and you're homeless."

"Goodness. What drama. Would you like a drink with your meal?"

"I'd like some advice."

"Red or white?"

"Remember Noo, the Thai forest monk? He's in a coma. It's as if he's given up on life but I don't know why."

"You don't know much."

"I know. So teach me. How do I bring him back?"

"We should have ice cream but the fridge is on the blink."

"Bpoo!"

"You really aren't very good at this, are you? Look. Isn't it obvious? The problem isn't him, it's his spirit."

"He's a Buddhist monk."

"So what? It doesn't matter what you call yourself. It doesn't stop the opposing spirits haggling over your soul. It doesn't carry any weight in the respective heavens and hells. If he's dangling there must be some unfinished business."

"How can I know what that is? Can you connect me to his spirit?"

"Do I look like a telephonist to you?"

"Please. He's been through a terrible ordeal."

"Then sort it out. You know what your problem is? You think *we're* in control. But here's a dose of veracity. I'm only here because you want me to be. You created me. We're all here because you put up this big psychic ROOM FOR RENT sign and you don't check on us at all. We're running riot, peeing on the carpets, breaking the windows and we get away with it because you can't keep your house in order. Don't beg, Siri. Show a bit of spunk. You want to help Noo, you go in there with your AK27 and you make a mess of his malevolent spirits."

"But how? Even you don't listen to me."

"I'm different. I'm out of control. Have you finished with your meal?"

Siri looked down to see a plate of feathers on the tray.

"How was it?" Bpoo asked.

"It was chicken, I asked for beef."

"Yeah, that's better. Spirits admire ornery hosts."

She handed him a laminated card. On it was a poem. He made the mistake of reading it. It was as awful and unintelligible as all of Bpoo's offerings.

Take to the sky

> *Why not? They used to say*

> *The safest way*
> *Then comes a bearded man*
> *A hidden blade*

> *Afraid of a lemonade can*

> *Exploding shoes*
Who's to know which one?

She started to walk back to the cockpit.

"It's forty-seven," shouted Siri.

"What is?"

"There's no AK27."

"Well, that's a relief. Can we go back to sleep now?"

Siri turned to his left to see Daeng, still in her turban, her eyes puffy with sleep.

"Did I disappear?" he asked.

"About half an hour. Where were you?"

"Aeroflot."

"I imagine a lot of people disappear on Aeroflot."

CHAPTER FIVE
Good Mourning

"All right. Here's the story," said Civilai. "I heard back from Inspector Phosy. He got in touch with his military contacts in Buagaew and, of course, they knew my Major Lien. His full name is Ailien Viaketh. As far as his colleagues knew he was on his way here as their delegate on the Olympic shooting team."

The old woman pushed him in the back for the tenth time. He turned and snarled at her but also took a step forward. He was, after all, a guest in her country.

"So I wasn't delusional," he continued. "Major Lien really did think he'd see me on the flight."

"Then what do you think went wrong?" asked Siri. He regretted not bringing a hat. The thought of getting sunburned beneath a July sun in Moscow hadn't occurred to him. Once they'd left the trees at the edge of the park there was no shade.

"It's almost as if everything was decided on the spur of the moment at Wattay," said Civilai. "Phosy found Major Lien in Vientiane staying with relatives, still in shock and very upset. He was hiding his puffy eyes behind dark glasses. He'd been ordered not to say anything but his sister walked Phosy to the gate. She was more talkative. She said some military officials had pulled him aside at the airport and said there was a problem with his application. Lien wouldn't tell her what. Phosy wondered what the Soviet security detail had found in the major's files at such a late juncture. He had access to the security office that kept the application forms of the military Olympic competitors. He found something in the major's record that could have had a bearing on his ouster. Major Lien had a criminal record."

"There are such things as criminal records?" Siri asked.

"Exactly! Everything from the old regime was destroyed and everything from our side is suppressed. There's no way the Soviets could have gained access to the military files of a senior officer."

The old woman jabbed him in the back again and he and Siri shuffled forward a few more paces. A guard with a pistol in a holster walked beside the queue looking at everyone's feet. Probably just a routine footwear check.

"What was he supposed to have done?" Siri asked.

"Black marketeering. He'd organized the import of petrol from Thailand, as did army units up and down the western border. It was standard policy. The only way they could keep their vehicles on the road. Everyone knew they were doing it. And it wasn't even a crime if you consider we tore up the constitution in '75."

"So this was a trumped-up charge to keep Major Lien off the Olympic squad?" said Siri.

"Apparently."

The old woman nudged him again. He called on the spirit of the great naga to give him restraint.

"But if that were true and he was pulled at the last second, there would have been one member missing from the team," said Civilai. "But there wasn't. The colonel on the flight counted the shooters and there were seven accounted for. So somebody stepped in at the last moment to replace Lien."

"Which suggests the whole thing had been planned," said Siri. "That the replacement was there at Wattay ready to step into the vacant spot. Now why would anyone do that?"

"I hadn't been given the official list of shooters so I asked the colonel to make me a copy. He gave me a handwritten list just before we arrived at Sheremetyevo. Major Lien's name wasn't on that list. I asked the officer why it had been left so late to get me the names. I reminded him I was the team manager and I was responsible for the whole team, including the shooters. He cited the problem of domestic communication and the fact that the military units didn't get around to sending in the names of their candidates as requested. As you know you can get away with arguments like that in Laos because our inefficiency is legendary. You request documents and they arrive six months later. So it appears he didn't know who was on his own team until Wattay."

"You believe that?"

"No. It's as if they were holding out till the last minute so they could fiddle with the list."

"And the organizers would have been so relieved to finally get the seven names they wouldn't have bothered to check them too closely."

"Which leaves us with the fact that someone on the shooting team shouldn't be here," said Siri.

"And we can't find out who that is because our Lao soldiers have been whisked away to a Red Army base outside the city," said Civilai.

"And the question is, why go to the trouble of infiltrating the Lao Olympic squad?"

Still they shuffled and still the old lady prodded but after ninety-three minutes Siri and Civilai were at last in sight of their goal. Compared to the opulence of the Ukraina, the sarcophagus was disappointing. It had recently been renovated with tile-like slabs that made it look like a large outdoor kitchen cabinet.

"We'll have to wait till we're all together at the Olympic Village," said Siri. "The shooters will have no choice but to stay there. It won't be that hard to talk to them individually and find our interloper."

"We can do—"

"Shh," came a voice.

They looked up to see a burly guard standing beside the small entryway. In spite of the July heat he was dressed like an Arctic border guard in furs and earflaps. Most importantly he was armed with something that could have taken out a tank.

"But we aren't even inside yet," said Siri, in French. In such a situation he hoped that any foreign language would do the job.

"Shh," said the guard, holding his gloved index finger to his mouth.

"We can do something in the meantime," Civilai whispered. "Phosy's been working with the official photographer. He took hundreds of snaps of the team and the trainers at Wattay. Phosy's hoping he'll be able to cross-check and find the face that replaced Major Lien's."

"And do what?" Siri asked.

"Well, send it to us, for a start. We can—"

The armed guard took a step forward and punched Civilai in the shoulder. It wasn't playful. The old boys really didn't want to be sent to the back of a queue that snaked all the way across Red Square and into the park so they shut up and shuffled.

Visitors were told to enter the chilly mausoleum in pairs even if they'd come alone. The procession veered to its left and descended a marble staircase. Another left and a right passing somber guards, none of whom returned Siri's smiles. Then suddenly the bier was in front of them, bathed in a saffron glow. The pace picked up and there was Uncle Lenin, not flat out exactly, more propped up slightly as if he'd asked the nurse if he could watch television. His hands, or at least the hands they'd given him, were linked in a deflated prayer and his slightly orange face seemed to be concentrating. Siri wondered whether he was trying to solve the puzzle of how he'd ended up in a musty room being ogled by thousands of morbid mourners every day from eight till five.

A few more steps and it was all over. They reemerged into the daylight like passengers on a funfair ghost train bursting through the final black doors. The old friends broke away from their queue mates and squinted beneath a midday sun. Civilai prodded the old woman as she passed them but she didn't seem to notice. She held onto her beatific mask.

"Any idea why we queued an hour and a half to view a body?" Civilai asked.

"None whatsoever," said Siri.

CHAPTER SIX
The Friends of Socialism Ball

Vientiane seemed to have forgotten the euphoria of Olympic departure day and had returned to its doldrums. A joint Vietnamese-Soviet study had recommended Laos give up its ambitious cooperative rice farming program and Thai entrepreneurs were taking advantage of the open border policy by trucking thousands of tons of timber out of the country. In return, the Lao markets were filling up with shoddy clothing and Thai junk food—unidentifiable morsels in brightly colored plastic bags.

Inspector Phosy had looked at the photographs of the shooting team. One was taken on the bleacher with the seven shooters, their Soviet coach and their minder, Colonel Fah Hai. Then there was a series of photos of the athletes climbing the steps to board the flight. They'd been told to stop on the platform, turn and wave at the crowd. The shooters in their military dress uniforms and distinctive red armbands were easy enough to spot. By comparing the two sets, Phosy was able to find the man who had replaced Major Lien. Whereas all the other shooters smiled at the camera, this one frowned and looked down. He did not have an armband. His was a nondescript face with a military haircut. The only identifying feature, if it could be called such, was his unusually long neck.

Phosy had pointed it out to his young daughter at teatime and she'd compared the man to a tortoise whose long neck reached far out of its shell. She was many streets ahead of her age group linguistically. The inspector loved nothing more than telling stories to Malee and listening to her peculiar interpretations of them. The only person he loved more than Malee was his wife, Dtui. Yet still he found it hard to tell her so. To his first wife he'd confessed his love every day. He'd hugged his children so tightly they often complained they couldn't breathe. He'd told secrets and confessed his frailties because he was certain they'd all be together until the children had children of their own and he and his wife would sway together on rattan rocking chairs. But suddenly she was gone. She took his children to a refugee camp without a word. There was no trace of them. No way to find them. No knowing what he'd done wrong. So, although Dtui filled his heart he would never tell her so for fear she too would betray him.

The next morning he dropped Malee off at the crèche and went to the office of *Pasason Lao*. It was their official photographer who'd shared the Wattay pictures with him. The inspector had an idea but he needed cooperation from the newspaper editor, Savang, who answered directly to the Ministry of Information. Phosy sat with Savang and the Vietnamese media adviser and pitched them an idea. The families and friends of all the Olympic heroes had turned up at the airport to wish them well. But one man, one army marksman, had been ignored by the crowds. No loved ones had come to see him off. He'd stood in the shadows until it was time to board the flight and here was his photograph, looking sad and lonely. Who was this modest Lao hero? Didn't he deserve the same plaudits as everyone else?

The Lao editor hated it. His was a newspaper of information, he said. Of statistics and figures. There were occasional interviews with model socialists who led by example. There were facts. There was propaganda. What it most certainly was *not* was a Thai-like sensationalist broadsheet that ran tacky competitions and gimmicks.

"Absolutely not," he said.

The Vietnamese adviser smiled. He pointed out that the *Pasason Lao* was distributed weekly to post offices and learning institutions but that nobody actually read it, mainly for the reasons that Savang had just outlined. An unread newspaper was a metal safe that nobody could open, he told them. You had to give the combination so the contents could be enjoyed. What it needed was a little human interest on the front cover. The nameless hero angle was exactly the type of thing he'd been trying to introduce since his posting at the newspaper. And as he was a Vietnamese adviser whose advice few Lao dared question, it was decided that the photograph would appear on the front page of the newspaper two days hence.

◎ ◎ ◎

An announcement came over the intercom that the flight would soon be leaving and the passengers should stow their tray tables and return their seats to the upright position. But neither the tray nor the seat was adjustable. The intercom voice was clearly that of Auntie Bpoo. As was his

habit, Siri sat back and waited for the show. He was currently upside up. The aircraft began to move, the engines
booted, the force pushed him back into his seat and they
were airborne. In fact there were no other passengers and
no visible crew members. It was one of Siri's least entertaining dreams.

He thought about the last conversation he'd had with
Bpoo. She'd told him, not to put too fine a point on it, that
he was a wimp. She'd said this other world he glimpsed
from time to time was of his own making. If so, that must
have included this private Aeroflot. He was traveling in
a metaphor. She said he had to take control but didn't
mention how to go about it. Perhaps this was his chance
to steer his own ship.

He unfastened his seatbelt and started to walk toward
the cockpit. The voice over the intercom told him the
seatbelt sign was still on and he should immediately return
to his seat or there'd be trouble. He ignored it. He'd show
them who was a wimp. He was taking control. He heaved
open the temple door and, as he'd expected, the pilot and
co-pilot seats were empty. Through the front window he
could see a mountain getting nearer. It was his moment.
He sat in the pilot's seat and noticed there was no joystick.
In fact there were no dials or meters or switches at all.
There was just one red button. The other side was making
it easy for him.

The mountain was getting closer, so close he could see
goats on ledges and ice melting. The button began to glow.
Control was at the tip of his finger. He pressed the button
and . . . a small ceiling fan began to rotate above his head.
It had barely reached full speed by the time the aircraft
slammed into the side of the mountain.

He came to in the Ukraina's twenty-four-hour restaurant. His nose was pressed up against a grand Ionic pillar. He looked from side to side. There were no diners. The staff sat at tables knitting or reading novels. A guard in pale blue with a non-threatening truncheon in his belt was standing behind the doctor with a look of pity on his face. He mimed his rendition of a drunken man staggering to the elevator and sleeping off whatever had got him into such a terrible state.

A week after their arrival in Moscow, the boxers and runners were no more likely to win medals but they weighed a lot more. Everyone complained of the Soviet plot. They were being poisoned with butter and lard and sugar and sweet pasta. Yet none could refuse to eat the stodgy meals served free at the Ukraina restaurant. The very fact the food was free made it desirable. Families back home were starving and here was a buffet full to bursting. Like squirrels storing nuts, the Lao filled themselves with carbohydrates for the days after their return home. They'd be able to live off the fat through the harshest of dry seasons. They were starting to take luxury for granted and had already tired of riding the elevator.

Maen the conceited boxer boasted that he'd bedded two of the hotel staff and had set himself a target of eight. Khamon the walker had gone out every day to pace the twenty kilometers of his race walk along the banks of the Moscva River and study the terrain. Chom the rat catcher had been to the older suburbs and was fascinated by the number of stray dogs around the city. Roger had explained that Muscovites of old were wont to have guard dogs. As the small dwellings of the city were ploughed into the foundations of ever-taller skyscrapers, the dogs were let loose and today's strays were the descendants of those discarded guard dogs. Not even the intensive facelift for the Olympics had been able to rid the streets of their dogs.

In their free time, Nut and Nah and the other sprinters had taken to the water, where they enjoyed free ferry rides along the eighty-some kilometers of river that wound its way through the city. Of a morning, the Soviet coaches would take them to a nearby tartan track where they'd learn the art of ejecting from starting blocks and pushing their chests forward to gain advantage at the tape. In that matter the lady runners already had a disadvantage when compared with the buxom Europeans. The boxers pummeled sandbags in a high school gymnasium and were introduced to ropes that did not chafe. But most importantly they were taught the English numbers from one to nine and told that once face down on the canvas they should listen and not attempt to get up until the last number was called. There was a reason why they were flat out and that reason would repeat itself if they attempted to get to their feet.

On their last night at the Ukraina, the hotel sponsored a reception for all the virgin country athletes who'd stayed there. They were three days away from the opening ceremony and everyone would be moving to the Olympic Village, which was finally complete.

Madam Daeng was admiring her latest turban in the mirror when the door burst open and Civilai, out of breath, entered the room.

"A gentleman would knock," she said.

"Sorry," he said. "Where's Siri?"

"Defecating," she said.

"Finished," came a voice from the bathroom. Siri emerged wearing a towel around his waist that dragged along the floor. "What's up?"

At that moment, Dtui also entered through the open door of the suite.

"I'm here," she said.

"Listen, all of you," said Civilai. "I want us all together because something important has come to light. Dtui, please shut the door."

"We're in a Soviet hotel room," said Siri. "If it's important, shouldn't we speak on the balcony or turn on the bath tap or something?"

"You read too many spy novels," said Civilai. "We're Lao. What threat do we pose to the Union of Soviet States?"

"What's happened?" said Daeng.

"I've just heard from Phosy," said Civilai.

"That's more than I have," said Dtui. "How is he?"

"I didn't ask him," said Civilai, "but he—"

"Did he send his regards to his wife, by any chance?" she asked.

"Look, this is important," said Civilai.

"Sorry," said Dtui.

"Phosy put a photo of our imposter on the front page of *Pasason Lao*," said Civilai.

"Nobody reads that," said Siri.

"Which is why it took so long for someone to notice it," said Civilai. "A post office worker in Houaphan recognized the shooter and contacted the newspaper to claim her prize."

"What was it?" asked Daeng.

"The prize? I don't know. A coconut or something. It doesn't matter. The man in the photograph was her cousin. His name is Sompoo. That name is not on the handwritten list the colonel gave me on the flight; neither is it on the official Games roster list which was issued this morning."

"So Sompoo is on the team under an assumed name," said Daeng.

"Didn't they give you photocopies of the identification cards of the shooters?" asked Siri. "You are the team manager."

"I know that, but it seems the military doesn't. My request for team member IDs has been lodged since before we left Laos. I've had no response."

"Did Phosy come up with anything about Sompoo?" Siri asked.

"A lot," said Civilai. "The battalion he was attached to in Huaphan was trained in guerilla warfare to counter the threat of Chinese incursions on the northern borders. There are a lot of Vietnamese troops up there convinced the Chinese plan to invade Laos as a stepping stone to get to Hanoi. Sompoo is evidently one of their best men."

"So he's a trained killer, a gunman with Vietnamese connections," said Daeng. "Why would they send him to Moscow?"

"To kill somebody?" said Dtui.

"They have gone to a lot of trouble to get him here," said Daeng.

"All right," said Siri. "Although it's far more likely his wealthy relatives wangled him a trip to Moscow for a holiday, let's pretend he's here to assassinate somebody. I'd need a lot of convincing they'd send someone to commit murder on Soviet soil. Who would the target be?"

"The obvious target would be a high-ranking Chinese," said Civilai. "At least that's who I'd shoot."

"But the Chinese have boycotted the Games," said Daeng. "And we knew a while ago that they would, but Sompoo still came."

"Right," said Siri, "I doubt he's here to bump off a Russian given that they're the only friends we have at the moment. And he's not going to come all this way to put a bullet in the head of any of us in the Lao delegation. I paid two visits to the bathroom at Wattay airport. He could have shot me there."

"Me too," said Civilai.

"So, do you think he's here to eliminate somebody who's coming for the Games?" Dtui asked. "An athlete or official?"

"It's what the Palestinians did in Munich," said Civilai.

"They made a political point by taking Israelis hostages and killing them," said Siri. "Vast audience. But can we introduce some common sense here? What political point does Laos have to make on the world stage? It would be a disaster for our country and our reputation in the world."

"Then it's simple," said Daeng. "We tell the Soviets about our suspicions and they send him home."

"We don't have any suspicions," said Siri. "We're just making this up. It would be unfair to have Sompoo kicked out if he was here legitimately. What if the major was bumped for something more serious than buying petrol? What if Sompoo's here at the invitation of the Soviets? His background means nothing. How many on the shooting team don't have guerilla training? They're all expert gunmen for a reason. Until we have something concrete to show them I think we'll be making fools of ourselves to go to the Soviets with this."

"If he's so innocent why's he traveling under someone else's name?" Dtui asked.

"I'm not saying he's innocent," said Siri. "There's certainly something fishy going on. But we need to know what that is. Tomorrow we'll be at the Olympic Village with the shooters. We're all obliged to wear our picture IDs. This is what we do. We find our mystery shooter, Sompoo, and we keep him under surveillance. There are four of us. We can take shifts. If he breaks away from the pack we follow him. If he does anything naughty we'll have something concrete and we can go to the authorities."

The Friends of Socialism Ball was held in the Ukraina's function room. There was a stage at one end and a tribute band called the Meatles (the Moscow Beatles) was providing the music. The athletes from the virgin countries had nodded at one another in the funfair elevator and the lobby and the training grounds but no actual communication had taken place. Maen the conceited boxer had used the language of love to woo a gymnast from Mozambique but everyone else had run headfirst into that linguistic iron curtain.

But at the ball things were to change. Each team had its own Roger and even before the alcohol started to flow it had become a ball without borders. Bung, the Lao bantamweight, had a group of Angolans enthralled with his animal impressions and one of the Jordanians was a remarkable magician. The interpreters were working overtime and were by far the most popular characters there. Some athletes found it possible to dance without alcoholic stimulation and others refused to imbibe as it would set back their chances at the Games. Many were tippling secretly. Only the team officials, prancing around like teachers at the prom, failed to appreciate the source of this sudden elation. Most team leaders had insisted alcohol should not be available at the ball but that edict had not made its way to the hotel managers. Booze was everywhere.

The Lao delegation naturally had no alcohol restrictions. When the cocktail waitresses arrived with their Sterling silver trays and daringly short skirts they became the athletes' darlings. The dancing grew more eclectic as the evening wore on, as much fun to watch as to participate in. It astounded Siri how his country's best athletes could be so lacking in coordination.

"Our team has no rhythm," he shouted above the din. "How can we run if we can't hear a beat? The world's best sprinters are those raised to the sound of the tom-tom."

He was about to go into a physiological explanation but was interrupted by Chom the rat catcher, who pushed into the administrative circle with his arm around a man darker than coal.

"You won't believe it," said Chom. "This is Sammy. He's from Botswana."

"And why would we not believe that?" shouted Daeng. Her turban had started to get a little itchy and she'd taken to poking a wooden meat skewer up through the band to scratch her scalp.

"Absolutely believe it," said Siri. "Classic Botswana."

"No," said Chom. "What I mean is you won't believe what Sammy does for a living back in Botswana."

"Something to do with elephants?" Civilai guessed.

"We were getting to know the other ethnics," said Chom, "and Roger was doing the introductions. And I announced that I'm a vermin eradication officer and Sammy here jumps up and shouts, 'That's what I do too!' Except he said it in English and it took a while to get back to me. Who'd have thought it, eh? Two rat catchers at the same party."

"The odds against it are immeasurable," said Daeng.

"Incredible," said Siri. He looked up briefly to see conceited Maen heading for the exit hand-in-hand with the gymnast. The boy looked over his shoulder and winked at his fellow boxers. Siri had no respect for men who ticked off their conquests on public scorecards. The boxer had no class and he was headed for trouble.

This was the last thought that passed through Siri's mind at the Friends of Socialism Ball. Dtui turned back from the dance floor.

"Where did Siri go?" she asked.

"Oh, you know the doctor," said Daeng. "He's always disappearing."

She was surprised how often she could get away with that statement. Nobody ever took it literally.

CHAPTER SEVEN
Get Carter

Morning coffee at the Good Luck restaurant was a religion far more sacred than Buddhism for the retired cadres in Vientiane. The place was open-air and set back from the street with a small area under a tarpaulin in case it rained. It was somewhere the disillusioned could rekindle their socialist fire, where they might find evidence that communism was still working. Often it was just a gathering place for grumpy old men.

But on this sunny July morning there was a surprising atmosphere of joy. A Thai gunboat had drifted over to the wrong bank of the Mekhong and a Lao river guard had picked off the captain with one shot. The Thais claimed the boat was in neutral territory but everyone in the Good Luck knew Lao guards couldn't shoot that far. The Thais demanded an apology and compensation even though they knew they were in the wrong. The Lao told them to get lost.

Consequently, Thailand closed its border crossings once again and ceased its exports of goods. Within a week the markets were empty and the new Thai prime minister was joining China in its diatribe against the Vietnamese lackeys across the river. It was exactly what the old cadres needed to cheer themselves up. This purely economic love affair with their lifelong enemies had turned their stomachs. They resented the condescending Thai attitude to "poor Laos." Thailand had signed an international agreement allowing right of passage to landlocked countries but had never observed it for the Lao. Yet the Thais were happy enough to accept 930,000 megawatt-hours of electricity from their northern neighbors at budget prices. The old soldiers were sick of kowtowing.

So on the day Inspector Phosy joined them for breakfast they were already abuzz on thick Lao coffee, sweet condensed milk and nationalism. It wouldn't take much to nudge the conversations around to the topic the policeman had come to learn about.

They greeted him warmly. He knew many of the old men and had fought beside and behind a number of them in the battle for independence.   "What brings you down to the geriatric ward?" asked one old soldier in a Lenin cap.

"My wife's off in Moscow," he said. "I haven't eaten for a week."

"Wives have no right to go gallivanting around the world," said a crusty old fellow with flakes of skin on his dark green epaulettes.

"That's right," said Lenin Cap. "A woman should be at home where she belongs."

And those two comments explained well enough why the Good Luck was an exclusively stag location. Even Mint, the owner, a wiry old fellow with saggy eyes, joined in the applause. Phosy ordered coffee and baguettes.

Thanks to the to-do with Thailand there was no butter. He settled for Lao-made strawberry jam, which was basically pink sugar granules.

"Moscow, you say?" A shadowy character in a trench coat leaned across his table. He had a grey beard trimmed short.

"Olympics," said Phosy.

"Competing, is she?" asked Lenin Cap.

Phosy laughed. "You obviously haven't seen my wife," he said.

"Sporting prowess isn't something you can necessarily recognize by appearance," said Trench Coat. "Look at the Sumo wrestlers. If one of them walked down Lan Xang Avenue the tykes would be throwing sticks and calling them 'Fatty.' But at home they're great athletes."

"And look at Vilyphone Virachat," said Flakey.

They all looked at him.

"Never heard of him," said Lenin Cap.

"Sixth battalion flyweight boxer. Skinny as a blade of corn."

"And he beat everyone?" asked Lenin Cap.

"No," said Flakey. "Never won a match. Had no right calling himself a boxer."

"Thought so," said Lenin Cap. "You never do catch the point, do you?"

"You speak for yourself," said Flakey through the laughter that surrounded him.

"Ignore him," said the owner. Mint was wearing a once-white singlet that had taken on the appearance of abstract art over the years.

While Phosy ate, the boys flitted between subjects, got angry, fought, made up, joked and laughed a lot. He could see why Civilai had suggested a visit to the Good Luck. It wasn't long before the inspector had an in to his topic.

"Fifteen times they've tried to kill him," said a small oval man in a tracksuit. "Fifteen times and his bodyguards prevented most, but it was good fortune that's kept him alive. He's blessed."

"Or the assassins are hopeless," said Lenin Cap.

"He's a god on earth," said Oval Man. "He was a great warrior and great warriors earn credit on the battleground. He's indestructible."

Phosy knew only too well of the assassination attempts against the president. He'd investigated most of them. There had been eight that he knew of. Four of them were sponsored by insurgents across the river or across the Pacific.

"Who would you kill?" Phosy asked nobody in particular.

"Say what?" said Trench Coat.

"Let's say you were in Moscow with all those world leaders and politicians. If it was for the sake of the republic and you had a pistol in your hand and only three weeks left to live, who would you—"

"Get Carter," said Flakey. "He'd have to go first."

"He won't be there," said Phosy. "The Americans have boycotted the Games."

"Then Mao," said Flakey. "He's a troublemaker. Knock him off and all those idiot generals and there'd be none of this expansionist bullshit."

"He's not going either," said Lenin Cap. "No Chinese."

"Plus he's already dead," said Trench Coat.

"No Chinese, no Americans?" said Flakey "Well that's no fun."

There was more laughter.

"Come on," said Phosy, "you're an intelligent bunch of fellows. Whose sudden demise would benefit Laos or Vietnam?"

Everyone had his favorites, from middle-ranking Soviets who wanted to see finances withdrawn from third world countries to staunch anti-communists like Taipei. One quiet gentleman asked if it would be all right if he shot Margaret Thatcher if only because he didn't like the idea of a woman being prime minister.

"I wouldn't limit myself to visitors of the Games," said Trench Coat.

"What do you mean?" Phosy asked.

"Just that there might be Lao or Vietnamese living in Moscow that deserve a bullet."

"What would a Lao be doing living in Moscow?" said Flakey.

"I'm just saying," said Trench Coat.

Despite the odd burst of senility, most of the opinions were sensible and well-considered. The most confident of the old men had plenty to say and their points were interesting. But Phosy had been trained to notice those in the shadows who kept their thoughts to themselves but gave off a sort of aura. One such man was sitting at the back not drinking his coffee nor eating his bread. His eyes followed the conversations as if his mind were recording everything. Phosy decided to bring him in to the dialogue.

"Comrade," he said, "what thoughts do you have?"

The man was old and shriveled inside his clothes as if he were getting smaller by the minute. He looked out from his collar and smiled a mouth of brown teeth.

"None," he said, but Phosy felt that was untrue.

Twice more he tried and failed to bring forth the old

man's point of view. The breakfast broke up at eleven although some stayed for lunch. The others climbed on bicycles as old as themselves or headed off on foot to their dormitories. Brown Teeth had a bicycle but it only had one pedal so it wasn't so hard for Phosy to catch up to him on his department Vespa.

"Off home?" he asked.

"It's not a home," said Brown Teeth. "It's a dog kennel."

"You're a veteran," said Phosy. "Why don't you apply for a house?"

"Name's been on the list for five years. They keep slotting in more deserving patriots above me. "

"I'm sorry."

"Me too. Look, why don't you leave me alone? I have nothing to say to you."

"You didn't have any thoughts on who you'd assassinate back there."

"No."

"Why not?"

"It's a hypothetical game I'd sooner not play."

"What if it wasn't hypothetical? What if there's a military man in Moscow with orders to kill someone?"

The old soldier stopped and squinted painfully as if the rusty cogs were changing position in his head.

"Does this have something to do with the photo in the newspaper?" he asked.

Phosy was surprised he'd make that connection. "You read *Pasason Lao*?" he asked.

"Somebody has to," he said. "So, does it?"

"It might."

"Readers were told to contact police headquarters if they recognized him. You're from police headquarters."

"That's very observant of you."

"You've got a loose cannon in Russia and you want to know who he's there to kill. Did you get his name?"

The old man's face seemed to relax as if Phosy had removed some obstacle from his life.

"Yes," said Phosy. "Sompoo. Do you have any idea why he might be there?"

"I might."

"Is he—"

It was a crack rather than an explosion. The gun was fired from distance. A sniper. Phosy instinctively threw himself to the ground and made himself as small a target as possible. Two shots hit the old man, one in the back of the head, the other between the shoulder blades. Phosy looked up to see a burnt sienna smile on the man's face even though his nose and eyes were nothing but an exit wound. He fell sideways onto the grass verge, still mounted on his bicycle.

CHAPTER EIGHT
It Takes a Village

Dorothy and Toto could not have been more awestruck by Oz than were the Lao team on their first day at the Olympic Village. To a Lao mind, a village was a community of bamboo and grass huts with pigs and chickens running wild and naked children playing in mud pools. It most certainly was not what they discovered hidden deep in a 264-acre park in the southwest of the city. The village was a henge of eighteen blue and white skyscrapers towering over landscaped gardens. There were banks of apartments and covered pools and sports fields and gymnasia. There was a huge civic center and restaurants and bars. By comparison the Ukraina had been a hardship posting. Whoever christened this a village wanted their head examined.

Previous Olympic research had taught that athletes preferred not to travel too far from their accommodation so the Soviets had brought Moscow to the village. Roger smiled as he listed the facilities in his beautiful Lao.

"We have," he said, "in no particular order, three cafeterias open from five in the morning till midnight and one more for non-sleepers which is open twenty-four hours. There are smaller Russian tea houses and ice-cream parlors and milk bars which also serve alcoholic beverages. We have hairdressers and barbers, manicurists, pedicurists, and cosmeticians. Photographers will take as many pictures of you as you wish at leisure and whilst competing and they may be picked up at the service kiosks free of charge. We have a lost property office, and a fax and telephone exchange. In the cultural center we have concerts and assorted entertainment every night you're here. There are three cinemas showing feature films, documentaries and cartoons, respectively. There are TV viewing rooms, a reading library, individual and group music listening booths, slot machines, rooms reserved for religious observance with a spiritual leader of your choice, and a dance hall with discotheque music. All of this information plus a lot more can be found in your program" (he held one up) "which I have personally translated into Lao. Any questions?"

The group was too stunned to respond. Much of what Roger told them had soared hawk-like over their heads, as many of the facilities were not even figments of the imagination for the Lao. But they could smell fun a kilometer off and they knew they'd landed on their feet by being included on the Lao Olympic ticket.

"We didn't even die and here we are in Communist heaven," said Siri.

"It was Karl's vision," said Civilai, "a pinball table and hot tub in every home."

"I bet they're really pissed the Americans aren't here to see it all," said Dtui.

The accommodation only brought them slightly down

to earth. The rooms smelled of paint and wallpaper paste with a sub-aroma of hopeful potpourri. The color coordination may have adhered to some cultural principle but Madam Daeng had never been a fan of purple and green as a duet. Civilai's pink and royal blue suite didn't seem to worry him at all. The light switches were three-quarters of the way up the wall and the room fridges deep-froze the drinks but nobody on the Lao team was likely to complain. They were several years away from Nirvana but this preview made them eager to experience the main feature.

When the orientation was over, Madam Daeng called Maen the boxer to one side.

"Bad news," she said. "They've segregated the women. All your potential conquests are behind barbed wire."

"No problem, Auntie," said Maen. "When a woman gets the scent she'll find me. I don't have to hunt."

"Yes, I thought I could smell something," said Daeng. "But listen. If I hear you've touched any of our girls—so much as a tickle—you'll find a vacant space where your balls used to be."

He smiled his arrogant smile but she opened her shoulder bag where the sharp end of a meat knife protruded from her event program.

Inspector Phosy was lost. He'd asked all the "who, how, why" questions and had received nothing helpful in return. He'd walked back along the road from the scene of the shooting but could see no vantage point for a gunman. Even if someone from the restaurant had felt threatened by his questioning or his contact with the old soldier there was no way they'd get their hands on a rifle. As far as he could remember, none of the old boys was carrying a violin case. None drove cars so there was no chance of taking a weapon from the trunk. And who would take a gun to a coffee shop anyway? There was no phone for the drinkers to call someone to come from outside.

The obvious course was to find out all he could about the old soldier with brown teeth. At the moment he knew nothing. All he could wonder was whether the shooting was connected to the discussion at the restaurant. Had the old soldier been singled out for some other reason? But that was the type of coincidence he usually ruled out early in an investigation. There was another possibility he chose to ignore: that the gunman was not aiming at the old man at all.

Each national Olympic committee or NOC had been allocated a meeting room on the second floor of whichever building they'd been billeted in. At the center of the room was a conference table so large there was barely enough space to pull out the chairs. It was outside Siri's parameters of *sabai*; too regimented, too dull, too far from a drink, so in his quest to find an alternative he discovered a very comfortable milk bar on the eighth floor. It was called the Nebesa Milk Nook. It had armchairs and ottomans and alcohol and a personable bar man called Sergei. He was tall and swarthy as a pirate. It was at the Nebesa that the Lao administrators set up base. Like small, septuagenarian gods, Siri and Civilai could summon anyone with official business to meet them there. They'd put a notice and a map on the door of the assigned meeting room.

Sergei never seemed to go home and on their first afternoon in the village he was delighted to bring them cocktails of his own design. They were currently engaged in a very early happy hour. Nebesa had a white telephone on a long cord and with it, Sergei was able to contact anyone they wanted or order anything they needed.

"Shouldn't you be out coordinating or something?" Siri asked Civilai.

"My role is decorative," said Civilai. "Not quite as decorative as General Suvan, who rarely knows what country he's in, but more like the US President, whose decisions are all made by somebody else. My only purpose is to take flack when something goes wrong. I just dress nicely and smile a lot. And what about you? Shouldn't you be tending to the injured and dying?"

"Brother, in this one complex they have more medical expertise than in the whole of Southeast Asia. If we were to fall down drunk there'd be an ambulance here in twenty seconds."

"We're on the eighth floor."

"A helicopter then. They'll hoist us out through the window and we'd be in rehab before we regained consciousness."

"Which reminds me, I think it's time you had a cup of coffee."

"You of all people are telling me to sober up?"

"Just a warning that for the next six hours you'll be observing our assassin. You have to relieve Dtui at six."

"Really? Whose idiotic idea was that?"

"Yours, Siri."

"Well, we found him easily enough at the orientation, false name and everything. What's he calling himself?"

"Nokasad."

"Can't we just phone their coordinator, Corporal . . ."

"Colonel Fah Hai."

"That's him. Can't we just phone him and tell him to keep an eye on our Sompoo alias Nokasad and let us know if he runs off and shoots someone?"

Civilai called over to Sergei, "Two strong black coffees please."

"Why are you having coffee?" said Siri.

"While you're hiding in a tree watching an assassin I shall be entertaining your wife."

"You cad."

"We can't leave her alone on her first night at the village. I shall take our two attractive administrators for dinner."

"You may have to wait a while for Daeng. She's having a facial."

"A what?"

"I know. I think my wife's been replaced by an alien. Turbans and fashionable clothes and makeup. If I were a psychologist I'd suggest she's crying out for help and I'd know what to do about it."

"Are you neglecting her—you know—in the nest?"

"Certainly not . . . and it's no business of yours what goes on in my nest."

The topic was curtailed with perfect timing by the arrival of a pageboy in a pale blue uniform. He jogged up to Sergei and handed him an envelope. The bar man brought it to Civilai.

"To Comrade Seeweela," he said.

"That's almost me," said Civilai and signed for the delivery. From the envelope he removed a very long telex message and started reading.

"I thought the point of a telex was its brevity," said Siri.

"Shh," said Civilai.

"Ah, there's a job for you at the mausoleum."

"Shit," said Civilai once he'd reached the end of the message. He told Siri about Phosy's meeting with the old man and the subsequent murder. The inspector was following up on the identity of the dead man. He also mentioned the suggestion that the intended victim might be a Lao or Vietnamese resident in Moscow. This was a scenario they hadn't considered.

"This isn't the most cosmopolitan city in the world," said Civilai. "I can't imagine there's a Vietnamese or Lao community here."

"And it's the last place on the planet the royalists would have fled to," said Siri. "But I suppose it's worth following up on."

"We need Roger," said Civilai and gestured for Sergei to bring the phone. "I have to go to the communications center and answer this telex," said Civilai, dialing the pager number he had for their guide. "I'll meet Roger there and see what he can do to find us a list of foreigners in Moscow. Dtui will call here just before six to tell you where she is so you can start your surveillance. If you're lucky our assassin will be attending the big pre-opening ceremony bash in the garden tonight like the rest of us."

Roger was still pumped up from the magic that had enlivened a language he'd studied alone in a tape laboratory. He was full of the stories he'd learned from his new Lao brothers and sisters that day. But Civilai had no time for stories.

"Roger," he said.

"Yes, uncle."

"How difficult would it be to get the names and nationalities of all the foreign residents in Moscow?"

"Not difficult at all," said Roger.

"Really? I thought Moscow was all about secrets and paranoia."

"Perhaps it was in the fifties and sixties," said Roger, "but it's not like that anymore. They dragged all the spies out from under the beds. In fact it's quite boring here. That's why the Games are so important. It gives us something fun to do. And this is the age of openness and honesty. There's a lot we can share."

"Really? Then why did you send all your students to distant provinces during the Games?"

"There are plenty of students at the village or volunteering around the venues," said Roger.

"Hand-picked to be sure they won't be expressing any anti-Soviet sentiments," said Civilai.

"There are no anti-Soviet sentiments," said Roger indignantly. "We've come to expect your generation to continue seeing a lot of half-empty cups, uncle. We don't blame you. You grew up in paranoid times."

"So if you asked for those names you wouldn't get into any trouble?"

Roger laughed. "There's an information booth downstairs, uncle. Their only purpose in life is to tell the athletes anything they want."

CHAPTER NINE
Great Kelly

The pre-opening ceremony party was more splendid than anything the Lao had ever experienced. There was a concert by a singer whose name was far too long to remember followed by live chamber music in the open air. There was unlimited finger food and, of course, drinks. There were fireworks and jugglers and tables with artisans showing traditional crafts. The athletes and officials from each country were dressed in their national costumes and languages became irrelevant. It was all about sparkle. So many flashbulbs popped it was like the opening night of a Hollywood movie.

"If you don't like it, just tell me," said Daeng.

"Of course I like it," said Siri for the umpteenth time.

They were walking arm in arm along the broad concrete pathway in the grounds of the village. They were smiling at strangers, humming along to the music they had no cultural allegiance to and remaining no more than twenty meters behind Sompoo the shooter, who strolled with his teammates.

"I mean, I can change it," said Daeng.

"No, really. It's grand," said Siri.

Madam Daeng had returned from the beauty salon that evening . . . a redhead. Perhaps "Fanta Orangehead" might describe the color better. Her hair, not yet long enough to cover her neck, had been teased into a hundred small springs that made her head look like a piano stool that had split open. She wore a mauve polyester trouser suit and heels that put her several centimeters above her husband. But, worst of all, she was hiding behind somebody else's face.

"There are women here with engineering degrees who specialize in cosmetics," she said. "Two of them work on your face at the same time. It's incredible that both halves look the same at the end of it."

"That's wonderful," said Siri. "Are you sure you wouldn't prefer me to take the late surveillance? I haven't really been overworked here."

"No," she said. "Why? I requested the late shift."

What he wanted to say was that he doubted she'd be able to blend into the surroundings given how colorful she'd become. But he decided to keep that to himself until he could determine what particular help she was crying out for.

By midnight few of the athletes had retired. They knew they'd be unable to sleep with all the excitement they'd felt on the first day at the village. The shooters were seated at picnic tables drinking. Sompoo was still with them. The military had put a ban on spirits but didn't consider lager to be alcohol. Only Sompoo drank lemonade.

At 6 A.M. Siri awoke with a scream having dreamed an African witchdoctor was leaning over him with a knife. He'd left the light on when he went to bed and it was actually Daeng whose nose was close to his.

"Nightmare?" she asked.

"Not exactly," said Siri.

"I handed over to Civilai," she said. "But the boys are all in their rooms sound asleep.

"Daeng?"

"Yes, love?"

"I miss you."

"I missed you too."

"No, Daeng," he said, propping himself up on the pillow. He'd decided during his spell of surveillance that honesty trumped diplomacy. "I mean I miss *you*."

"What are you saying?"

"Why are you doing this?"

"Doing what?"

"All this. The clothes, the shoes, the hair, the face mask. None of this is you."

"Oh, Siri. You don't want to be promenading around Moscow with a frumpy old lady in a *pha sin* skirt."

Siri took her hand. "Actually I do," he said. "I love my frumpy old lady in or out of her *pha sin* skirt. She's my beauty. Where did she go?"

He'd seen her cry twice in their time together and on one of those occasions she had a bullet in her. But a tear broke free of its waxy mascara blockade and rolled down her cheek. It drew an almost perfect vertical black line before disappearing under her chin. That, for Madam Daeng, was hysteria.

"Oh, Siri," she said. "I just want to make myself attractive for you."

"Then don't do all this," he said, wiping away the

mascara line with his thumb. "Attractive for me is the puffy
eyes I see when you wake up in the morning. It's the panic
when I walk into the bathroom without knocking and you
try to cover yourself with a face flannel. It's the smile you
share with me when you see a baby, the menace in your
glare before you attack someone, the feel of your hand
on my chest when you're checking that I'm still alive.
Nobody does that like you."

"But you fantasize about other women."

"I do not."

"Then what about Great?" she said.

"Great, what?"

"Your darling, Great Kelly."

At last it clicked.

"Daeng, surely you haven't been doing all this because
you were jealous of a Hollywood movie star?"

"You talked about her for a week, Siri. Great this.
Great that. How elegant she was. How she'd married
a prince. How she turned heads everywhere she went.
Dtui showed me a picture of her. How could an old Lao
girl compete with that? You said she was your perfect
woman."

Siri took her in his arms and held her more tightly than
ever before.

"Daeng, you are adorable," he said. "Thank you very
much for trying to make an old man happy. But this isn't
the way. Grace Kelly came up in conversation because Civilai and I were putting together a cast for the movie we'll
never make. It was a flight of fancy. I didn't say she was my
perfect woman. I said she was my perfect leading lady. You
walked in at the wrong moment. I wouldn't begin to know
what to do with her if she turned up on our doorstep. You

are far more attractive than she will ever be because she is fantasy and you, Daeng, are natural."

"Really?

"Usually. So I want you to go to the bathroom, shampoo those rosy piglets out of your hair, wash off the war paint, take off those noisy clothes and come back to bed *au naturel.* Then I'll show you what type of woman a man wants in his life."

They were awoken an hour later by a loud knocking at the door. Siri stayed in bed because he'd just performed the septuagenarian equivalent of an Olympic marathon so Daeng went to the door. She found Civilai standing in the hallway.

"I think I've made a mistake," he said.

The three sat at their en-suite kitchenette table with cups of tea and Civilai told them what had happened.

"When Daeng phoned me to take over her shift I closed my eyes briefly," he said. "When I opened them again half an hour had passed. I had no choice but to go and check that the shooters, in particular, our Comrade Sompoo, were still in their rooms. It was getting on for 7 A.M. and I thought they'd be having breakfast but I forgot they'd had a late night. When I got to the third floor the door to their apartment was ajar. It appeared they hadn't yet grasped the concept of security. I have a map of the athletes' sleeping arrangements so I knew that Sompoo shared a room with the youngest shooter, Boom. Their room was off to one side and Boom was there but Sompoo's bed was empty. There was nobody in the bathroom. I went to the balconies on either end of the corridor but he wasn't there having an early morning smoke. All I can think is that he was coming down in the elevator when I was going up. What should we do?"

Siri shrugged.

"Sit back and wait for news of an assassination," he said.

◎ ◎ ◎

From the dead soldier's ID card Phosy had learned that the old man's name was Pinit Saopeng and that he had spent most of his later military career as an undercover officer on secret missions originally with a clandestine guerrilla movement famously known as Group 959. Like Phosy, he had worked on covert operations during the French and American occupations and there wasn't exactly a library section the policeman could go to find information on such things. Even the Defense Ministry archives were classified. Phosy had requested any files that had been cleared by the security division but he knew he had little hope of putting all the pieces of Pinit's life together. He did, however, have an address.

The old man had described his home as a dog kennel but even dogs had views. The Party had shown its gratitude to Pinit by giving him a concrete box to see out his grey days. It was like a cell in a block of cells and the wall of the adjoining block was six centimeters from its louver window. There wasn't even enough of a gap for a breeze to negotiate its way in. He had a straw sleeping mat, an old Soviet fan, a transistor radio and a basic table and chair. The only thing out of place was a stack of books and magazines against the far wall. In 1980 Laos there was not a great deal of reading going on.

Beside the bed was Pinit's collection of *Pasason Lao*

newspapers. Phosy knew there'd be nothing learned there. The magazines were all Thai, mostly political and anti-communist. They were banned on the Lao side and not easy to come by. Phosy wondered whether Pinit had them merely as reading material to stimulate his old mind or if the old man had sympathies toward Thailand.

The books were more eclectic. There were a number of languages, none of which Phosy could understand. He spoke Lao and some Vietnamese and several hill tribe dialects but had no European language skills. He did recognize enough to know that some of the books were in English, Thai, German and Russian. And it was the Russian connection that interested him most. The day before, when Pinit had made the connection between the photo in the newspaper and the suspected assassin in Moscow, the old man had seemed . . . what was it? . . . relieved in some way. Perhaps he was glad that Phosy had been able to put a name to the rogue soldier. Did Pinit know a hit was planned over there? Was Phosy reading too much into his own instinct or did the old soldier know who the target was? Was that the reason he was silenced?

Phosy put the Russian books to one side. He'd have someone go through them later and write a synopsis for him. Thai and Lao were close enough that he could tell the Thai books were all fiction. A literate Lao had nowhere to go for reading pleasure in a bookless country. But the ministry bloodhounds would still have branded Pinit a subversive if they'd ever raided his room. At the bottom of the stack were four children's books in Russian. They were dated in the early 1940s, which suggested they meant something to the old soldier. One of them had a handwritten message inside the front cover. That too Phosy would have somebody translate.

The inspector looked inside the wonky wooden closet. From the rail hung one black civilian suit, one long-sleeved white shirt, one pair of camouflaged trousers and a light, waterproof jacket. Beneath these were socks and underwear and a pair of gloves. One pair of military boots stood to attention inside the door of the room. Nothing was new. Not a great reward for a lifetime's dedicated to the revolution.

As an investigator of many years' experience, Phosy had learned to look in all the places a man with something to hide might stash his secrets. There were no floorboards or ceiling panels, no desks with false bottoms. He went to the communal bathroom along the hall, looked in the cistern and the water tank and felt for loose tiles. They were all loose but hid nothing. Back in the room he walked one final circuit before collecting his books. He looked again at the view from the window. All he could see was non-rendered brickwork. He removed the louvers from the window frame one by one to get a better look at the wall. With no sun to bleach it, the grouting around the bricks was still grey all but for one area. Its frame was a lighter shade to all the others. He ran his finger along the edge of the bricks and sniffed at his finger.

Toothpaste.

"He might have gone for a jog," said Dtui.

"Or a walk on the roof," said Daeng. "Insomnia."

"Or he might have been out casing the scene of the shooting," said Siri.

"Or actually committing the crime," said Civilai, still feeling guilty for his failure.

The four were seated in the B block cafeteria with stodgy Soviet breakfasts in front of them. Two tables away sat the shooting team with Sompoo in the middle telling jokes.

"This really is a fine time for an assassination, you have to admit," said Siri. "The local TV stations have nothing but Olympic news and smiling citizen interviews. I can't even imagine a murder report finding its way into the newspapers for the next three weeks."

"We should still get Roger to check the papers just in case," said Daeng.

"Why are you so sure he's done something wrong?" said Dtui.

"And when did you join the 'innocent until proven guilty' camp?" Civilai asked.

"You know, I watched him for six hours at the shooting range yesterday," said Dtui. "He was friendly and relaxed. He was polite and dedicated. I didn't spot any homicidal tendencies."

"That's exactly why hired assassins are so successful," said Civilai. "They merge. They're the type about whom you say, 'I can't believe he was a killer.' They're calculated and calm under pressure. They don't wear T-shirts with their occupation printed on them."

"I doubt he'll do anything silly today," said Daeng. "The eyes of the world will be on us here. There'll be more security people on the streets than the country's ever seen before. It's a big day."

A big day it certainly was. After breakfast, everyone would be ferried to the central Lenin Stadium to prepare for the opening ceremony. They'd be participating in the greatest show on earth. The predictions were that it would be live on television in one and a half billion homes around the world and even the boycotting nations would see the highlights. America's NBC had paid eighty-seven million dollars for the coverage rights but North America would view no more than five minutes of Olympic news a day.

The Lao administrators were already in a froth, but the arrival of Roger cranked up the excitement tenfold. He was jumpier than a flea in a dandruff drift. He shook hands with everyone twice, pulled a spare chair from the next table and sat astride it with his elbows on the chair back.

"Not hungry?" he said, seeing the untouched plates of food on the table.

"It's delicious," said Dtui. "We're just a bit overexcited."

"I know. I know," said Roger. "Isn't it wonderful? Aren't we all doing a splendid job so far?"

"Splendid," said Civilai.

"You know how many people will be watching the ceremony?" Roger asked.

"We know," said Daeng.

"I don't suppose you had a chance to find me that list of foreigners?" said Siri.

"Oh, yes," said Roger and he produced a roll of paper from his inside blazer pocket. Like most Russian men he wore a shirt and tie that weren't really happy together. And they weren't on speaking terms at all with the jacket.

"Moscow is desperate to please," said Roger. "The research center claims it can answer any question the athletes ask with total candor. Anything—historical, political, cultural—all in record time. I showed them my official translator name card and within twenty minutes the printer was churning this out. Isn't it remarkable?"

◙ ◙ ◙

There were nine sheets in all and the font was small. Dtui and Daeng started to go through them.

"Not including tourists and business visas there are nine thousand and ninety names of long-term foreign residents in Moscow," said Roger. "Their status is marked beside the names. I've taken the liberty to underline all of the names I suspect are of Lao origin. That comes out around fifty. There are almost two hundred Vietnamese."

"Thanks," said Civilai. "That's a lot more than I'd expected. I think we should concentrate our limited resources on the Lao names. By the way, I don't suppose you listen to the radio of a morning?"

"Yes I do, uncle. Every morning."

"Anything interesting this morning?"

"These days it's mostly Olympic news," said Roger.

"Crime?"

"The Party's negated crime for the duration of the Games," said Roger with a smile. "They've sent all the drunks and addicts up country for a bit of a vacation. The hardened criminals are helping police with their inquiries for the next three weeks."

"So no murders on the radio?" Siri asked.

"Didn't mention any."

"Splendid," said Civilai.

"All right," said Daeng. "A lot of these names are connected to the embassy or trade delegation. Most are students. Then there are one or two with dubious spelling that we aren't sure about. So I suggest we send the whole list to Phosy."

"He can only research the Lao names," said Siri. "And

time's limited. I don't think we have the resources to check out the Vietnamese."

"Roger," said Civilai, "do you suppose your research department might be able to find more detailed information about all the Lao names on this list?"

"Actually they seemed quite bored," said Roger. "I'm sure they'll be delighted."

The clock struck four and a hundred trumpeters blasted forth a fanfare that was soon to be drowned out by the Soviet Anthem. Greek warriors and goddesses in blond wigs carried the Olympic flag of rings on foot into the Central Lenin Stadium with chariots in close pursuit. The Lao could only watch this on TV screens beneath the terraces because it was not yet their turn to perform. They were aquiver with nerves. All they had to do was walk; something they'd done without mishap since they were toddlers, but as they waited all the possible missteps came to their minds.

General Suvan, the senior Party representative, was petrified to the point that he decided he wasn't up to carrying the Lao flag.

"Look at my hands," he said. "Can't keep 'em still. I'm going to drop the bloody thing in front of a billion people."

So it was Civilai himself who took the pole position, although he wished he'd had the foresight to go to the bathroom beforehand. At the sound of a whistle, the Lao People's Democratic Republic made for the entrance ahead of Lesotho. It was probably the only time they'd lead anyone for the next fifteen days. At last they stepped into the late afternoon sunshine. It was like entering a new solar system. Cameras flashed and 103,000 voices rose to a deafening roar. Siri and Daeng had seen more than most but had never witnessed anything like it. Even the thought of preventing an assassination paled to a colorless irrelevance beneath the euphoria. They walked on unsteady legs around the track, waving and blowing kisses. They'd had seconds of fame here and there but this was their full five minutes.

When the countries were corralled at the center of the stadium the speeches began. Siri rolled his eyes. In Laos they'd be spending the next hour pacing on the spot praying for an end to the interminable dross. But he was pleasantly surprised. The Games chief organizer, the chairman of the Olympic Committee and the General Secretary of the Central Committee of the Communist Party of the Soviet Union all kept their remarks brief and the whole thing was over in five minutes. The crowd roared its approval and even President Brezhnev applauded himself for his brevity. The flag was raised and an unnaturally fit torch-bearer ran up an almost vertical ramp to light the flame. Several thousand birds were released and although a number may have been roasted in the fire it was agreed they'd bravely gone up in smoke for the motherland.

Two cosmonauts sent their good wishes via a live feed from space, which was probably the moment that extended Siri and Daeng's disbelief to its limit. From then on they could only have been in a hypnotic trance. The athletes were shepherded to the stands and several thousand dancers and singers and contortionists moved in to put on a most remarkable exhibition. Daeng reminded Siri of the trouble they'd had at the youth camps getting twelve children to march in step. Yet here were thousands of bodies moving as one, forming human blancmanges, defying gravity. Layer upon layer of men and women piled like psychedelic multi-story sea anemones. 8,400 Cossack warriors throwing their Cossack girlfriends into the air and, fortunately, catching them again. Then a lake of impossibly pretty blonde girls ebbed and flowed across the playing field. It was unimaginable that such a thing could be achieved by obedient performers under the guidance of a patient choreographer. Comrade Marx and Comrade Lenin could only have fantasized about such coordination.

"Let the Games begin," someone said.

CHAPTER TEN
Luxury Penthouse, Armed Guard, French Maid

Research showed that the speed of the average filing clerk in Laos was only slightly faster than the movement of an ice shelf at the South Pole. So rather than tempt fate by handing his list to a police department bureaucrat, Phosy decided to take it to the Good Luck restaurant the next morning. Given the occurrence at his previous visit he expected the old soldiers to clam up when they saw him but on the contrary the killing had reanimated some long-forgotten lust for life. They were more vocal than at his first meeting with them. Even more old soldiers had gathered there that morning to drink coffee and to toast one more fallen comrade.

When Phosy took out his lists it was like a feeding frenzy. The old men formed groups and had one member read out the names while the others made comments. Even if they'd never met the characters living in Moscow they'd recognize the surname and talk about the families. Many of the names were of relatives of the Central Committee who'd been sent away to study. There were comments about the unreliability of embassy officials and about the good fortune of old friends who were on a healthy Soviet *per diem*. But there was one name that seemed to stick in the craw of many of the patriots.

"Can I take back my request to shoot Thatcher and shoot this one instead?" said the same old flaky gentleman pointing at the name. "That's the one that's going to bring us all down."

It was never easy to separate fact from fiction at such a gathering but the consensus was that Manoi Zakarine, the eldest son of Thonglai Zakarine, was the most likely to be attracting unwanted attention. He was being groomed for a leading role in the Lao politburo. He'd been sent to the Soviet Union as a teenager and studied through high school to university level. He was currently a year into a PhD in political science, which he was studying in the Russian language. Undoubtedly he was a brilliant student and everyone agreed he would make a fine leader—but for one thing. He was vehemently anti-Vietnamese. Of course it would have been political suicide for Manoi to admit such a thing but the rumors were rife.

Every man at the Good Luck had been trained by the Vietnamese. They'd fought alongside Vietnamese troops. Even today, five years after the revolution, there were still forty thousand People's Army of Vietnam troops stationed on Lao soil. Every ministry, every department had its own Vietnamese adviser channelling Vietnamese policy into the Lao system. Every member of the politburo had deep, sometimes familial connections to Vietnam. Expressing doubts about Vietnamese integrity was probably not the wisest of career moves.

Manoi's father, Thonglai, was one of the Lao businessmen who had survived the coup. He had been generous to the Pathet Lao and had been invited to advise the cabinet on such issues as investment and business endeavors. When the government first admitted it was driving the country into bankruptcy it was Thonglai who established the first government/private sector joint ventures. And it was Thonglai who steered that sinking ship back into the black. Laos still struggled but Thonglai became more powerful.

He was the economic guru for all the top politburo men but he was a patriot. Laos was in his family bloodline back through generations beyond King Zakarine of Luang Prabang. He openly resented the fact that the French had brought in Vietnamese to run the country, that Vietnamese children had been given priority to study to high school level ahead of the Lao, that the Lao revolution to oust the French oppressors had been credited solely to the Vietnamese. But he was a patient man. He had three sons. One he sent to France to study, one to the USA and one, Manoi, to the Soviet Union. The first two sons had fallen out of love with their country of birth and established ties in the West. Each had excelled in his studies but only Manoi had carried his father's nationalism. Most agreed it was he who would be the flag-bearer for Lao autonomy. He would be the true Lao savior.

"Yeah, he's the one I'd shoot too," said Trench Coat.

"But why?" said Phosy. "Aren't you all patriots?"

"To the death," said Lenin Cap. "But we're afraid what might happen if we dissociate ourselves from our closest allies. We owe everything we have to them. It's only that relationship that stops China invading us."

"That's right," shouted some of the others.

So Phosy had his candidate for assassination in Moscow:

Manoi, the son of Thonglai the patriot. Now he needed to find a connection to dead Pinit Saopeng, the old soldier.

Behind the bricks opposite the old man's window, Phosy had found forty thousand US dollars in large bills wrapped in plastic. But the old man was hardly living a lifestyle that type of money could buy. Phosy had learned from the files that Pinit Saopeng had retired from military service in '75 and from there on there was no trace. He hoped the old boys at the Good Luck might fill in some of the gaps.

"What kind of man was Pinit Saopeng?" he asked nobody in particular.

Heads looked left and right but nobody answered.

"We were hoping you might be able to tell us," said Flaky.

"Secretive, was he?" said Phosy.

"No idea," said Mint, the owner.

"Come on," said Phosy. "You drank coffee with the fellow every morning. Surely you got to know something about him."

"Who drank coffee with him?" said Trench Coat. "We'd never seen him before you turned up. We thought he must have come with you."

❏ ❏ ❏

There are events that you can't stop talking about and others that you don't know how to start. And perhaps that was why the atmosphere on the bus back to the Olympic Village was so subdued that very early morning. The athletes and officials had taken part in something remarkable. Even the most cynical of viewers in front of their TVs

in Tokyo and Toronto would have to admit there had been
no Olympic Ceremony to match it.

Daeng held onto Siri's arm and couldn't wipe the smile
from her face nor calm the wag of her tail.

"Thank you for not disappearing," she said.

"That would have been a hell of a trick, wouldn't it?"
said her husband. "I doubt they'd be able to top that even
in Los Angeles in '84."

"I feel sorry for anyone who has to compete today,"
said Daeng. "I'm drained. I doubt I'll even make it to
breakfast."

"I could use a bed myself, but . . ."

As he no longer trusted Civilai to stay awake, Siri had
agreed to take the 12 P.M. to 6 A.M. surveillance shift. But
post-ceremony euphoria had dragged on in the stadium
and it was already well after midnight when they arrived
at the village. They watched Sompoo step drowsily from
the bus and, like everyone else, head directly to the dormitory block. Siri stopped in the foyer and kissed his wife
goodnight.

"You know, Daeng," he said. "there's only one thing
everyone watching the show today will agree on."

"And what's that?"

He took a step back and admired her glossy chignon
hair extension with its simple silver tiara, her silk blouse,
her heirloom blue *pha sin* skirt and her neat leather sandals. The mound of her tail was barely noticeable and her
face was scrubbed and glowing.

"That of all the thousands of beautiful women in the
stadium yesterday, none was as beautiful as you," he said.

Daeng put her hands together in a slow, sensual *nop* and
lowered her head. His original Madam Daeng was back.

Once alone, Siri went to the vending machine, realized he didn't have any tokens but didn't dare desert his post to get some. So he sat in the least comfortable chair and spent his next four hours making up Lao country song lyrics in his head.

Phosy sat in his police dormitory room watching his daughter sleep. Not for the first time he considered how little he knew or understood about the society he lived in. Pinit, the dead soldier, had turned up at the Good Luck for the first time on the day Phosy had chosen to go there. The suggested location had come in one of Civilai's telexes and Phosy had written back to say he would go there the following morning. The police department had a telex machine operated by a young lady who, supposedly, couldn't read western script. Phosy wasn't that hot on it either. He'd take the telexes to Inthanet, the puppet master who lived in Siri's house. Inthanet would translate them into Lao and write the reply in French. Apart from the possibility that Pinit's turning up at the Good Luck was an amazing coincidence—which Phosy dismissed immediately—there were three ways that anyone would know of Phosy's intentions. First was the chance that the telex girl allowed someone else to read the messages before passing them on to Phosy. Second was the scant possibility that Inthanet passed on the information to a third party. As Phosy put much faith in friendship he didn't want to give that likelihood much credence. Third was the possibility that someone in Moscow was intercepting the messages. That was his suspicion but it was a problem he couldn't address until the following day.

He then moved on to motive. Why was old Pinit at the

Good Luck? This he whittled down to two possibilities. One, that the soldier was there to find out what the police knew about the "loose cannon" in Moscow. If Phosy was getting too close there was a chance he'd be taken out of the equation. Someone had gone to a lot of trouble to get Sompoo to Russia. They wouldn't want an overenthusiastic cop spoiling all that preparation. So, that could mean the two bullets were intended for Phosy. That the sniper was just a lousy shot?

The second option was that Pinit had planned to meet with Phosy after the breakfast meeting and tell him what he knew. He'd started to talk when the bullets shut him up. But then again it was Phosy who'd approached Pinit, not the other way round. What if someone else had got wind of Pinit's intention and put two bullets in him to silence him? They'd analysed the bullets and found they came from an American M40, probably left over from the war. That was not a weapon for poachers or lucky border guards. Someone with a gun that serious shouldn't miss twice.

Then there was the room and the money. Had the old man intended to take him there and offer him a bribe to turn a blind eye to what he'd learned? Or was that just wishful thinking on Phosy's part? Forty thousand dollars could buy a nice life for Phosy, Dtui, and Malee. They could go overseas. Take jobs that didn't involve getting shot at. Open that cake shop in . . . He dragged his thoughts back to the room. Did the old man actually live there? The signs of habitation were scant, almost stage-managed. Was Phosy being encouraged to study the piles of reading material looking for hidden meanings? Was it all intended to tie him and his investigation in knots? Or was there really something there? The policeman regretted the absence of his think tank. So many of his cases had been solved by bouncing ideas off Dtui and Daeng and the two old codgers.

Malee farted then laughed in her sleep. She did it often. She was a born entertainer.

Phosy looked at the summary of the Russian language books he'd found in the old soldier's room. Two were basic Marxist-Leninist ideology. Three were technical: mechanics, electronics, water management. One was on first aid and there was a Lao–Russian dictionary, something Phosy had never seen before. It was unusual to find Lao characters in a book of such quality, or in any book at all for that matter. Of the four illustrated children's books there was one with an inscription in Russian inside the front cover.

To Bébé with love from Daddy. Don't forget me.

It was an odd thing to write to a child. It was as if the writer was absent or planned to be. Phosy leaned over his sleeping daughter and whispered in her ear.

"Don't worry, sweetheart. I'm not going anywhere."

◎   ◎   ◎

Sunday was a full day of events at the Games. Buses and limousines and diesel road trains shuttled the competitors from the village to their respective events. Each country had its own pool of vehicles but the drivers were instructed to give rides to anyone with an official name tag as long as they had room. Civilai had drawn the day shift and would accompany the marksmen to the Dynamo Shooting Range some fifty kilometers away in Mytishchy. They'd be there the whole day so it shouldn't be difficult to keep an eye on Sompoo.

As the other Lao competitors' events wouldn't begin

until the following day, Dtui and Daeng thought it would be fun to go to the boxing arena at the Olympiisky Indoor Stadium and admire world-class pectorals and abdominals. They were a little disappointed when they discovered Olympic boxers wore vests.

Once Siri had slept off his shift in a comfortable bed, he jotted down the various tasks he had to perform. First he would go to the Communication Center at the post office and pick up Phosy's daily telex. At coffee time he had an appointment with Roger at the Nebesa Milk Nook. This, he thought, might be followed by a sauna, a leisurely lunch with wine and a film or two at the cinema. There were no Lao performing that day so he didn't feel unpatriotic for having such thoughts. And the first feature film of the afternoon would be *Distant Journey*, a Czech film made in 1950 and directed by Alfréd Radok. He'd never heard of it. He wouldn't be able to understand the dialogue or read the English subtitles but he considered himself fluent in the intrinsic language of cinema. He and Civilai had discovered that particular voice in their study days in Paris and had been hooked ever since. They could have easily forgotten the Games and spent the entire week in a dark air-conditioned room watching the magic of cinematic genius.

Two telexes to Civilai had arrived from Laos. He and Siri had exchanged nametags so the doctor could collect them. The charmingly efficient clerk in baby blue fatigues looked at the name on the tag, compared it with the name on the telexes and didn't even bother to look up into the eerie green eyes of the little Asian man in front of her. Siri sat on one of the many overstuffed armchairs and read the messages. He circled the name of the PhD student in

Moscow and underlined a few pertinent statements. He went back immediately to the clerk to send his reply.

"Thank you, Comrade Seaweedeye," she said.

◙   ◙   ◙

Roger seemed a little upset not to be with the Olympians on the battlefield but he'd been assigned to take instructions from the Lao administrators so his smile never faltered. He had brought with him a roll of papers not much thicker than the original list.

"I'm so sorry, uncle," he said. "It seems the best the research department can do is provide the addresses and phone numbers. They suggested that handing over private information would be an invasion of privacy. But I get the feeling all the interesting stuff will be in a file at the Kremlin."

"So much for the new age of openness," said Siri.

"We wouldn't want the KGB to be unemployed, would we now?" said Roger.

Siri went directly to the name of Manoi Zakarine on the new list. There were two phone numbers and two addresses beside his name. They were written in Russian.

"Why would this fellow have two addresses?" asked Siri.

Roger took the list. "Ah," he said. "One is a student residence out near the People's Friendship University."

"He shares a dormitory room?"

"It's a sort of apartment building near campus. Students have that option if they can afford it."

"So the boy has money."

"It would appear so."

"And this other address?"

"Now this used to be a very exclusive address in the center of Moscow. Most of the apartments belong to the descendents of influential people. The rooms would be passed down through generations. A foreigner wouldn't be able to buy or rent such a place. It's a short walk from the river. If we were allowed a commercial real estate market it would be the equivalent of a building with a view of Central Park in New York."

"Then how can he list this as his address?"

"It would have to be a sort of loan, I suppose. The owner would allow someone to live in their apartment, perhaps while they're overseas or working officially in another province."

"But he would have been there long enough to list it as one of his official residences."

"Perhaps a favor from a friend?"

"Or a friend of the father," said Siri, recalling the information in Phosy's telex. Of course, Siri had met the old tycoon. He'd found little to like. The man would happily jump into bed with any faction, creed or religion if he thought there was a few million kip to be made. He was fickle even on a personal level and Siri doubted the tadpole had wriggled very far from the toad. Money passed down through the blood of generations. But Siri was open-minded enough to give Comrade Thonglai Zakarine's son a chance.

"Sergei," he shouted and signaled for the telephone.

Dtui and Daeng had enjoyed their morning at the boxing arena. It was a vast hall with seats that went so far back you could barely make out the number of boxers in the ring. To offset the distance there were huge screens that showed the action live at ten times its normal size. They sat with some of the runners and the Lao boxing team who had nothing to do that day but be mesmerized. The thought that later that week they'd be down there in the ring with the world's TV cameras trained on them would keep them awake at night. They were in awe of the skills of the boxers on display, all that is but conceited Maen.

"I can win this," he said.

His teammates mocked him playfully because they weren't bright enough to realize he was being serious.

"The only thing that can stop me beating the Jordanian is if they pay off the judges," he said. Daeng and Dtui had stopped listening to him long before. At the end of one fight, Dtui turned around to talk to Chom the rat catcher in the seat behind her.

"How's your Botswana friend?" she asked.

"Sammy? We only get to understand each other when Roger's around. But we compare notes through drawings and hand gestures. Personally from a professional point of view, I think he's a slave to technology. Far too reliant on gadgets."

"What do you use?"

"Stealth," he said, with a perfectly straight face.

Dtui held back a laugh. "Stealth?" she said.

"Study the enemy. Learn their weaknesses. Allow them to defeat themselves."

"I see," said Dtui.

"It's worked for me and my family for three generations. Back then it was for sustenance. Used to be plenty of good meat on a rat back then."

"Really?" said Dtui.

"They taste a lot like deer."

"I see."

"But with all the chemicals people put down you aren't brave enough to chance eating one these days."

"That's a shame."

"And then there's the Rat's Piss Fever," said Chom. "A lot of places seem to have that back home. That can kill you. Don't know if they have that here. We're looking forward to discussing it with Yusov."

"Yusov?"

"He's the vermin eradication officer for District eight, right here in Moscow near the village. Roger arranged it. I wouldn't be at all surprised if I can pick up a few tips to take home with me."

"I'm happy for you," said Dtui.

Conceited Maen was boasting about some dynamite-bodied blonde discus thrower he'd met after breakfast. He was deciding whether to keep the appointment they'd made or work on the cocktail waitress who'd slipped him her phone number the night before.

Dtui and Daeng decided to move on to some other event. They'd had enough of he-men. They were fine when you admired their oiled biceps from a distance but the closer you got the more you had to listen to them. And that was invariably a turn-off in anyone's book.

◙ ◙ ◙

Siri had sat spellbound through *Distant Journey* but had foregone the pleasure of watching *The Childhood of Maxim Gorky* because he had an appointment. He didn't have to take public transport. He could have clicked his fingers and a limousine with an attentive driver would have carried him off to anywhere on the planet. But after only two days at the village the service overkill was already getting to him. He'd become conscious of the force field around the village that kept depression out. The swanky department store and burger stands might have fooled most of the athletes but not a seasoned socialist like Siri. So instead he took the beautiful metro to Park Kultury and walked the rest of the way. The Royal Palace in Luang Prabang wouldn't have made it onto the short list of metro station design excellence in Moscow. He wondered how long a chandelier might last in a Lao bus station.

The block which housed Manoi's city apartment was only three stories. A height considered a waste of space in the rapid age of development. It probably dated back to the rebuilding boom after the great fire of Moscow in 1812. Roger had insisted there were no longer any elite districts and no exclusive buildings; that a toilet cleaner would have as much right to live there as a concert pianist. But, as apartments were passed down through generations, that would only work if the toilet cleaner's ancestors had been lucky with the lottery.

Siri leaned against the heavy glass doors and found himself in a small foyer with a deep carpet. The decorations were every bit as ancient and fussy as the old lady seated behind a large desk. Her motorcycle helmet hairstyle had been rinsed pink. An ornate plaque in front of her probably described her occupation but Siri couldn't read it. She spoke into a clunky walky-talky handset and even before he gave the name of the man he'd come to see, the woman had held up three fingers and pointed to the lift. It was a small cage, the type they used to lock up the criminally insane in France. Despite the poor state of his lungs Siri opted for the stairs. He stopped on the first two landings to catch his breath. He was planning to do the same on the third floor but instead he looked up to see a solid hunk of a man with tattoos. One was the outline of a cobra squirming from one wrist to the other. He was likely of Asian descent but everything else about him said Russian bouncer.

"Siri?" he said.

"Yes," said Siri.

When Siri reached the top step the man gestured for him to raise his arms. It was a very thorough frisking. When it was over, the bouncer nodded to the open apartment door. As he passed the man, Siri noticed a bulge in the back of his belt that probably wasn't a tail.

Manoi had perfectly timed his walk to meet Siri in the hallway. He shook the doctor's hand with two of his own; the politician's shake.

"Dr. Siri," he said. "I'm honored."

Manoi was the type of twenty-seven-year-old who was already on the threshold of middle age. He was overweight with a chin for each decade he'd lived. His hairline was retreating, his eyes were puffy, and his nose was latticed with veins. He was clearly an abuser of himself.

"Comrade Manoi?" said Siri. "I wasn't expecting you to know who I was."

"Are you mad, man?" said the youngster. "It isn't every day a national hero phones to make an appointment. My father talks about you often."

"Really?" said Siri, trying hard to retrieve his hand. If the father ever did mention his name, Siri was sure it would have been in a negative context.

"Absolutely," said Manoi. "I'm flattered to be receiving delegations from the Olympic team. Please, come this way."

The apartment was more spacious than most Vientiane markets. Manoi led him through a series of museum-like spaces, pointing out this and that famous artefact. They arrived at a comparatively small room with an enormous television on one side. It was naturally tuned to the Olympics. The picture window offered up a partial view of the trees that lined the river and the city beyond. A European woman in a French maid uniform stood to one side. She was attractive but heavily made up and not at all friendly. Manoi sat on a velvet sofa and Siri joined him. On the granite-topped coffee table sat two glasses containing a clear liquid. Manoi hoisted one, Siri the other.

"This," said Manoi, "is probably the most delicious vodka one can buy, yet it costs nothing. It's Stolichnaya. Only Russians know how to make vodka."

"It seems a shame to waste it on such an old man," said Siri.

"It will make you live forever," said Manoi.

All Siri could think of was the scene in *Arsenic and Old Lace* where the lonely old man is killed with a poisoned drink. Nobody knew where Siri was. He could disappear in the crime novel sense of the word and nobody would be any the wiser. There was no time to switch glasses so he knocked back the inexpensive vodka and survived.

"That's astounding," he said.

"Can't get better," said Manoi.

There were a few minutes of small talk about life in Moscow and conditions back in Laos, of the Olympic team and their chances. But Manoi hurried it through so he could get to his question.

"Why did you want to see me?" he asked.

Siri had planned a lot of lies in anticipation of that question; as a courtesy visit on behalf of the Lao Olympic

Committee, as research to get a feel for the life of a Lao student in the Soviet Union, as a potential business venture. Everything had depended on the impression Siri gained in the first ten minutes. Things had not gone according to his expectations. He'd imagined a cocky but confused youth squatting in a friend's apartment, living on a modest stipend until he graduated. No luxury penthouse, no armed guard, no French maid.

"There are rumors back home that somebody in Moscow wishes you ill," he said.

The young man didn't seem at all concerned. He held up the two glasses for the maid to refill.

"It's 1980," he said. "Have our countrymen still not reached a level of maturity at which they no longer listen to rumors?"

Siri considered that comment to have been directed at him.

"I'm afraid not. The committee felt it was a credible enough threat to ask me to come to see you."

"Any names or dates?"

That was Siri's moment. That's when he should have given the shooter's name and let the man sort it all out for himself. But there was something about the situation that made him fear, not for the life of the student, but of the assassin.

"Well, comrade," said Siri. "You know what rumors are like. Nobody wants to commit themselves to a name."

They waited for the second glass to be filled before Manoi said, "Exactly. But I want you to tell the committee that I am grateful they should be concerned for my safety. And I especially appreciate you coming here this evening. I feel more than ever the love and kinship of my brothers and sisters across the globe. We will never be intimidated by external threats because the Lao heart beats more strongly than that of any of her foes. To Laos."

They threw back their drinks and Manoi stood to signal it was time for his visitor to leave.

CHAPTER ELEVEN
It's How You Play the Game

Sompoo was scheduled to compete in the small bore rifle event in the morning of day three. Following advice from the Red Army minders, shooters would be confined to barracks the night before their event. Colonel Fah Hai didn't actually lock his soldiers in their rooms but he did order them not to leave and he checked on them from time to time. They ate their evening meals in their room kitchens. Fah Hai had gone to the Nebesa Milk Nook to explain this to Civilai. The old politburo man took the opportunity of this rare encounter to once again bring up the matter of the discrepancy in the shooter's names.

"It was a last-minute thing," said Fah Hai. "There was nothing we could do. The major was taken ill at Wattay Airport and our first reserve was there for such an eventuality. Of course we didn't have time to change the passenger manifest or the names on the list of participants. But you'll see the problem has been sorted out and we have his correct name on the Games' register."

Civilai knew the major hadn't been taken ill. He'd been taken out. And the name on the register was not Sompoo.

"Are you sure you've got his name right this time?"

"What do you mean?"

"Just checking. I am the team manager, you know."

"I know."

"Then why didn't you explain all this to me on the flight here?"

"I wasn't made aware of the change myself until after we got here," said the soldier.

"And why are you only telling me now?" Civilai asked. "We've been here for two weeks."

"With respect, comrade, this was an administrative matter that I dealt with directly through Soviet military channels. As your position is somewhat . . . ornamental I didn't see it necessary to trouble you."

Civilai had reached his limit. "Lad," he said, "did you notice the flag I was carrying yesterday?"

"Of course."

"Well, as long as you march behind the colors of our country and as long as I am the representative of that country you will tell me everything, no matter how troubling you might consider it to be. Is that clear?"

The colonel put on a stony face, saluted but said nothing.

"So the assassin is officially shooting under a false name," said Daeng.

"So it seems," said Civilai. "I'm sure we're breaking all kinds of laws and rules."

"But the name had to check out," said Siri. "Everything would have to match—the passport, the personal ID card, the Games pass. Someone's gone to a lot of trouble."

"I suppose the same people who stopped Major Lien from getting on the flight could have stolen the documents of the first reserve," said Daeng. "Then all they'd need to do is change the photo."

They were at their regular table in the Nebesa. Sergei had offered to make them cocktails but they'd settled on vodka over ice. This was work.

"The important thing is that they know that we know," said Siri.

"Who are they?" said Dtui.

"That's what we don't know," said Civilai. "But we do know they're monitoring our telexes."

"How do we know that?"

"Phosy's last telex sent regards to Comrade Daeng," he said.

"So?"

"It's one our codes," said Daeng. "He never calls me 'comrade.' It means our communication is being compromised."

"You and Phosy have codes?" said Dtui.

"Not many," said Siri. "We tend to forget them."

"Amazing how little a husband and wife know about each other," said the nurse.

"Dtui, it's not an affair," said Siri. "It's just a few little tricks we put together when we were on the trip up north last year. But the point is that someone's been reading our telexes. Everything we've shared with Phosy and everything he's told us are now general knowledge."

"Have we completely abandoned the possibility that the cousin misidentified the photo in the newspaper, that Sompoo is actually just a substitute, and that there is no planned assassination attempt?" asked Dtui.

"The colonel lied about Major Lien's being sick," said Siri.

"Less embarrassing than saying he was arrested for racketeering," said Dtui.

"Yes, Dtui, you're right," said Siri. "All of that is possible. But the fact remains that someone is reading our telexes and that has probably led to an incident in Vientiane that left a man dead. Even if everything else is of our own imagination we still need to find out what it is we're onto that's making everyone so jumpy."

"Then if we're putting together theories, what about this?" said Dtui. "What if someone else in the shooting squad is the assassin? What if they saw Major Lien at the airport and recognized him, or thought that Lien might recognize the assassin? What if he arranged with his people to get the major bumped from the flight and bring in the reserve? That would mean the reserve, Sompoo, is innocent and somebody else is planning a murder."

Everyone sipped their vodka.

"Damn," said Daeng.

"Didn't think of that," said Civilai.

"But that would mean . . ." Daeng began.

"We'd have to follow everyone on the shooting team," said Siri. "And as there are seven of them and four of us I think we'd be better off enjoying the entertainment and forgetting all about it."

They refilled their glasses, snacked on their free herring on toast and looked through the large window at the horrendously beautiful tower blocks all around them alive with electric lighting.

"I went to visit Manoi Zakarine," said Siri.

All eyes fell on him.

"You did what?" said Daeng.

"I got his address from Roger and went to say hello."

"You said you went to the cinema," said Daeng.

"And so I did," said Siri. "I went after the show."

"You really are a maniac," said Daeng, and pecked him on the cheek.

"Thank you."

For the next fifteen minutes he described his odd house call.

"Wow," said Dtui.

"And a French maid to boot," said Civilai.

"The uniform was French," said Siri. "She could have come from anywhere. But the point is he's living a very privileged lifestyle in Moscow, presumably on his father's money."

"The Soviets wouldn't tolerate it unless they were sure he'd be useful for them in the future," said Civilai. "It looks like they're nurturing a potential president."

"He's already behaving like one," said Daeng.

"And it seems he's confident in his own invulnerability," said Siri. "He didn't shed an eyelash when I said somebody might be after him."

"Then we've done our duty," said Civilai. "We've warned the target, we can't watch all the potential assassins, and we have an Olympic Games to participate in. So as there's nothing else to be done I suggest we order another bottle, relax and stop looking for problems."

"What about Phosy?" said Dtui.

"Ah, yes," said Siri. "That's another matter. We've dragged him into something unpleasant back home, that's for sure. I suggest the first thing we do is discover whether the security leak is at our end or his."

"How do we do that?" she asked.

"Find Roger," he said.

Phosy's method of testing the police department for leaks was simple. He had the telex girl transferred to the canteen and brought in his own Sergeant Sihot to man the telex. He then arranged for another old friend, Seksan at the abandoned French embassy, to act as translator. If the leaks continued he'd know they were at the other end.

The money continued to worry him. Yes, he'd thought about that money a lot. Forty thousand dollars sat locked in the drawer of his desk. He hadn't yet reported it. He feared that as soon as it became the property of the state it would lose its appeal as evidence and become someone's travel expenses. Wealth annoyed him. He was angry that influence and power often existed only as a result of the amount of money a man had. He lived in a country where the majority of the population had no ambitions for wealth or power. Their prayers to the respective gods and spirits were not that they might become rich but that their children might be free from disease and have enough to eat.

The money in his desk was more than any of them would see in a lifetime and it was unfair that someone might consider it a fee. For no particular reason, he'd got it fixed in his mind that the forty grand was put aside to pay somebody off. Very few people in Laos would have that kind of cash to pay for any legitimate service. As money attracted money he decided to step into the inner circle of the unusually wealthy. He went to the telephone office and dialed the number for Grassroots Joint Venture Company Limited. A secretary answered and he asked to speak to Comrade Thonglai Zakarine. The secretary asked who he was and he gave his name and rank. She suggested the director might be able to fit him in the following Tuesday.

Phosy laughed.

"That's a terrible shame," he said, "because I'm on my

way to your office right now on police business. I'd sooner speak to your director but if he isn't available I'll interview the employees one by one, starting with you. We're short staffed here so it might take a few days to get around to everyone. I hope that won't interfere with your day-to-day business. And, before you ask, yes, I have a stamp of permission from my superior because I'm investigating a murder."

He hung up without waiting for a reply and sighed. There was nothing at all to connect the Zakarine family with events in Moscow or the murder of the old soldier. Everything hinged on the opinions of a group of old patriots who drank coffee together and had a problem with rich and influential folk. If Phosy ever did put in a request for a warrant he knew with certainty that it would be refused. Some individuals were politically inaccessible. But, regardless, he climbed on his lilac Vespa and headed out to Tanaleng. He was already way out of his depth.

Apart from one as-yet-unreported murder, day three at the Olympics went rather well. Over breakfast, Roger solved the mystery of the leaked telexes.

"It's nothing sinister," he said, enjoying a runny fried egg with puffy white bread. "If someone phones home, a record of the call, the time, duration, and called number is sent to the National Olympic Committee of the respective country as a courtesy. Or perhaps it's to show the participating country how generous we are to provide free telecommunication services. In the case of a telex, the official merely prints out a copy and sends it to your chairman."

"Otherwise known as General Suvan," said Siri.

"Exactly," said Roger.

They knew the general's habits only too well. He was notoriously untidy. He'd leave all that unfathomable printed data lying around, since he'd have no idea what to do with it. When the piles got too high he'd throw them in the trash. And then there was his issue with "companion-ship." Wherever he traveled he had an open door policy. All the Lao competitors were obliged to pay him regular visits at his suite. He was particularly fond of young men, although there was no evidence that this partiality was of a sexual nature. He adopted young people and had them make his tea or run errands for him. So every man and woman in the Lao squad and any number of outsiders would have had access to Civilai's telexes. It was time to fall back on the telephone.

There were two Lao boxers in action on day three. Dtui, Daeng, the other boxers, the runners and the walker returned to the Olympiisky arena to cheer them on. And their enthusiasm was contagious. The first fighter was Prathip, a light flyweight who wore his tem-ple tattoos proudly. The Lao cheered his every punch, inciting others in the audience to join in. As Marx had apparently said, "it's how you play the game," and Prathip bowed out with dignity. His smile earned him a particularly loud cheer as he left the ring, delighted it was all over.

Before the second Lao took to the ring, they had to withstand a blow-by-blow account of conceited Maen's seduction of a beautiful blonde Russian the night before. They had to listen to Chom the rat catcher's disappoint-ment about his meeting with Yusov the Soviet vermin eradication officer, who seemed far too dependent on poison and wasn't prepared to give any advice to the two Olympic rat catchers. In fact he wasn't a very likeable character.

The second fighter, Khampet, was the light welter-weight and the eldest man in the squad. He lasted far into the second round, which was every bit as good as winning the world title. The Lao were on their feet screaming even when the referee lifted the hand of the winner. Khampet had come second and his supporters wanted the world to know how great that was.

Civilai was at the shooting range in Mytishchy, not to tail an assassin but because everyone else had opted to watch the boxers and he felt obliged to give support to the shooters. Sompoo, shooting under the name Nokasad, was competing in the small bore rifle. Civilai had to admit that shooting was not the quintessential spectator sport and *small bore* was a very apt description. The competitor lies down or stands up and shoots. Nobody dies, no bottles explode, there's no sideways glance at an opponent as you race for the tape. Civilai watched with no enthusiasm as Sompoo lay on a green mat, concentrated and began to squeeze the trigger. When it was over the soldier stood, shook hands with his opponents and went for a Pepsi. Like Dtui before him, Civilai had seen no homicidal leanings. But in his mind was the other theory, that any one of the Lao team could be the killer.

Siri would have loved nothing more than to watch the boxing or the shooting live but as he was passing the cultural center he'd noticed a poster advertising *Knife in the Water*, a Polanski film from 1962. He knew how the day would end: a lot of enthusiasm but no medals, no assassinations, and no medical emergencies. So he stepped into

the air-conditioned cinema and was still there three feature films later.

In 1980 there was little opulence in Vientiane beyond
the extravagant but unoccupied palace at the end of Lan
Xang Avenue and one or two glittery temples. And to be
honest none of these would have caused a ripple of envy
in the minds of any visiting European royalty. Outward
demonstrations of wealth in Vientiane were discouraged
and considered in poor taste. The government was still
hanging on to the pretence that all men were equal. Yet
beyond the ferry at Thadeua, where the boats now sat
idle, awaiting a change of heart from the Thais, there was
forested land with no signposts. And one might pull onto
a dirt track there and drive to a gate that was latched but
not locked. Beyond it, one might come to a paved road
that led to a lushly landscaped property.

And that was where Phosy found himself that afternoon,
staring at a luxurious two-story house and a separate office
block. On the deck of the house sat an old man in a rocking chair that wasn't rocking. Phosy recognized his face
from official functions. This was Thonglai Zakarine, financial adviser to the politburo. His was a face whose features
had to compete with a tract of liver spots and whose hair
was plastered to a broad skull.

Phosy stepped off his Vespa and walked up the concrete
steps to the concrete balcony.

"How did you find the place?" asked Thonglai.

"I've been here before," said Phosy.

The old man didn't offer his hand and Phosy didn't
bother to *nop*.

"I don't remember you," said the old man.

"You weren't here. Some of the Thadeua kids had broken into your outhouse and stolen some motorcycle parts. My director ordered me to come and investigate."

"It doesn't sound like you were too pleased about it."

"I'm a detective. I have better things to do than chase juveniles."

"And why are you here now?"

Phosy sat on the balcony wall. "I'm sure your secretary told you," he said.

"Something about a murder?"

"A man named Pinit," said Phosy. "He'd just made comments about you and your son before he died."

As the man was dead, Phosy didn't see what harm a small lie might do.

"What sort of comments?" said Thonglai.

"I'm afraid I can't tell you."

"You can't tell me what a dying man says about me? Am I implicated in some way?"

"We're looking into a number of possibilities."

"And by 'we' you mean you."

"I beg your pardon?"

"The chief of police knows nothing about this inquiry. I phoned him after your rather rude call to my office. I have his number because we play *boules* together."

"It takes a long time for ongoing case reports to make it to the director's desk," said Phosy.

The chief of police knew as much about police work as Phosy knew about offshore oil exploration. It didn't surprise Phosy at all that these two might be *boules* buddies.

"Why would you be so sensitive about a police inquiry?" Phosy asked.

The old man glared at him. "As a tax payer I expect

minor public officials such as yourself to contact me through the appropriate channels."

"I didn't have two weeks to wait."

"I have more important things to do than meet policemen."

"Then why are you here waiting for me?" asked Phosy.

"What?"

"You're a busy man. You know my boss. You could have told him to call me off. You could have pretended to be overseas. You don't want visitors without an appointment yet here you are waiting for me on your rocking chair. Is there something you'd like to tell me?"

The man smiled and began to rock.

"Perhaps," he said.

"Then I wouldn't mind a glass of water."

CHAPTER TWELVE
Enter Elvis

Day four of the Olympics had promised to be the most relaxed for the Lao squad. They had no events and no teammates to cheer so it was every man and woman for him or herself. A lack of surveillance on the shooters had not, as far as anyone knew, led to a spate of killings. Civilai had postulated that given the bubble of happiness the Soviets had created around the Games, there could have been a massacre of epic proportions but news of it would not make it to the general public.

Despite the feast of sporting events going on everywhere the old boys had thought they might step into the cinema to see Eisenstein's *Battleship Potemkin*.

"Ah, you have a friend now," said Avgusta, the Ukrainian projectionist. She spoke several languages, one of which was French. She was a sturdy lass in her twenties and she had kindly explained the plot and nuances of the movies Siri had watched for the past two days.

As Civilai often boasted—with no empirical evidence— French was his language of seduction.

"I'd much prefer to be sitting in the dark with a pretty girl like you," he said.

Siri sighed.

"It would remind me of the days my grandfather took me to the cinema when I was little," said Avgusta.

Siri laughed. "Well done," he said.

"I've been married to the same woman for fifty years," said Civilai.

"Then you should be ashamed," said Avgusta, flicking the projector switch and dimming the lights. "Flirting with an innocent young girl in the dark."

"That told you," Siri chuckled.

The countdown flashed onto the screen, followed by the credits, then all at once a grubby ship's crew was seen but not heard complaining about maggots in their meat. Already the Lao were lost in the magic. It was a shame they couldn't read the English subtitles, but not a catastrophe. They'd allow full rein to their imaginations, then have Avgusta fill in the gaps when it was all over.

But they were only twenty minutes into the story when the door opened at the rear of the room and somebody shouted to Avgusta in Russian. At first Siri and Civilai didn't allow themselves to be distracted, but there was nothing they could do when the film suddenly stopped and the house lights came back up. It was like being dragged from the arms of a loved one. They turned to see Agvusta standing beside a Soviet police officer in a stiff collar.

"Sorry," said the girl. "You have to go with this man."

"Why?" said Civilai.

"He won't tell me," she replied.

Lao legs were apparently too short for the liking of the guard because he kept stopping and gesturing for the old men to keep up. As they had no idea where they were going or why, Siri and Civilai elected to keep a more leisurely pace. They arrived at the Village Security Office located on the ground floor of the women's block. The guard led them directly to a back room where they found Daeng, Dtui, Roger and General Suvan surrounded by a gang of serious looking characters in suits and uniforms. Siri immediately felt guilty because he normally was.

"What's up?" he asked.

"We have no idea," said Daeng. "Sorry to drag you out of the film. We thought this might be serious."

"They haven't told me anything," said Roger, who was starting to look as if he might lose control of his bladder at any second. The Soviets were standing together mumbling like extras in a low-budget stage production. Nobody seemed prepared to step into the spotlight.

"I don't like this," said Suvan, the old general. "I don't like it at all."

Finally the door opened and a middle-aged man with a greying Elvis hairstyle entered with some haste. He was dressed like a high-school teacher in jacket and stay-press slacks and a sizeable gut hung over his belt. He looked around at the Lao and smiled. If it was meant to put everyone at ease, it didn't work.

"Thank you for coming," he said in heavily accented English and sat down at the only desk in the room. Everyone else sat on folding chairs and benches. He opened a file. "I'm afraid we have a serious problem," he said, switching to Russian. He looked up from the papers in front of him. "I should be hearing a translation by now."

Nobody spoke.

"Who is the interpreter into Lao?"

Again nobody spoke. One of the large Soviets pointed at Roger.

"Him," he said.

"Boy," said Elvis. "Do your job."

"Yes, comrade," said Roger. His voice eked from the back of his throat sounding like that of a young girl and he stammered his translation.

"As I say, there has been a very serious incident," said Elvis. "It involves one of your citizens. I am Senior Detective Volkov from the Moscow Criminal Investigation Department, which perhaps will tell you how serious this matter is. Over there we have Comrade Sokolov of the KGB, and Comrade Mihylov of the Foreign Ministry. There has been a murder committed by a Lao citizen who is a member of your Olympic squad."

Siri and his team did their utmost to look surprised. Each of them had a favorite candidate for the assassin role. Apparently the hit had been successful but the killer had not made a clean getaway. It was shameful for the Lao squad but at least they'd learn who the murderer was. Siri saw it as a positive that the Red Army had adopted the Lao shooters because they'd have the power to make the incident go away. The killer would be sacrificed but it wouldn't become an international incident. He just found it a little surprising that there were no military officers in the room.

"Before eleven P.M. last night," said Elvis, "one of your boxers, Maensai Khamdeng, murdered a young Russian woman in an apartment in Khamovniki District."

Elvis waited for a response but the Lao were too stunned to react. Maen—Mr. Conceited himself—had lost his cool and killed one of his beauties. What a mess that would be.

"How do you know?" asked Civilai.

Elvis looked up to see where the question was coming from. He replied to the translation.

"A neighbor saw Mr. Maensai arrive with the woman at nine P.M. yesterday," he said. "The doorman witnessed him leave hurriedly a little before eleven P.M. He was suspicious and went upstairs and found the door to her apartment ajar. Inside he found the victim dead in the living room."

"The weapon?" Daeng asked.

"No weapon has been found," said Elvis, "but there were multiple stab wounds to the stomach. In fact, the details of the police inquiry are not relevant to this meeting. Of course every effort will be made to document our findings in the report that will be sent to your government. But I'm sure you'll agree that this is very embarrassing for your nation."

"Very, very embarrassing," said General Suvan. "I must offer you our most sincere apologies."

"It is also uncomfortable for us," Elvis continued, "as you are one of a few socialist countries and we invited you personally to the Games. We are not saying that justice will not be done in this case. A murder is a murder. But we are prepared to keep the matter between you and ourselves. We may be able to extradite the killer to your country to be dealt with according to your laws. But we see no reason why the press should be notified."

"That's most kind of—" General Suvan began.

"So, you've decided Maensai did it, then?" said Siri.

Elvis looked at the questioner. "Who's he?" he asked.

"The team doctor," said Roger.

"Is that so?" said Elvis. "Well, being a doctor I doubt he knows that much about police matters. All that I can say is that the evidence against your boxer is overwhelming."

"Where is he?" asked Daeng.

Again, Elvis asked for the identity of the speaker.

"The team doctor's wife," said Roger.

"Then tell her he's at a secure location and that she doesn't need to concern herself about his nutrition."

"That's not good enough," said Civilai. "A suspect has rights, even a foreigner in the Soviet Union. He must be allowed representation. He has the right to give his version of events. I insist I see him."

"He's the team manager," said Roger.

"But not a lawyer," said Elvis.

"Actually, he is," said Roger, who had memorized the CVs of everyone in the Lao squad.

"Some toilet paper degree from his country?" said Elvis.

"A degree in law from the Sorbonne," said Roger.

Elvis smiled his doubt but Civilai stared coolly back at him.

"Then congratulations," said Elvis. "You may see your client."

Before Civilai's scheduled meeting with Maen, the think tank put its heads together at the Nebesa Milk Nook.

"What do we know?" asked Daeng.

"He's a conceited son of a bitch," said Dtui.

"He has the looks and the charm to carry it off," said Daeng.

"But not the language," said Siri.

"So unless he got really lucky and found a girl who studied at the same unwanted languages faculty as Roger, this relationship was based on hand-signals and lust," said Daeng.

"Are Russian women really that shallow?" asked Dtui.

"Being Russian's irrelevant," said Daeng. "There's romance and there's sex. Western women are more prepared to pursue the latter for the thrill of it. More like men, in other words."

Siri looked at his wife. He didn't need to ask why she knew such a thing. There were no secrets between them about her spying days and the sacrifices she made for her country. And she'd never lied to him about her sexual cravings at that time or beyond.

"So then the theory is that a local girl meets a handsome Asian boxer, an Olympic competitor, and she wants to sample his wares," said Civilai.

"Delicately put," said Siri.

"So she takes him home."

"That's relevant," said Siri. "It happened at her apartment. What kind of girl has an apartment in Moscow without a granny and ten relatives living with her?"

"She might have been a competitor," said Dtui. "He'd been boasting about meeting a blonde athlete in the village the day before."

"Then we need to know where the Soviet athletes are staying and whether they were given individual accommodation," said Daeng. "If not there might be roommates."

"And the knife," said Siri. "The doorman saw Maen leave in a hurry. Was he carrying a knife?"

"I doubt someone like Maen would have the foresight to remove the murder weapon," said Dtui.

"If not, where did it go?" said Siri. "And was there blood on him?"

"And how did he get back to the village?" said Daeng.

After Civilai had left, Daeng thought about that whole stream-of-consciousness brainstorming session. Many questions had been asked but one had not. Nobody had thought it necessary for Civilai to ask Maen whether he was guilty. They all assumed he was not. Maen was unpleasant and vain but he was a lowland Lao representing his country. They all knew in their hearts that the boy was innocent.

Phosy had precious little time from his busy caseload to visit Noo the forest monk but Mr. Geung would come by police headquarters every day to update him.

"Still un-un-unconscious," he said.

Either from his dealings with Dr. Siri, or from the codes of Down syndrome that nobody had yet been able to decipher, Mr. Geung had become spiritually aware. He could feel other people's pain, and love and insincerity. But he couldn't express them. He knew that Comrade Noo was dying, but not from his injuries. He knew the monk had lost something, but the concept of faith was too abstract. So he told Phosy that Noo had lost his feet and couldn't stand up. He should tell Comrade Siri as soon as possible. It made perfect sense to Geung but none at all to Phosy.

The inspector had no resources to look for Noo's feet and he was struggling to find a safe way to communicate with Moscow. In his final telex, Civilai had written directly,

"Half the planet has access to our telexes. No more secrets."

This left the inspector cast away from his support group. It was a pity considering he had such good news to pass on. Thonglai, the father of Manoi, had offered rewards to any of the Lao in Moscow for information leading to proven threats against his son's life. The old man knew there were dangers.

"No snippet of information can be too small," he'd said. "Nothing is without value."

To emphasize this he'd assured Phosy that his role as coordinator would not be forgotten. Any charity or personal projects he cared to nominate would be generously supported.

He'd added, "Phosy, like me, you are a father. I care for all my sons as much as you do your daughter. We wouldn't want anything to happen to them. But one of my boys is set to achieve prominence. I cannot emphasize how great our country might become under the guidance of patriots returning from study overseas. My boy in Moscow loves his country but there are those who see him as a threat to outside concerns. He is fearless, which puts him in even more danger. I need ears and eyes everywhere. I am afraid, Phosy. I'm afraid as a father who might lose a son but even more afraid as a Lao who might lose a great commander. Work with me, Phosy. We will be of benefit to each other."

Phosy had driven his Vespa back into the city. Had it been a Harley Davison he would have gunned the engine and kicked up dust onto the roadside vendors. But it was a Vespa and Italian scooters didn't lend themselves too keenly to wrath. Instead he'd clenched the handle grips so tightly they'd changed shape. It wasn't just the money. The bastard could buy an Olympic team, change history, realign the planets with his damned money.

"You're a father," he'd said, not as paternal bonding but as a warning. What Phosy heard loud and clear were the words, "You take the money or your daughter has an accident." Phosy had met his kind before and he wasn't likely to lose control in front of the great entrepreneur. He still had deals to negotiate.

"I'm having trouble contacting my people in Moscow," he'd said. "The international phone line in . . ."

"Say no more," said Thonglai, and Phosy had said no more. The next day a team of telephone engineers had arrived at his office and put in a direct line.

"No operator," said the engineer. "Perfectly secure."

Now all Phosy needed was a way to confound the secret listeners at the perfectly secure service.

"He's in a bad way," said Civilai. "It took forever to get to see him."

It was late evening. The village was still buzzing from the news that a Hollywood movie star had accepted the Republican nomination to run for the U.S. presidency. Russian seers predicted that this was just the beginning of nature's vengeance for the American boycott of the Olympics.

"Have they harmed him?" Daeng asked.

"No bruises I could see," said Civilai, "but you wouldn't recognize him from the arrogant boy we learned to dislike as far back as the pre-Games. They've put the fear of hell in him. He can't understand anyone or make himself understood. The guards treat him like a wild beast who violated their little sisters."

"Okay, so what's his version of events?" asked Siri.

"He met the girl on day two," said Civilai. "The day after the Opening Ceremony. She was a competitor. She showed him the athletics pictogram on her nametag. She used sign language to say she was a javelin thrower. She was wandering around the village after breakfast and they smiled at each other and somehow they agreed to meet in the evening. They were driven to an apartment building."

"Games car?" Daeng asked.

"Taxi," said Civilai.

"Did he remember where the building was?" asked Siri.

"He's a fighter from the jungle," said Civilai. "One concrete mountain's the same as the next. He said when they arrived they had to walk up the stairs."

"How many floors?" asked Siri.

"Five, and hers was at the top. On the way up, a neighbor came out of her apartment and ranted. He said it was as if she'd been waiting behind her door for the girl to come back. The neighbor yelled. The girl yelled."

"It wasn't a Games dormitory?" said Dtui.

"Old, old building, he said. Just a run-down apartment. The girl lived there alone," said Civilai. "There were no signs of family. No photos or old-people souvenirs. There was only one bedroom that was barely decorated."

"Did he notice anything in the bathroom?" asked Daeng. "Other toothbrush? Medicine?"

"I don't know," said Civilai. "Who'd ask questions like that?"

"Someone who wanted to solve a crime," said Siri. "Any detail might be vital."

"Well, excuse me for not cramming a thorough interrogation into half an hour," said Civilai.

"Keep going," said Daeng.

"They did their thing in the bedroom," he said.

"Any social niceties?" asked Siri. "No foreplay? Glass of wine? Music?"

"From the front door to the bed," said Civilai. "She seemed to be in a hurry for it. They made love but she wanted it violent, if you know what I mean."

"Discipline?" asked Daeng.

"Just wanted him to knock her around a bit. She hit him and goaded him to hit her back. He wasn't really into it, he said, but he made a few token slaps and it was all over. She turfed him out. It wasn't what he was used to. He walked back down to the lobby. The downstairs neighbor didn't put in an appearance. There was no doorman. Maen went to the street and realized he had no idea how to get back to the village. But he had his village ID. He flashed it at someone in a truck and the driver brought him home."

"And what about last night?" Siri asked.

"Well, according to Maen, there was no last night. He said he met some North Korean gymnast yesterday evening, they went for a walk somewhere in the park, got drunk on vodka, screwed in the bushes and fell asleep."

"But that was the night of the murder," said Dtui.

"He claims he wasn't there at the Russian's apartment that evening."

"Then why do the police think he was?" asked Siri.

"The downstairs woman claims to have seen him come back with her last night. The doorman said he saw him leave in a hurry an hour or so later."

"Why wasn't there a doorman the night before?" asked Siri.

"He's a sort of superintendent," said Civilai. "Does a bit of everything. The night before he was fixing a leaking pipe in one of the apartments, so he didn't see Maen at all. He was still busy when the couple came back last night. But he saw Maen leave and identified him immediately from the photo the police showed him."

"Wait! What photo did they show him?" Dtui asked.

"This is where the evidence starts to pile up against him," said Civilai. "They found his ID card in the girl's apartment on the night of the murder. They say he must have been in a hurry to get out of there and forgot it."

"But if he's telling the truth he'd used his photo ID to get back to the village on Sunday night," said Daeng.

"So the only way it could have been in the apartment is if he really did go back with the Russian last night," said Dtui.

"And to make matters worse," said Civilai, "the police located the North Korean gymnast and she'd been in bed with diarrhea all yesterday evening so there goes his alibi."

"Confirmation of that?"

"North Korean team doctor," said Civilai. "And when they showed her the photo the girl said she'd never met Maen and vehemently denied having sex with him. She said she was saving herself for Kim Il-Sung, the glorious leader."

"Aren't we all?" said Daeng.

"It doesn't look good for the boxer," said Dtui.

"What do we do next?" Civilai asked.

They downed their vodkas.

"We have two avenues to pursue," said Siri. "One is the fact he'd met the Russian girl in the village so she had to have a village ID. The security is tight here so she couldn't have just walked in off the street. We've learned from experience that you can't stroll twenty meters without someone snapping a photograph of you. I doubt the police will hand us a photo of the dead girl and it would help to know what she looked like. So we should check out the photographs from Sunday morning and see if we have the boxer and the javelin thrower together. We know roughly what time they met after breakfast and when they met again in the evening. We might get lucky."

"We need to go to the building where she was killed," said Daeng.

"That's my second avenue," said Siri.

"And how do we find that?" said Civilai. "Maen couldn't remember where it was."

"They went there by taxi," said Siri. "The taxi rank is outside the security perimeter. Somewhere we should have a picture of Maen. And if we find a photo of the girl we can show it to the drivers until someone remembers taking them. They're more likely to remember a pretty girl. If we don't find any photos we just ask the drivers if they recall taking a pretty blonde Russian and an Asian boxer for a tryst on Sunday night. I get the feeling a red-blooded Moscow taxi driver would be less than delighted to watch one of his women flirt with an inferior."

"'Being a doctor I doubt he knows that much about police matters,'" said Daeng in a Russian Elvis accent.

"How do you think the Soviets will react to a bunch of foreign tourists re-examining one of their cases?" asked Dtui.

"We aren't tourists," said Siri. "We're Olympians."

There were so many photographs they could only pin a few of them onto the corkboards at the kiosk. They were beautiful colored prints so crisp and detailed they made the Lao instamatic look like a mallet and chisel. The bulk of the photos lay in long fat drawers. The athletes hadn't yet got around to claiming them.

"We're looking for the morning of the twentieth," Dtui told the girl behind the stand.

If she was surprised to hear an Asian speaking Russian she didn't show it. Dtui had a knack for languages. She'd taught herself English when there was still the chance of an American scholarship. Then she relearned all her old medical texts in Russian when she thought she might have a chance to study forensic medicine in the USSR. But then came the baby and there went the chance.

The girl looked at the catalogue and opened the second drawer from the bottom. It was full. The date and time were recorded on the bottom right-hand corner of each print. Dtui and Civilai sat on two small bathroom stools the girl provided for their comfort and started to go through the photos for day two.

"Maen claimed to have met the girl after breakfast," said Dtui. "We were all in the canteen early so we should start looking at around six-thirty."

She got lucky almost immediately. She found the first photo of Maen timed at 7:10 A.M. He was alone and hamming it up for the photographer, doing his "staring off into nothingness" look. Dtui had to admit he was a good-looking man. Sixty photos of post-breakfast strollers later, they made a second breakthrough. In the foreground of the picture, three Indian Sikhs in turbans were posing in front of a fountain. In the background, an attractive blonde was sitting on the fountain lip admiring the sculptures. As the focus was on the Sikhs she was a little blurred. But it could have been her.

There were no pictures of the hunt or of the capture but at exactly 8:15 A.M. the blonde and Maen had been photographed together. She held his arm and they were walking through the landscaped garden laughing. She was a foot taller than him. In the first picture they had been unaware of the photographer who'd snapped them candidly from the side. In the second picture the javelin thrower looked angrily at the photographer but Maen beamed a boastful smile. That was the photo they needed;

a beautiful, perfectly focused couple. The kiosk girl wrote the reference number in her catalogue, removed the negatives and told Dtui they'd be able to make second copies in twenty-four hours. She seemed unconcerned that neither Dtui nor Civilai were in the photo.

Dtui went off with the original prints to talk to the drivers at the official village taxi rank. Civilai decided to remain behind at the kiosk. He no longer had a specific date or time in mind but he did have a theory. He would begin his search on the day before the opening ceremony—what he supposed would be called Day Zero. He sat back down on the plastic stool and began thumbing through the thousands of photographs.

CHAPTER THIRTEEN
Asians Is Asians

Siri and Daeng stood in front of a dirty grey five-story building in Severnoye Chertanovo, an area known for its depressing prefabricated skyscraper apartment blocks. Soon this old architectural relic too would be knocked down and replaced by something even uglier. Siri looked up at the weather-beaten bricks and the smoky window panes. In a fourth-floor window was the scary face of a wizened old crone frowning down at him. He poked out his tongue at her. A village van pulled up at the curbside and they watched Roger climb down from the back seat. Roger was a smart lad and Siri knew he didn't have to explain why they'd arranged to meet him here. He could have opted out but he didn't.

"How did you find the place?" he asked, shaking hands with both Siri and Daeng.

"We didn't," said Daeng. "It was Dtui. She took photos of Maen and the javelin girl to the taxi rank and in ten minutes she had an address. Dtui phoned us and we phoned you."

"You know when I was last in the Soviet Union," said Siri,

"you couldn't even get a tour guide to crack a smile. Now you just have to click your fingers and the locals would do anything for you."

"I told you, uncle," said Roger, "it's the new spirit of openness. The world is our friend."

"You know, if you'd sooner not be here we'd quite understand," said Daeng.

"My Lao brother is in prison," he said. "What kind of relative would I be to leave him there?"

Daeng kissed him on the cheek and he blushed puce.

The building was dilapidated but still inhabited. When they forced their way into the foyer through the bulky glass doors they weren't surprised to find nobody manning the reception desk. It was obvious the caretaker had a lot to keep him busy. Siri looked at the steep staircase and sighed. There wasn't even a lift to decline. They began to climb, allowing the doctor a rest on each landing. The stair carpet was of no identifiable color and it smelled of potatoes. Paint was peeling from the ceiling like impoverished Christmas decorations and the wooden banister had been worn into waves by generations of hands.

On the fourth floor balcony one door stood open and a woman with many decades of ugliness behind her stood blocking their path. It was the crone from the window.

"More Asians?" she said.

"They're not moving in," Roger assured her.

"What do they want?" she asked.

"This is the President of Asia and his wife," he told her.

"Asians is Asians," she said.

Daeng asked Roger if this was the neighbor who'd identified Maen. He asked her.

"It appears so," he said.

"Ask her what she saw."

"She says if you're press she can't tell you."

"We're not press," said Daeng.

Easily convinced, the woman told Roger what had happened.

"The Russian girl arrived with that Asian on Sunday," she said. "I told her it was sinful what she was about to do. She yelled filth at me and I yelled filth back at her."

"How did she know what they were planning to do?" asked Siri.

"It seems this wasn't the first time she'd brought young gentlemen home," said Roger. "But actually she means 'mixing races with God's lesser beings,' not so much the sex."

"I see," said Siri. "Did the blonde mix races very often?"

"Brazen, she was," said the ugly woman. "I saw her with all types."

"And she was with this Asian creature two nights?" asked Daeng.

"Didn't see them arrive yesterday," said the woman. "Must have come during my nap time. But I saw him leave right enough."

"And she's sure it was the same man?" asked Daeng.

"Nothing wrong with my eyes," said the woman.

"And did she hear any sounds from upstairs?" asked Daeng. "Any arguments or screams?"

"Huh?" said the woman. "This building was erected by Peter the Great himself. You could fire a cannon in here and nobody would be any the wiser."

They thanked her and started up the last flight of stairs. But after two steps Daeng stopped, opened her shoulder bag and took out her purse. From one of the flaps she removed a photograph.

"Ask her if this is the man she saw leaving the apartment," she said to Roger.

He took it from her and held it up in front of the woman's face. Her glasses were hanging from a beaded lace around her neck. She put them up to her eyes, perused the photo and nodded.

"She has no doubt that's him," said Roger.

While he was picking the lock of the door to the murder scene, Siri asked casually, "You have a picture of Maen in your purse?"

"And how would you feel if I did?" Daeng replied with a smile.

"Some curiosity as to how you got hold of it, and perhaps questions about your sanity," he said.

"What woman wouldn't want a photo of a gorgeous, fine-bodied young man in her purse?" she said and held it up for him to see. Siri smiled.

"That would be me," he said to Roger just as the door clicked open.

They stepped inside.

"And it would appear there isn't a milligram of doubt that the thirty-four-year old Dr. Siri Paiboun was seen fleeing from a murder," said Daeng.

"Why, that's splendid," said Roger. "You have discredited a key witness."

"Why do you have a forty-year-old photo of me in your purse?" Siri asked.

"You should be flattered that I have any photo of you at all," Daeng said. She shut the door and they looked around the room. The only natural light came from the bathroom, as it was the only room with a window.

There wasn't much to see. The living area had a three-piece suite in some maroon vinyl-like material, a coffee table, a standard lamp. The kitchen was no more than an alcove beside the bathroom door with a sink, a single gas range, a cumbersome refrigerator—currently unplugged—and an empty wall cupboard. The bedroom was separated from the living room by a flowery cloth curtain on a rail. The only furniture in the bedroom, apart from the bed, was a large, ornate wooden chair. The wallpaper behind the bed didn't match that on the other three walls. But there was a remarkably tacky op-art portrait of Lenin made of multicolored reflective glass.

"She wasn't exactly living a life of luxury," said Daeng.

"If it were a picture of me at seventy-six I'd be flattered," said Siri, still preoccupied with Daeng's purse.

"Perhaps she was a prostitute," said Roger.

Daeng smiled. "You don't have much experience with prostitutes, do you, Roger?" she said.

"Well, I . . . no, not a lot," he said. "Actually, none. Why?"

"Because if you did you'd know that a beautiful woman could live a much more splendid lifestyle than this. And she'd know better than to go to the Olympic Village and come home with a poor boxer. She could have chosen a yachtsman or a horseman or one of the European government representatives. If nothing else, a hooker has a well-honed business sense."

"A photograph of the thirty-four-year-old me suggests you're living in the past," said Siri. "That you'd have preferred it if I hadn't aged."

"So why do you think she was living in a place like this?" Roger asked.

"We hoped we might find the answer to that by taking a look around," said Daeng. "But this place is devoid of clues. It's not unthinkable that it's a short-term rental apartment and the girl really was here to compete in the Olympics. But there are no clothes. No equipment. No personal effects. Perhaps she was just a boxing groupie and she rented a room for a little nooky."

"It's quite likely the police took everything away," said Roger. "You don't know how Soviet police work. I'm certain they would have already found the legal owner of the apartment. I wouldn't want to be in his shoes. Subletting is a very serious offense."

Siri stood in the bedroom admiring the glass Lenin.

"No," said Daeng.

"No, what?" said Siri.

"We have no room for it. Not in our luggage or in our life."

"It's very attractive," said Siri. "And we all know you prefer the new and the colorful to the old and dingy. But I wasn't planning to steal it. I'm just uneasy about this room."

"It's the tape outline of the body on the linoleum," said Roger. "It gives me the willies, too."

"No, son. It's not that."

On their way out of the building they were perhaps fortunate to bump into the caretaker/doorman. He looked moldy, as if his old clothes and old skin had been left in a damp dark corner for too long. Daeng showed him the young Siri photo.

"Yes," he told Roger. "That's him. Saw him run out of here yesterday like a scared chicken."

"Did he have a knife?" Siri asked.

"Didn't see one," said the man.

"Any blood on him?"

"Nah! Didn't see no blood."

"But you're certain this was the man?"

"Never forget a face, me."

"Asians is Asians," said Daeng as they stood in the street waiting for a taxi.

Civilai had been in the photo booth for most of the day. He'd paused for lunch but brought his cafeteria tray back to the kiosk so he could continue to search. He was astonished at the number of photographs after only four days. A team of developers must have been working twenty-four-hour shifts at some hidden lab. The problem with finding what he was looking for was that he didn't really know what he was looking for—or rather he knew but was aware he might never find it. Hypotheses could be annoying like that.

But it was shortly after his lemon meringue pie dessert that he found what he wasn't sure he'd been looking for. He'd been going through the photos of the day before the majority of athletes arrived, Day Zero minus One. Some teams had made special arrangements due to travel connections and had come a day early. Most of the facilities had yet to open so there were competitors and officials walking around with nothing to do. And it was on one of those aimless strolls that he found his Russian javelin thrower again. She was smiling at a well-built, dark-skinned man in sunglasses who was a head shorter than her. He had the type of blond hair that could only have come from a bottle.

Civilai went through all the photos for that day and found one more picture of the blond man. He was in a group. There was no Russian in sight but the team's uniforms stood out proudly. Blondie was from the Bahamas. Civilai had what he needed. He took the two photos to the village map and discovered that the Bahamian team was billeted in building E. Roger was off somewhere with Siri and Daeng so Civilai had no translator. But he reasoned French was a common enough language in the Caribbean. He was certain to find someone who'd understand him.

His arrival at the Bahaman meeting room was very Olympic. The five officials at the conference table looked up when he entered and immediately noticed the "team leader" category B card hanging around his neck. They stood to shake his hand and smiled and said things, none of which amounted to communication.

"Does anyone here speak French?" Civilai asked.

"I do," said the only female in the room. She was as rosy as an apple and her uniform was much too tight for her figure.

Civilai introduced himself and they shook his hand one more time and invited him to sit. On his way there he'd decided to go for the jugular. He took out the photo of the blond Bahamian with his teammates and passed it around.

"I'm looking for this man," he said, pointing at the blond.

"It's Juno," said one of the officials.

"Light middleweight," said another.

But then, as if a dark cloud of apprehension passed over them, they lowered their heads and said no more. The team manager stiffened. There was a flicker of something resembling shame and Civilai knew his day hadn't been completely wasted.

"Is he in the building?" he asked. "I'd like to see him."

"No, he's not," said the French-speaking woman. "Why do you want to meet him?"

Civilai weighed the truth in his mind. It was a little too heavy.

"If our boys make it through the first two rounds they'll meet in the semi-finals," he said. It was a lie but he was relying on nobody there having studied the fixture list. "It's a Lao tradition for opponents to get together before a battle and wish each other good luck."

It was a tradition he'd just made up but the group seemed fractionally more relaxed. He reached into his jacket pocket and took out the second photo. This was the one that would confirm or deny his theory.

"I have another picture of him," he said.

He put it on the table where everyone could see it. Juno and the Russian woman. Civilai looked from face to face. Everybody held the secret but nobody spoke. One man who had been silent since Civilai's arrival stood and walked out of the room. He glared at the Lao as he left.

"He just walked out," said Civilai. "Just disappeared."

"That can be annoying," said Daeng.

"You didn't confront them with your suspicions?" asked Siri.

"I don't have any suspicions," said Civilai. "I just had a theory that this woman was preying on poor athletes from small countries. There are no Soviet athletes staying at the Village. But there was our Russian javelin thrower strolling around after breakfast. Why did she settle on the smaller weight classes like Maen when there were so many full-sized heavyweight boxers to choose from?"

"We ruled out prostitution," said Roger, who had been officially drafted into the think tank.

They considered all the possibilities while Sergei delivered a new batch of cocktails.

"And that only leaves the groupie theory," said Daeng. "She had a thing for small boxers. And that's even more likely now that she approached another one."

"And it gives us another suspect for the murder," said Siri. "The Bahamian has a brief affair with a beautiful woman and thinks it's love. He goes back to her apartment and she's with another man. He lies in wait till the new fellow leaves and kills his lover in a fit of jealousy."

"But who was she with that last night?" Daeng asked. "Maen swears it wasn't him."

"He might be lying about being there because he knew he'd be accused," said Civilai.

"Well, that ploy didn't work, did it?" said Dtui. "He might as well have told the truth."

"What if our Russian found herself another boxer?" said Siri.

"You think she's going for a record of her own?" Dtui asked.

"You think she'd be successful catching a man every night?" said Civilai.

"Are you serious?" said Daeng. "A big, beautiful blonde putting out sexual vibrations to a boy from the village? It's the type of fantasy they talk about around the bonfires."

◙   ◙   ◙

At exactly 4 A.M. on the morning of day five, Siri sat up in his bed the way they do in the movies—an act rarely witnessed in real life.

"How stupid could I be?" he said.

Daeng was only half awake beside him.

"Where have you been?" she asked.

"Nowhere," said Siri. "I've been right here thinking about windows."

"That's lovely," she said, hoping he would take his window thoughts back into the land of nod. But, as had happened many times, she turned her head to find her husband putting on his trousers.

"We're going somewhere, aren't we?" she said.

◎ ◎ ◎

At exactly 4 A.M. on the morning of day five, Civilai also sat up in his bed but didn't say anything because he was alone. But he did get up and put on his trousers because he'd worked it out too.

◎ ◎ ◎

Siri and Daeng roused the courtesy twenty-four hour Olympic Village shuttle driver. They flashed their IDs and showed him a bit of paper with an address on it. It took him a while to come around and recall where he was but eventually he sighed, put in his false teeth and headed off in the opposite direction to the city.

◎ ◎ ◎

Civilai walked down the emergency staircase because he still didn't trust elevators after midnight. He went to the boxers' apartment suite, the door of which was wide open. He walked into Maen's room and turned on the light. Anou, the roommate, emerged from a deep sleep like a sloth pulling itself out of a barrel of Vaseline.

"He hasn't come home yet," he slurred. Word of the arrest hadn't made it down to the competitors. Civilai knew the Soviet police would have already searched this room when everyone was off at events. But they wouldn't have been looking for what Civilai needed.

"Where's Maen's stuff?" he asked.

Anou swayed.

"Maen's stuff?" Civilai repeated.

"It's all gone," said Anou. "Think he must have run off with that Korean."

Civilai looked through the drawers, the closet, under the bed. There was nothing. The police had erased the boxer. Not that far down the line, nobody would remember who he was.

"Damn," he said.

He was about to turn out the light and leave when he looked at the back of the bedroom door. Two ID tags hung from the hook. He took them down and looked closely at them.

"My ID," said Anou. "It's where we hang 'em."

"Then who does this other one belong to?" asked Civilai.

"Some guy, I guess. No idea."

The photo was of a slim Asian man with long hair. Civilai let out a whoop.

"It isn't Maen," he said.

"No. Can't think why it's there," said Anou.

"I can," said Civilai.

He went over to Anou's bed, grabbed the boxer's

ears and gave him a kiss on the forehead. It was fine. He wouldn't remember it next time he woke up.

It was too early still for the crone on the fourth floor to respond to the sounds from the crunchy staircase even though the sun was already rising. The building's front door had been simple enough. A quick insert of an Olympic Village Souvenir Shopping Card and the latch was unfastened. It didn't surprise them how easy it was. This was a building you'd want to break out of, not into. On their earlier visit, Siri had left a wedge of paper lodged between the crime scene door and the frame, so re-entry was no problem either.

"For me it was part of the training," whispered Daeng. "But tell me again where a doctor learned the art of breaking into people's houses."

Siri closed the door behind them.

"Paris," he said.

"You were housebreaking to cover your school fees?"

"Not exactly. One of the speakers at a Communist Party conference—it might have been Ho himself—suggested we take advantage of our study opportunities and sign up for apprenticeships that might further the cause of the revolution."

"And you took housebreaking?"

"I saw myself more as a detective solving mysteries for the insurrection, but there were no courses so I trained with a locksmith on weekends."

They were in the bedroom tapping the walls with their knuckles. They'd established that the rear wall was made of hardboard and that the wallpaper there was comparatively new compared to the rest of the apartment.

"And when exactly did this revelation come to you?" she asked.

"The seed began to germinate when we were down on the street yesterday looking up at the old woman," he said. "Her apartment was directly below this one. Why did she have two windows and this apartment have just the one? The answer was obvious. Ah, here it is."

Siri was on his knees in the corner of the room. He knew there had to be a trap door or a flap and he found it behind the padded chair. There was a small rectangle where the wallpaper didn't exactly match. He pushed at its center and there was a click. The hardboard rectangle fell forward.

"Nice carpentry," said Siri. "Wasted on blackmail."

He scurried through the space on his hands and knees. The actual rear wall of the apartment was three meters beyond the hardboard partition. To the left there was a window blocked with cardboard. He peeled it off to get some light there. The video camera stood on a tripod directly behind Lenin's Op Art two-way mirror. A still camera, an expensive Leica, was on a stool beside it. On a small table sat trays of developing solution and distilled water. Several still photographs hung from strings across the room. Siri and Daeng started to unpeg them and put them in their shoulder bags. The jig was up.

◙ ◙ ◙

In spite of everything that had already happened on day five it was only breakfast time at the Olympic Village. Both Siri and Civilai had returned to the dormitory eager to share their news. They met up in the canteen. Roger was enjoying his first Olympic hangover and was on his third cup of coffee. Dtui was tackling a Russian breakfast. But food and drink very quickly gave way to elation. Siri gave Daeng the privilege of describing their return visit to the crime scene. They'd recorded everything on their instamatic but had not yet reported their findings to the police. They needed to discuss the potential pitfalls before doing so. And if they were being honest, the discovery did not necessarily clear Maen of any guilt. There was still a murder to account for.

Civilai believed he could help in that regard. He told them of his early morning visit to Maen's room.

"There was nothing there," he said. "The police had removed all his belongings. But behind the door hanging on a hook were two official nametags. One was his roommate, Anou's. But the other was not Maen's. That's why the police didn't take it. But what was that tag doing there? Nobody recognized the man in the photograph. The name and country code on the tag clearly indicated he was Vietnamese. So I started to expand my theory. Maen said he'd used his nametag to get a ride back to the village on Sunday night. But what if the Vietnamese had forgotten his name tag at the Russian's apartment the night before? What if Maen picked up the wrong tag? He wouldn't have checked it."

"Right," said Daeng. "He goes to the room with the girl. They do their calisthenics. She asks for a little rough and tumble. He obliges in some small way. He's a boxer. Violence isn't such a big deal. The cameraman takes his movie and a few photographs. That's all they need. She tells him to leave. It's dark. He gets dressed. He reaches under the bed, finds the Vietnamese boxer's tag and puts it on. When you're expecting to find something you don't look at it too closely."

"But his own nametag is in the bathroom or wherever," said Dtui.

"He goes to the street and flags down a truck," said Siri. "The driver sees the Olympic ID so he gives him a ride home. He doesn't have any reason to compare the man in the photo with the man beside him."

"Asians is Asians," said Daeng.

"Exactly," said Civilai. "The Vietnamese in the photo was all hair and smiles so he could very easily have been mistaken for our boy. In fact, Maen wakes up the next day and continues to use the wrong nametag. He has his date with the North Korean and comes back to the dormitory. He puts his nametag behind the door and goes to bed. Next thing you know he's being dragged out of the room by the police with no idea what happened."

"Oh, Lord, I am surrounded by genius," said Roger.

"Not yet you're not," said Daeng. "Genius is when we find a way to put all this conjecture together and prove it. Genius is when they release our boxer."

"But it's simple, now," said Roger. "We just go to the police and tell them what we've found."

"That's the end plan," said Civilai. "But first we need to collect a little more evidence."

"And we'll have to set up an insurance policy or two so the police don't ignore us," said Siri.

"But why would they?" said Roger.

"They haven't been very thorough in their investigation so far," said Siri. "In fact once they had their suspect they stopped digging. It's as if our man's life wasn't important to them. Admittedly they were under no pressure to investigate the crime because they'd already planned to snow over it. Now here's a small gang of country bumpkins about to tell them they did a bad job. And we'll be giving them new evidence about a crime committed by their own nationals against IOC country members. They won't like that."

"Do we actually know what the blackmailers intended to do with their films?" asked Roger.

"I think so," said Siri. "They focus on smaller countries. Innocents like us. Someone claiming to be from the police or the KGB meets with the NOC representatives from those countries. He plays up the embarrassment angle just like Elvis did with us. He brings photos of a pretty Soviet athlete bruised and bleeding and shows the film of their boxer beating her up. The shame for their country would be too much for them to bear. The National Olympic Committee asks how it can avoid the disgrace. The negotiations begin. A sum of money is agreed on and the NOC arranges for a transfer from its embarrassed government at home."

"How do you know all this?" Roger asked.

"I don't," said Siri. "I'm guessing."

"But he's a really good guesser," said Daeng.

"Then how can . . . what can you do to make sure our police listen to you?" asked Roger.

"To be heard," said Daeng, "you have to be loud. And many voices are louder than one. So you increase the population of shouters."

"I'll go to see the Vietnamese," said Civilai. "And I'll talk to the Bahamians again. From their reaction to me yesterday I get the feeling they've already been approached by the blackmailer. It shouldn't be hard to convince them we're all in this together. In fact I imagine they'll be grateful to hear it was a sting."

"But who did it?" asked Roger. "Who murdered the girl?"

"It's looking bad for whichever Asian she took home on Monday night," said Siri. "But that isn't our problem. What's important is that we can remove the evidence against Maen. The name card. The unreliable eye-witnesses. They don't have any proof that Maen was there at the time of the murder. That should be enough to get him released."

"I don't know," said Dtui.

"You don't know what?" said Siri.

"I'm sorry to rain on your fireworks but isn't it still possible Maen went back for seconds on Monday?" she said. "That he was pissed off she'd thrown him out the night before and went back to murder her?"

There was a moment for thought.

"It's not impossible," said Daeng. "But it didn't happen."

"How do you know?"

"Because I've killed people," said Daeng. "I know what it takes."

There was only one Lao to cheer on day five. One more boxer. All the Lao athletes except for the shooters went along to Olympiisky to support Siwit the bantamweight. The boxing crowds had started to look forward to bouts that involved Lao fighters because the atmosphere was party-like. Only the Soviet supporters failed to let their hair down. They looked on mystified. What joy was there to be had from losing?

The administrators and Roger had stayed behind at the Village because they'd set up a meeting. They'd insisted that Elvis and his team attend. On the telephone to police headquarters Roger had used the expressions "international outrage" and "humiliation for the Soviet Union."

As there were three NOCs in attendance and the Lao had
threatened to call in the press the police had little choice.
But even so, Elvis took his time. It was midday before the
entourage arrived. The door burst open and the Senior
Detective and his herd of suits and uniforms quickly filled
the room.

Instead of taking the seat offered to him, Elvis pointed
at Siri and Daeng and spoke gruffly to the men in uniform. Two of them stepped forward. Roger asked for an
explanation.

"He wants to arrest you," said Roger. "A police car detail
saw you leaving the murder scene building early this morning. They took your photograph."

"You'd better warn him," said Siri, "that if anyone lays
a hand on my wife it will be at the end of a broken arm."

Once their translators had passed on the policeman's
intention, the Bahamian and Vietnamese delegates got
to their feet and blocked their path. There was a tense
moment when two of the plainclothes men reached inside
their jackets but sanity arrived in the unlikely form of
Roger. He held up his hands and said, "Your men have
made a terrible mistake. If you refuse to listen to these
people there will be a scandal you'll never recover from."

"These two foreigners broke into a crime scene which
had been marked off-limits by the Ministry of Internal
Affairs," said Elvis.

"And it's just as well for you that they did," said Roger.

He pointed to the pin board on the wall with its display
of Siri's instamatic photographs freshly developed by the
ever-helpful kiosk ladies. They had asked no questions.

"How are you going to explain that your detectives
missed this?" asked the translator.

Elvis and his backing group walked to the wall and studied the photos. He recognized the apartment and could clearly see the false wall, the trap door and the camera set-up. There were some twenty-four pictures in all.

"We've mailed copies of all of them to our countries just in case these get lost," said Siri.

It was as if the air had been let out of the Soviet delegation. They sat at the meeting table muttering amongst themselves. Their arrogance was gone.

"Tell me," said Elvis.

The young Russian translator was very thorough and spoke slowly so the other translators could keep up with him. Dtui did her best even though the vocabulary was a way beyond her ability. In fact, Roger was so succinct the Soviets had no need to stop him speaking so they could ask questions. They sat opposite like overly-large grade school children at story time. When the tale was told Elvis whistled like a kettle and shook his head. That was when Siri handed over the prints from the Leica they'd found in the hidden room.

CHAPTER FOURTEEN
The Twenty-Kilometer Amble

"How are you, boy?" Civilai asked.

The boxer looked stunned. The cockiness and conceit were gone. Maen put his hands together in a deep, respectful *nop* and bowed in front of each of the Lao team administrators. He cried uncontrollably, which drew tears from Dtui and Roger. One condition of the release was that he told nobody of his arrest for murder. If anyone asked, he was to tell them he'd been staying with a girl. Given his state of mind after two nights in a Soviet prison, they doubted he'd be boasting about such a thing ever again.

The Soviet investigation was ongoing and the Lao had agreed to keep mum about the blackmailing. The police were in no position to set conditions but it was clear any leaks might damage their inquiries. Elvis promised to keep Siri and his team informed of developments. It was a promise the Lao would have to see to believe.

In the van on the way back to the village Civilai asked Maen, "Do you want us to cancel your fight tomorrow?"

"I don't know," said Maen.

"I'm guessing incarceration isn't the best preparation for a world event," said Daeng.

"I've been thinking about it," said Maen. "I was sure I was going to die. All the time in there when I had nothing to do but imagine what might happen to me, I wished I could have my time over. You know? I wished I could ask the ancestral spirits for a second chance."

"No harm in starting a new life with a good memory," said Dtui.

"Even without all this I wasn't going to win my fight, but if you don't mind I'd like to try."

"You'll have the loudest supporters in the stadium if you do," said Daeng. "We're being nominated for the Crowd of the Year award."

Maen's smile faded quickly but his eyes shone.

When she got back to her room, Dtui found a note from the telephone exchange. A Mr. Phosy had tried to call her on three occasions. He would call again at 8 P.M. Moscow time. Her heart sank with fear for her daughter. It was 7:50. She hurried downstairs and across the Square of Nations. By eight she was sitting on one of the comfortable armchairs watching the wall of phone booths where colorful and noisy athletes shouted across oceans in a fruit cocktail of languages. There were tears from those who missed their families, laughter, frustration, elation. Nobody cared who was listening. Every heart was out there on public display.

"Mrs. Dtui," came a voice over the speaker.

Dtui went to booth number seventeen as she was instructed and picked up the handset. It was unnecessarily heavy and she wondered if that was a deliberate ploy to limit the length of calls. Her stomach was swarming with the ugliest of butterflies.

"Hello?" she said.

"Dtui, it's me."

His voice was so close she could have reached out and caressed his cheek.

"It's Phosy," he said.

"I know," she said. "Is Malee all right?"

"She's fantastic," he said.

She was relieved but irrationally mad at him for causing her this grief.

"She asks about you every day."

"Listen, Dtui. I've been very lucky and a kind gentleman called Comrade Thonglai Zakarine has put in a direct telephone link from my office so we could keep him informed of the wellbeing of his son, Comrade Manoi, who's a student in Moscow. His father has heard rumors that someone might be out to harm Manoi. Could you tell Comrade Daeng and Siri that if there's any news they should call me at this number, immediately? If the telephonist didn't give it to you, the number is 8567999."

Dtui repeated the number.

"Your Auntie Arpy says hello and hopes you're continuing your studies and having a good time," Phosy continued. "Oh, and I'm afraid Comrade Noo might be on his way out. Mr. Geung says to tell Siri that the monk has lost his feet. And . . ."

"Yes?"

"Well, I guess that's everything. Give my best to everyone."

"Phosy, I—"

And the line buzzed and died right there in her hand. She felt the telephone get heavier.

"All right," she said loudly in English for the neighboring booths to hear. "Yes, really. Don't worry."

She laughed loud and long.

"Yes," she yelled. "I love you too."

Day six was a proud one for the Lao team. Siri's namesake, christened Siri II to avoid confusion, boxed mid-morning. He made it to the end of the bout. A hundred and eighty grueling seconds. He lost on points by a huge margin to an enthusiastic Iranian but he'd given everything he had and more. The Lao supporters were noisier than ever. Someone had found a drum and the Lao athletes and supporters sang along to the beat and cheered and danced in their seats. The bongo countries, Cuba and Brazil and the like, picked up on the Lao vibrations and the boxing commentators had to yell into their microphones to be heard.

This was followed by a mad rush to the Lenin stadium for the heats of the men's two hundred and eight hundred meters. The Lao had a competitor in each event. The supporters' club had picked up a few straggling Americans and Chinese and one confused Japanese lady in her forties. It appeared that nobody had told her Japan would be boycotting the Games. As she and the others had no team of their own to cheer they became honorary Lao for the day. After an x-ray, the drum was allowed into the stadium and the supporters began their concert from the second it arrived.

Chom the rat catcher waved at them from his starting blocks of the two hundred meters. He'd seen his first starting block three weeks earlier at orientation. He wasn't so confident in spikes, either. He would have happily taken them off and run in bare feet but polyurethane wasn't nearly as friendly as grass. The pistol shot resounded around the half-full stadium and Chom kept a close watch on the backs of his competitors as they headed off. But when he crossed the finish line the cheer from the stands was even louder than that for the winner. It was what the drafted American fans started to refer to as "The Lao Cheer."

It would be heard again ninety minutes later when Kilakone the high-schooler ran the eight hundred meters. He led from the gun and hit the inside lane in the lead after the first turn. Photographs were taken at that moment which would become famous back in the Lao PDR. But Kilakone had run the first two hundred meters faster than he had ever run in his life and still he hadn't shaken off his opponents. He'd sprinted the whole way, perhaps hoping his body might respond to his enthusiasm. By three hundred meters he was neck and neck with the runner from Burma. They were ten meters behind the field. Were it not for the sound of the Lao Cheer from his countrymen and women in the stands he might not have bothered to complete the second lap at all. The Burmese retired so Kilakone did not officially come last and every head in the Lenin stadium turned to see what had happened when he crossed the finish line to an enthusiastic ovation.

But two minutes later the Lao supporters were gone, hurrying back across the complex to the boxing arena where Maen was about to compete in the featherweight qualifier. His Mongolian opponent had more the appearance of a wrestler than a boxer and in the buildup he seemed excited and disoriented. But at the sound of the bell he attacked like a fighting bull, and Maen's role in the ring was more that of self-defense than of competition. He did get in two respectable punches in the first round, which were met with shouts of *olé* from the Lao-friendly crowd. The referee stopped the fight in the middle of the second round even though Maen gave the impression he could have withstood no end of punishment. He left the ring to a resounding Lao Cheer. For a man who'd spent two nights in a Soviet jail it had been a magnificent performance.

Fatigued from their sleuthing, Civilai and Siri had foregone the pleasure of watching boxers and runners and had instead joined Avgusta for the matinee showing of *Merry-Go-Round* from Hungary and an afternoon showing of *The Loves of a Blonde*. But they had reluctantly passed up the opportunity to watch the evening screening of *Andrei Rublev* because they had decided instead to watch a man walk. Even though they'd pumped up the egos of every member of the team with their patriotic rhetoric, in their minds there was only one athlete in the squad they considered to be a serious contender. Inspired by the atmosphere at the stadium there was no telling what Khamon might achieve. But, of course, that didn't prevent the old boys from making fun of the sport.

"Is it before or after the hundred-meter dawdle?" Siri asked.

"It's next on the agenda to the three-kilometer stroll," said Civilai.

But however slow the event, they liked and admired the man who had performed his way onto the Lao Olympic team. So they joined the ever-expanding Lao crowd in the Lenin stadium. They'd only see the beginning and the end of the race in the flesh but an enormous screen would cut back and forth between the walkers and ongoing field events. Nobody on the Lao cheer squad was particularly interested in watching a bearded Englishman toss a metal ball twenty meters.

"Really useful that in battle," said Siri. "The enemy would need extremely poor reflexes to be hit with one of those."

"How was the film?" Daeng asked.

"The first was a little too *avant-garde* for me," said Civilai. "Brilliant but of no entertainment value whatsoever."

"Yet you sat through the whole thing?" said Daeng.

"You'd have us leave and insult the director?" said Siri.

"Was he there?" she asked.

"Just us and the projectionist," said Civilai. "But directors are very sensitive. They know when people walk out of their films."

"Even when they're dead," said Siri.

"You're at the greatest sporting event of your lives and you sit in an empty cinema watching movies you don't understand," said Daeng. "You do know you're both complete idiots, don't you?"

"Not complete yet," said Siri.

"We're working on it," said Civilai.

They were interrupted by the crack of a starting pistol. The twenty-kilometer race walk had started. Thirty-four men waddled around the stadium like ducks. They would complete one lap before leaving through the huge stadium doors to begin their scenic walk along the riverbank. The Lao Cheer was buried beneath the stadium roar. Time seemed to be less than urgent to the walkers. They ambled along the back straight toward the exit. Even the Lao with binoculars had trouble picking out Khamon in the pack. But still they chanted his name and beat their drum. And, all too soon, the walkers were gone. The large screen followed the leaders for a few minutes, then switched to the ladies' high jump.

Civilai turned to Dtui. "So what exactly did Phosy say?" he asked, continuing their attempts to decipher the policeman's phone call from the previous evening.

"I can tell you what he didn't say," she replied.

"That," said Siri, "would be an endless list. Let's stick to his actual words."

She talked them through the phone call again.

"Ah, so he called her Comrade Daeng once more," said Siri. "He doesn't trust the telephone system either. We should be careful what we say."

"We don't exactly have anything to say, do we?" said Daeng. "Haven't we given up on assassination theories?"

"Certainly not," said Civilai. "We still have a possible assassin in the squad. We just don't have the resources to follow everyone."

"I don't see the shooters here," said Dtui.

"Their dormitory's empty," said Civilai. "The Red Army has invited them to enjoy a week at the barracks at some other place I can't pronounce. They kindly let me know this morning after they'd left."

"How far is it?" Siri asked.

"Still inside the city limits," said Civilai. "If there is an assassin in the group there's nothing stopping him jumping on a train."

"We'd drive ourselves barmy trying to keep track of all the participants," said Siri. "Let's just focus on helping Phosy solve his Vientiane murder."

They were drowned out by the screams of the Lao crowd around them and their international fan club. The drummer beat his drum. Daeng squeezed Siri's arm and he looked up at the big screen. Already the race walkers had settled on a pace and the field had stretched out. A group of thirty had progressed to the front. The lead camera was on a truck beside the front three of these and amongst them, shorter than the other two, was Khamon.

"Look at him go," said Civilai.

The Lao flags waved and the supporters cried out his name and nobody else in the stadium knew what the fuss was about. But the Lao had drawn attention to themselves. One stadium camera found the drummer and zoomed in on the vociferous group. And there they were on the big screen and probably on TV around the world.

The Lao screamed their delight and danced an impromptu *lamvong* conga line around the drum, waving at themselves on the screen. Peels of good-natured laughter rippled around the stadium. This was replaced by a Lao groan of disappointment when the main screen returned to the high jumpers. An Italian with legs comprising eighty percent of her body was about to take her final jump but the Lao weren't interested.

"He's going to win it for certain," shouted Chom the rat catcher, maps of sweat seeping through his T-shirt. "And I'll miss it."

"How so?"

"Interview," said Chom, modestly.

"What for?"

"It's just TV," he said, attempting to keep the smile off his face without success.

"You're going to be on TV?" said Daeng. "That's great."

"I'm a bit nervous, to tell the truth," he said. "It's only a community thing, they said. They talk to professional people here for the Olympics and they ask how we do things at home compared to the Soviet Union. I'll be with my mate from Botswana."

"Are you taking Roger?" she asked.

"No, auntie. The TV station's got its own interpreters. I'll tell you later how it went."

He hadn't been gone a minute when the stadium screen returned to the race. The Lao contingent looked up with open mouths like fish staring at a lure. The coverage began with the second camera car showing a competitor being disqualified for walking in some illegal manner. The Lao feared that their man might have fallen to the same fate. But then the picture returned to the front three, who had stretched their lead. There was a ten-meter gap to the fourth-placed walker. Leading the three was an Italian. He was followed by a Belarusian and, to the delight of the crowd, a Lao. The Lao Cheer made up for its tardiness with its volume. There were those who thought there must have been a murder rather than a miracle as the Lao men and women screamed with delight.

Once again the camera singled out the Lao supporters and caught an overjoyed Dr. Siri and Daeng doing their moves on a seat. For those who had never heard of Laos, this was a fitting introduction.

"He looks really comfortable up there," said Civilai, glaring at the screen.

"Wouldn't it be something if he won?" said Dtui.

"Don't hex him," said Civilai.

"He seems to be the only one wearing a T-shirt," said Siri. "All the others are in skimpy singlets."

"Perhaps he's cold," said Daeng. "He trained in the tropics. We have to assume he knows what he's doing."

The camera truck followed the three walkers with the river in the background and small pockets of onlookers in their "might be seen on TV" fashions. They'd covered five of the twenty kilometers and Khamon looked as calm as a lull in a monsoon.

The cameras returned to the high jump accompanied by another groan from the Lao and a laugh from the crowd. There were allotted seat numbers but during the qualifying rounds nobody seemed to care where you stood or sat. Or, at least, the ushers didn't know how to control a gang of excited fans. The organizers just wanted the place full for as long as possible. They'd given free tickets to the trade unions and the military but it wasn't easy to fill a 100,000-seat stadium.

Siri and Daeng returned to order.

"What were we talking about?" said Siri.

"Phosy," said Dtui.

"Right, what else did he say?" said Daeng.

"He sent regards from my Auntie Arpy," she said.

"And you don't have an Auntie Arpy," said Daeng.

"No, but after we talked last night I remembered a game we used to play with our friend Ou at the Lycee."

"May she rest in peace," said Civilai.

"Oh, she is," said Siri.

"Well, Ou studied in Australia," said Dtui. "She liked to drink. She had a lot of friends. There was a drinking game they played over there. I suppose, not so much a game as a mental exercise. One night she came over to our place and she taught it to us. It's stupid but it's really effective. It's called Arpy."

"How does it work?" said Siri.

"It's a sort of way to disguise your language," said Dtui. "In front of every vowel sound you insert the word 'arp.' So, in English the phrase 'I love you' would become 'arp-I larp-ove yarp-ou". It takes a while to work it out but once you get the flow you can become fluent. It's great when you don't want people to know you're talking about them. It's harder for the listener but because you know how it's put together you can deduce what's been said."

"Does it work with Lao?" Civilai asked.

"Of course," said Dtui. "Every language has vowel sounds. That night at the dormitory we played it in Lao. So, 'I love you' would become "karp-oy harp-uk jarp-ow.' See?"

"Then that's the language you and Phosy can use to pass on our secret communications," said Siri.

"Well, look, I could teach you three easily enough."

"Old dogs. New tricks," said Siri.

"I don't—" Dtui began but she was interrupted by another yell from the crowd as the coverage of the race continued on the big screen. Khamon was no longer in the front three. The trailing group had caught up with the leaders and positions had been juggled. The Lao was still in the group but had dropped back to around tenth position, twenty meters behind the leader. He still looked fresh and, well, what was twenty meters in the Olympics? The Lao supporters screamed and waved their flags. The stadium reacted. The camera found its favorite group once more. They'd become a feature. It was a pity so few people back in Laos had a functioning TV.

The evening crawled in on the back of a pink sky and every five minutes the screen showed the progress of the walkers. Khamon lost touch with the leading group but whenever they caught sight of him in the pack the Lao Cheer would urge him forward. But then came a time when Khamon no longer featured on the screen at all. He was so far back there was no camera to film him. The terraces grew sleepy with occasional bursts of applause for jumpers and tossers but the race had lost its appeal. His teammates feared the worst. Khamon had given up or had been disqualified.

The next stimulation for the drowsy supporters was when the stadium door opened to the sound of a cannon firing and a single trumpet fanfare. The first of the walkers, a lanky Italian, entered the arena. He was met with a tumultuous reception and a slightly begrudging Lao Cheer. There were those in the squad who still chose to disbelieve the drama they'd seen on the screen. TV was fantasy to them and not always credible. They fixed their gaze on the gate, expecting Khamon to charge into the stadium, but all they saw was a Russian and an East German followed by an assortment of wobbly walkers. But no Khamon.

"Should we go and look for him?" Siri asked.

"It was a great beginning," said Daeng. "He did us proud whatever happened to him."

"He did that," said Civilai.

All the surviving walkers completed the race. According to the announcement, two had dropped out and seven were disqualified. The field events continued and the Lao considered going home for a drink. But they owed it to the walkers to give a final cheer to the winners. After forty minutes the medal platforms were carried out to the track and three adorable women in ethnic costumes stood before it.

The Chairman of the Soviet Race Walk Association began presenting the medals to the winners. He was about to shake hands with the Italian when there came a disturbance from the far side of the stadium.

There were strict rules on what constituted lawful walking but nowhere in the annals was there a rule which stipulated how long a competitor had to complete the race. So it was that, unaided and still observing the accepted technique, the last walker entered the stadium to begin his lap of honor. The officials hurriedly cleared the track of debris. All eyes were on Khamon. His first hundred meters was met with polite applause. Many of the Lao were on their way to the exit with their drum. But once the screen found their man on the back straight the supporters quickly regrouped and yelled their approval. The applause rose to a cheer and by the time the Lao had reached the final straight even the announcer's voice was drowned in the deluge. A close-up of Khamon's smiling face towered above him. He performed a half-pirouette to wave at the crowd, which probably infringed some regulation, but there wasn't an official on the planet who would disqualify him now. The winners, still on their podia, applauded the Lao as he passed them. Someone had found a measuring tape and had strung it across the finishing line. Khamon walked into it with his arms raised and a smile that made the front page of newspapers around the world. Khamon had become the most popular loser in the history of the Games.

CHAPTER FIFTEEN
A Lopsided Man

In the good old days of cinema you'd get value for money. There'd be a newsreel and a cartoon, perhaps a short Western and an interval before the main feature. This gave you time to buy ice creams and sugary drinks from a lady with a tray hanging from her neck. Sometimes her bosoms would be too large to see everything on display. At least that's what Siri remembered from the picture houses in Paris.

In order to keep the seats full, cinema owners began to show more and more short dramas known as cliff-hangers. These were so named after a common episode ending where the hero or heroine was left hanging from a cliff, usually from a feeble branch. The only way you'd know whether your favorite star survived this impossible situation would be to come back the following week, which Siri always did. In all his years of study he didn't lose one star.

But all that experience doesn't prepare you for a cliff-hanger of your own. Here he is in the cockpit of a doomed Aeroflot aircraft with the ceiling fan whirring overhead and a mountain looming up ahead. The audience gasps. His death is impending but he doesn't have the option of coming back the following week to learn of his fate. Then he sees it—the handbrake. He dives for it. It sticks. He looks around for oil but there's no time. The mountain is just meters away. He yanks at the handbrake one more time . . . and it works. The aircraft screeches to a halt with the nose cone nudging the rock face. He sits on the floor for a moment to catch his breath and savor the adrenalin rush.

He'd almost completely forgotten Madam Daeng. He knew she'd be angry. They'd been on their way to a performance by the Moscow Classical Ballet State Concert Ensemble at the Village cultural center. She knew that ballet and floral crochet held the same fascination in her husband's mind so he assumed she'd say he disappeared deliberately just to avoid it. He didn't, of course. Not consciously anyway. He just hoped not too many people witnessed his passing to the other side. It never got easier to explain.

So here he was in the cockpit of his large Soviet metaphor. He knew from experience he had limited time to ask questions and interpret the answers. Auntie Bpoo could have simplified all these encounters by just sending him daily memos but she was a pain in the backside. She'd told him he was the master of his own afterlife. It meant nothing. Stopping the plane in mid-air should have given him more confidence but he still doubted himself.

He opened the cockpit door and there in the front row of business class sat Comrade Noo enjoying a martini. This was a disaster in itself. Siri only ever saw people in these cameos who were dead or as good as. The family back in economy—the only other passengers—was undeniably in the former category. They were a tangle of misplaced body parts and gore and discontent. Somehow they'd managed to press the attendant alert button, which flashed above their heads.

Siri ignored them and sat beside Noo.

"Noo?"

"Siri? Peanut?"

"No, thanks."

"You need to fasten your seatbelt."

"We aren't moving."

"Right."

Comrade Noo sipped his martini.

"I didn't think you . . ." said Siri.

"Desperate times," said Noo. "I might even have a joint later. Amazing what you can get in business class."

"Are you . . . ?" Siri began.

"Not yet."

"That's a relief."

"Really?"

"Of course," said Siri. "Why would you doubt that? I don't want you dead."

The disjointed family in economy was getting rowdy.

"Quiet back there," Siri shouted.

"I've failed," said Noo. "All that damned tree-sitting and dirt-digging and muck-raking. What good was it? What did it achieve? I'm better off dead."

Siri thought about Mr. Geung's message. Noo had lost his feet. He looked down and, sure enough, Comrade Noo had nowhere to put his shoes. Somewhere in his subconscious the monk was losing his faith. That's why he was sitting beside Siri in business class. He was in search of a guru and here they were frozen at the top of a mountain. Nothing subtle about that. Siri got it. He was supposed to be Noo's seer. It was probably time to give the monk a blast of wisdom that would inspire him back to life. But Siri was no philosopher. Philosophy didn't ever stop you getting hit by a bullet. You needed someone to shout "duck." What Comrade Noo wanted was a coach. He remembered the Notre Dame trainer's words to Ronald Reagan.

"Noo," he said, "sometimes when the team is up against it and the breaks are beating the boys, tell them to go out there with all they've got and win just one for . . . Dr. Siri."

Noo looked blank and Siri realized he hadn't chosen the most appropriate movie quote so he added a few lines of his own. He had no qualms about mixing sports metaphors.

"Noo," he said, "every game you enter, you leave a trail of goodness and honesty behind on the field. The little people love you because you speak for them. You stand up to the bullies. The oppressors beat you this time but it was a low-scoring round in a bout you'll go on to win with a knockout. I want to be proud of you out there on the field. The team's counting on you."

He wasn't sure whether Noo got it. But the monk nodded, put down his martini, and walked to the emergency door on two perfectly functioning feet. That was a good sign. He read the instructions, pulled the red lever, opened the hatch and stepped off the plane. That was less of a good sign in Siri's mind.

"Eh, you," came a voice from economy. "We need some attention here."

Siri was in control of the flight. He'd pulled the hand-brake so he felt obliged to look after his passengers, even the poor ones. He walked along the aisle to the

troublesome family. There were blood and guts everywhere. They still hadn't sorted out whose parts were whose.

"Can I be of service?" Siri asked.

"You certainly can," came a familiar voice from somewhere beneath the seat. "If you aren't going to turn down
the air-conditioning the least you can do is provide a
blanket."

"Certainly, sir," said Siri. "Would you like individual
blankets or one large one? Or how about a plastic garbage
bag?"

It was when he leaned down to turn off the flight
attendant light that he saw the remains of a French maid
uniform.

"I don't know," said Siri.

He and Daeng were having a stodgy breakfast in the
cafeteria. It was day seven. The Lao delegation was torn
between supporting their competitor in the woman's hundred meters at the stadium and the two soldiers in the
rapid fire event at the Sportivnaya Range. The events were
on at the same time. So the supporters had worked out a
roster and half went to the range and half to the Lenin
stadium to encourage Nah, the elder sister. She had an
ant's hope in a buffalo stampede of qualifying for the next
round.

Siri and Daeng had woken up with hangovers and were
not likely to spend the morning in an enclosed space
where people were firing guns.

"What do you mean you don't know?" said Daeng. "Is
he dead or not?"

"We need to contact Phosy to be sure," said Siri.

"But?"

"But there's a chance I might have talked him out of . . ."

". . . of dying?"

"It's possible."

"Bravo. So that makes you . . . what? A brown belt?"

"I don't think shamans have belts."

He looked once more at the sausage on his fork and put it back on the plate.

"But you did actually talk to him," said Daeng.

"Yes. Back and forth. It was thrilling."

"You won't forget me when they have you over there on the other side full time, will you?"

"We might even be there together some day."

"I'd rather not. You're much more accustomed to inspecting body parts than me. You're sure it was them?"

"The maid's uniform was the first clue. Then I found the bouncer's wrist tattoo. It was a cobra. I'm pretty sure it was them."

"But there was nothing to identify the student, Manoi?"

"Nothing I recognized. But there were certainly three bodies. It seems likely one was him. And the voice seemed to be his. His head was under the seat. I wasn't about to forage around in all that offal to get a confirmation."

"You realize how tricky this is."

"Absolutely."

"The son of an influential deal broker in Laos is killed. The only way we know this is because my husband met the victims in a . . . ?"

". . . supernatural event."

"In a supernatural event onboard an airplane frozen in mid air. And they were dismembered. And as your other world corresponds to events in the real world we have to assume they are actually dead. And that they died in a horrific manner. But how can we confirm that? The television and newspapers only report good news. We can hardly go to the police and make inquiries without incriminating ourselves. In fact we don't even know how they died."

"I've been thinking about that," said Siri. "Remember yesterday when the leading walker arrived at the stadium? There was the sound of a cannon. We assumed it was part of the entertainment."

"You joked that it was probably an electrical junction box blowing up," said Daeng.

"It happens all the time back home and it was comforting that not even the Soviets had been able to solve all their technological faults."

"Now you're having second thoughts?"

"Yes. I mean, who's going to go to the trouble of firing a cannon for a walker? Even at the Olympic Games. What if it was an explosion in Manoi's building? The apartment block he lived in wasn't so far from the stadium. What if Manoi and his staff were gathered in front of the TV watching the race, and bang?"

"Siri, the worst an exploding TV can do is spray a little glass."

"I don't mean it was an equipment malfunction. I mean, what if someone planted a bomb there?"

"How would they get it past the tattoo man?"

"He wouldn't need to. Manoi lived on the third floor. If the killer had access to the second floor he could have piled up a stack of dynamite directly underneath Manoi's apartment."

They both stared at Siri's sausage and pondered.

"If it was a bomb, the authorities would assume it was an

act of terrorism," said Daeng. "Their first reaction would be that it was one of the restless Soviet states making a statement. They'd bring in the KGB and the anti-terrorist units."

"And to thwart the terrorists they'd say nothing about it," said Siri. "But there'd be a huge behind-the-scenes inquiry and they'd identify the victims and pick up on the Lao connection. We might not be their chief suspects but we'd certainly be on their list. In fact they might even be able to place me at the apartment on that first day."

"So eventually they'll come to see us," said Daeng. "We've already given them grief over the blackmail scandal so they'll be delighted to pin something on us."

"That blackmailing was hardly our fault," said Siri. "In fact we made them look better. I imagine they'll come to us to ask for our help in solving this murder as well."

"Siri, there are times I believe you see yourself as the main character in an international mystery series," she said, "flitting off here and there to solve crimes. You aren't as indispensible as you think you are, my husband. I want you to promise me you won't offer them advice this time. When they come I want you to perform that expression you do so well."

"Which one?"

"The look of total surprise when they tell you about the murder."

Siri tried it.

"That's the one," said Daeng. "But if they appear not to know you were at the apartment I want you to offer up that information anyway."

"Tell them? Why?"

"Because in a good Communist country there are spies

on every corner. They have a photo of us leaving the blackmailer's apartment. Someone could have seen you at Manoi's. You have to assume they know everything."

"Not so much that they could prevent an explosion, obviously," said Siri.

"And I think we should consider Inspector Phosy's position," she continued. "He made contact with the young man's father. He was worried. He asked us to help. We failed. He isn't going to be pleased about that. I recommend we send Phosy some suggestions as to how he might sidestep any possible repercussions."

"I'll get Dtui to compose an Arpy message."

They were interrupted by Chom the rat catcher, who'd spotted them across the cafeteria and come running in their direction. He was as stoked as a furnace.

"Comrade doctor, comrade auntie," he said. "You won't believe what's happened."

He sat down at the table and shadow-boxed away his excess energy.

"I thought you'd be going to the track with everyone else," said Daeng.

"I was going. I was going," he said, "when this guy from the Soviet Social Newsletter stops me at the front door. He's with Roger. He tells me they're proposing to have a competition."

"I assume he wasn't talking about running," said Siri.

"No," said Chom. "In the newsletter interview I was talking about Comrade Civilai's idea that there should be an Olympics for rat catchers."

"I don't think that was exactly—" Siri began.

"So Yusov the Russian rat catcher picks up on that and tells the newsletter editor he'd win hands down if there was such a competition. Real boastful he was. So the newsletter editor says, "Why don't we do it?" They asked Sammy from Botswana at the TV interview yesterday and he's really up for it. And they found me this morning and asked if I'd compete. Naturally I jumped at the chance."

"You can't be serious," said Daeng.

"Deadly," said Chom.

"And how are they going to organize such a thing?" asked Siri.

"They'll sort that out at the newsletter," said Chom. "What do you think?"

"We're very happy for you," said Daeng.

"I'll want some of that good old Lao Cheer," said Chom.

"Oh, I'm sure you'll get that," said Daeng.

"Great," said Chom and threw playful air punches at the old couple.

He stood to leave but Siri said, "Why didn't they ask you at the TV interview yesterday?"

"What?"

"You said they asked the Botswana fellow if he'd join the competition. Why didn't they ask you then?"

"Oh, I missed that," said Chom. "Got on the wrong train going in the wrong direction. But never mind. I don't have a face for TV."

And their sprinter merged with the early morning crowd. Siri and Daeng looked at their half-ignored breakfast.

"How do you suppose we might go about finding a decent bowl of noodles in Moscow?" Siri asked.

"Information desk," said Daeng.

They found a French speaker at the desk. They collected

Dtui, Civilai and Roger, climbed in a mini-van and twenty minutes later they were at the Kabul Noodle Bazaar on Arbut. It sounded and looked a lot worse than it was. It was decorated in a style Civilai liked to call, "Fill up all the walls with bad posters and hang unrecognizable stuff everywhere." From the atmosphere you'd never know the Afghans were being invaded by the Soviets. It didn't stop them making damned good noodles or serving them with a smile.

Both Dtui and Civilai knew with various degrees of certainty of Siri's relationship with the spirit world. They'd both seen evidence although Civilai cultivated his logjam of denial.

"All tricks," he'd say.

But Roger? Well, Roger sat with one strand of noodles dangling from his mouth as Siri described his meeting with the assorted parts of Comrade Manoi and expounded on his theory that a future Lao president had been assassinated. When the translator had first introduced himself at Sheremetyevo Airport, the Lao administrators had assumed he was KGB. Siri and Civilai considered it *de rigueur* for Soviets in professional contact with foreigners to work as informants. They hadn't completely shaken off that belief but Roger's intervention at the blackmailing meeting had, at the very least, brought him into their camp. And if he was a spy what damage would it do for the Lao to confirm for him that they were demented and therefore harmless?

Yet Roger was clearly fascinated by Siri's account. His education had not been limited to language. He'd learned of Laos' history and geography but had been most fascinated by her alignment to the world of the spirits. Perhaps that element had first enticed him to learn a language only .0009% of the world understood.

"So, to summarize," said Civilai. "A Lao student, his bodyguard and his pseudo-French maid might or might not have been blown to bits by someone on our team. We have no bodies and no news reports but still you would have us track down the culprit?"

"That's correct," said Siri.

"Wait," said Roger. "I need to savor the greatness."

"No time for sarcasm," said Siri.

"No, I think he might be actually savoring the greatness," said Daeng, staring into the translator's wide eyes.

"No, why, yes, yes," said Roger. "No question about it. This is way beyond the life development I expected when I selected Lao as my major."

"Then while you're riding on this magic cloud," said Civilai, "what chance is there you might ferret around and pick up rumors about a building explosion?"

"I'll go there right now," he said, the noodle still dangling from his mouth.

"We don't want anyone to think we sent you," said Daeng.

"I'll be the most discreet of bystanders," said Roger. "Don't worry."

"Then go forth, brave Roger, and find us a murder scene," said Siri, and he wrote down the address. In two minutes Roger was out in the street looking for a taxi. They watched him through the greasy window.

"So, we trust him, right?" said Dtui.

"After the story he's just heard I imagine he's on his way to a mental asylum to make an appointment for us," said Civilai. "Either that or he's as mad as us."

"I vote that he's as mad as us," said Daeng. "And I'm something of an authority on madness."

"Then let us turn our attention to the perpetrator," said Siri.

"Of the murder that, as yet, does not exist," said Civilai.

"We can eliminate most of the competitors because they were with us at the stadium at the time of the explosion," said Daeng.

"Except for the shooters," said Dtui. "They weren't there."

"But you know we didn't exactly do a roll call," said Civilai. "Anyone could have slipped in and slipped back without us noticing. We were all distracted by the race walk. And if there was a bomb it might have been on a timer. It could have been set at any time."

"I don't think so," said Siri. "The killer would have wanted to be sure the victim was in the building. He wouldn't go to all this trouble only to find Manoi was off at the *boulangerie* buying baguettes. He'd have been there watching."

"We have to find out what the shooters were doing on the evening of the race walk," said Daeng.

"Why are we bothering to do the job of the local police?" said Civilai.

"Because, firstly, when the authorities discover that a Lao was killed, I'd like to be one step ahead of them," said Siri.

"Me too," said Daeng.

"And secondly," said Siri, "the boy's father entrusted us with the wellbeing of his son. We did a lousy job. If we can come up with results it might placate the old man and keep Phosy safe."

"And how do we go about discovering the whereabouts of the soldiers yesterday afternoon?" said Civilai.

"We ask them," said Daeng.

Not for the first time, Malee was sleeping in a hammock beside the roll-out bed of Gongjai the reformed prostitute. The child was growing up in a number of perilous situations and Phosy didn't like it. Laos was too small. Information was too cheap. Life was too temporary. You could change any decision, reverse any conviction, steer public opinion with just a few US dollars or the threat of harm to a family member. So Phosy had sent his daughter to Siri's official house, just to be sure. And just as well. It was on Phosy's first night alone that the stranger arrived with the news the inspector had been dreading.

Phosy was usually the last to bathe in the communal bathroom. He rarely arrived home before dark and often when the moon was peeking down through the broken tiles on the roof. That night he'd ladled enough water on himself to drown a turtle. The sweat and grime washed off but the slime of bureaucracy clung to him. Again he thought of the forty thousand dollars in his desk drawer and the breathing space that much money could give a man.

He reached for his towel but it wasn't on the nail where he'd hung it. He looked around and that was when he saw the lopsided man. He wore Phosy's towel on his head like a turban.

"Sorry to disturb your ablutions," said the man. He was distorted. It was as if two men of different builds had been sliced down the middle and reassembled as one. His muscular side leaned against the doorframe.

Phosy wasn't easily embarrassed or intimidated.

"You can either stare at my groin for another minute and regret that nature didn't endow you so kindly," he said, "or you can toss me the towel."

"I'm a messenger," said the man.

"Then give me the message and throw me the towel, you asymmetrical freak."

"Don't give me an excuse to hurt you," said the man.

"I'll take that as a threat," said Phosy. "That's a shame. We could have been such good friends."

"Comrade Thonglai is very disappointed with you," said the man. "He just learned that his son has been killed. You were entrusted with his safety and you failed. If you don't find out who was responsible in the next few days, you never know what might happen. Heaven forbid your family meets the same fate as Comrade Manoi."

He removed the towel from his head, threw it to Phosy and turned to leave. He'd looked much better in a towel.

"Can I just summarize?" said Phosy. He wiped his feet before wrapping himself in the towel.

"What?" said the man. He stopped and looked over his shoulder.

"Your boss's son was killed," said Phosy.

"That's right."

"And because I couldn't prevent it, despite being seven thousand kilometers away, my family is in danger?"

"You got it."

"Then you're under arrest," said Phosy.

"Yeah, right."

"No, I'm serious," said Phosy. "Threatening a police officer is a crime."

Lopsided turned toward the policeman.

"No," he said. "You know what a crime is? This is a crime."

He pulled up the flap of his safari shirt to give Phosy an uninterrupted view of the pistol in his belt.

"You're right," said Phosy. "It is a crime. Threats with a weapon. Put your hands up."

"Don't push your luck, policeman."

With dry feet and the advantage of surprise, Phosy was on the messenger before the lopsided man could react. He had him on the tiled floor, bounced his head a couple of times and relieved him of his weapon. Something might have broken after that: a finger perhaps or a nose. Statistics showed that eighty percent of domestic accidents occurred in the bathroom.

Dtui chose day eight to go in search of the shooters because they didn't have anyone competing on that day. She was given a route map by the ladies at the information booth and she set off with a plastic box containing her secret weapon—sticky rice and mangos. At the Kabul Noodle Bazaar they'd learned where to buy glutinous rice and the nurse had risen early that morning to produce a batch. At the Cherkisovsky Market she'd found mangos. They came from Vietnam and cost a fortune but the Lao administrators decided they were worth the investment. They were part of the range of exotic fruits and foodstuff that had found their way into Moscow for the games to pad out the empty shop fronts.

Dtui had been nominated for the role of military liaison for a number of reasons. She could speak Russian, which gave her a better chance of getting through the gates. She was married to a policeman, so she wasn't intimidated by men in uniform. And she was pretty and chubby like the sisters and wives and mothers of the men on the shooting team.

As it turned out, getting into the barracks had been simple enough. She went to reception and told them she had some sweets for the Lao team. They copied down her ID number and name and gave her directions to the recreation room. She'd been expecting something less convivial. The shooters were playing games or watching the Olympics on TV. When they saw her they gathered around and suddenly she was with a group of seven lads from any village she'd ever been to. They were funny and honest. They sat in a circle eating their sticky rice and mango, missing home and telling Nurse Dtui their secrets.

"We'd sooner be with the rest of you at the village," said Sompoo.

He was long-necked and clumsy looking but he was surprisingly open considering he'd not met the nurse before. Not at all the assassin they'd pictured.

"We're negotiating to get back there for the last three days of the Games," he said, "but it's not easy. The Red Army provided our weapons and sent us trainers so they feel kind of responsible for us. Once our events were over they insisted we accept their hospitality out here."

"It's good though," said a spiky-haired youth named Boom. "They arrange activities for us. Church tours and stuff. They're kind."

"We've been watching the events on TV," said Ming, the eldest of the shooters. He was lanky and had the type of smile a single Dtui would have swooned over. "And we're over the moon at the support you've all been giving the team. That walking race was the greatest."

Dtui felt guilty. She'd been sent there as a spy, to

observe, to ask questions and use her instincts. She'd been told to identify a likely assassin but she could see none. The only man missing from the group was their leader, Colonel Fah Hai. He'd begged off the sticky rice feast, claiming to have a stomach bug. He'd been unpleasant from the beginning. If she really had to identify a potential killer, his would be the name at the top of her list. That was until they started talking about the twenty-kilometer race walk. Just mentioning it started a buzz of excitement.

"Wasn't that something?" said Sompoo.

"I'd given up on Khamon," said Ming.

"At the start he'd looked so strong," said Sompoo. "I thought he was going to win the bloody thing."

"And then it's all over and the doors open and there he is," said Sompoo's friend, Boom, "smiling and strolling along. I'd have given him a medal just for that."

"And there was a close-up of the Lao flag and all you lot dancing and cheering," said Sompoo. "I've never felt so proud. And the world's watching and they're all saying, 'Those Lao, they never give up.'"

"I cried," said Boom.

"Me too," said Dtui. "It was a shame none of you could get to the stadium. You'd have loved the atmosphere."

The soldiers stared guiltily in the direction of the only man not to have spoken since she arrived. He was probably in his late twenties but his face looked old and wise. His eyes hid behind two curtains of curly black eyebrows. He blushed at the sudden attention.

"Sitti was there," said Boom.

"Shut up," said Ming.

"We can tell her," said Sompoo. "She's not going to give anything away, are you Big Sister?"

"Not a word," she said.

"Sitti went AWOL, you see?" said Sompoo. "He just jogged out through the gate wearing his tracksuit as if he was training. The guards didn't know what to say. And he kept jogging all the way to the station."

"And you went to the stadium?" Dtui asked.

Sitti nodded.

"Brought us back souvenirs," said Boom holding up his brand new Marx-Lenin wristwatch. "A dozen of the things."

Dtui smiled. "How did you get back in?" she asked.

"Same way he left," said Ming. "They'd changed the shift by then. Didn't know he'd been gone half the day and most of the night. Wish I'd done it too."

"Great atmosphere, wasn't it?" she said.

Sitti nodded again, obviously embarrassed.

"He doesn't talk much, does he?" said Dtui.

"He's shy," said Ming. "A man of actions rather than words."

"Why didn't you come up and sit with us in the west stand?" Dtui asked.

Sitti thought about the question for a while. "You were attracting too much attention up there," he said. "Last thing I wanted was my face on the TV screen for all the officers here to see."

"Good point," said Dtui.

She remembered from her visit to the firing range that Sitti was a pistol shooter. There was nothing menacing about him. He was just a sweet, shy soldier. But he was the only one in the group with no confirmable alibi for the evening of the explosion. An explosion that, as yet, was unsubstantiated.

"Did Colonel Fah Hai watch the race with you?" she asked.

There were a number of sideways glances and winks.

"The colonel prefers to hang out with the Soviets," said Ming. "He speaks the lingo. So he watches all the competitions up there in their officers' mess."

"We only see him when he's taking us to events or activities," said Sompoo.

"You don't like him much, do you?" said Dtui.

Their smiles answered her question.

CHAPTER SIXTEEN
Little Boxers All the Same

"Phosy!" came a voice from above.

The inspector was about to head off on his moped but his boss, Comrade Oudomxai, leaned over the third floor balcony and beckoned him upstairs. The chief of police was not a policeman. He was an accountant and he was one of the main reasons Phosy was so seriously considering floating himself and his family across the river to a camp in Thailand. He arrived in front of Oudomxai's office winded from the jog up three flights.

"Phosy, have you arrested anyone in the past twenty-four hours?" asked the chief. He was a wide, solid man of little substance.

"No, sir," said Phosy. "Can I go now?"

"No. I . . . there has been a query," said Oudomxai. "It comes from a very high source."

He glared at Phosy who stared blankly back at him.

"I'd like you to consider your answer very carefully," said the chief.

"That was my answer," said Phosy. "If I'd arrested somebody they'd be in one of our cells and their name and the circumstances would be documented in our log book."

"One would hope so."

"So?"

"So one of our officers claims to have seen you . . . apprehending somebody last night."

"*Apprehend* meaning?"

"Drag forcefully into a car."

"Time? Place?"

"In front of the police dormitory at around eleven P.M."

"And by 'officer' you mean the rarely sober guard who mans the police box in front of our building? He's the only one likely to be present at that hour but it sounds like he wasn't totally conscious. Damn, that means we have to dismiss yet another guard. Perhaps if we offered a higher salary . . ."

"Are you saying he's lying?"

"Perhaps just confused," said Phosy. "Firstly, I don't have a car. Secondly, my wife's off in Moscow so at eleven P.M. I was helping a young woman get home from a bar before curfew, if you know what I mean. I was concerned she might have epilepsy so I stayed with her at her place to make sure she didn't swallow her tongue."

He nudged the chief in the arm.

"The complainant said—"

"What's his name?"

"That's not your concern. The complainant states that his assistant went to see you yesterday evening on some administrative matter and he did not return."

"Well, that's it, then," said Phosy.

"That's what?"

"This missing assistant went to see me. I wasn't there.

He was about to leave when somebody in a car mugged him and dragged him into the back seat. The drunk guard woke up temporarily from his stupor, spied the abduction and assumed it was an arrest. End of story."

"Except there's no assistant."

"Probably dead," said Phosy. "Muggers who can afford a car don't leave witnesses."

The chief clearly had coronas of doubt and confusion slowly rotating around his mind.

"If that's so . . ." he began.

"Yes?"

"I'm putting you on this case. I want that man found."

"If he's still alive I'll personally deliver him to his boss," said Phosy. "Who did you say the complainant was?"

"I . . . didn't. Just bring him to me."

"Yes, sir. Can I go?"

"Yes, dismissed," said the chief.

Phosy saluted. The chief didn't know how to respond.

It doesn't count as an arrest if you're being held in a room above a noodle shop. The lopsided man was handcuffed to a pipe and had a backward balaclava on his head. Every hour or so, Mr. Geung's fiancée, Tukta, would lift the mask to below his eyes and squirt coconut water into his nose. It was an uncomfortable way to receive nutrients but the messenger was vile mouthed and it was an unpleasant experience to remove the dishrag from between his teeth.

Phosy sat silently opposite him and considered his plan. If it went wrong he would no longer be a police-man and the money burning a hole in his desk drawer would find a purpose. If it went right, there would be one hell of a shake up in Vientiane. He composed the next Arpy conversation in his head. He'd call in an hour. He wouldn't tell his wife about the threat to Malee and the fact she was being looked after by their friends. He wouldn't specifically mention the messenger. But he'd urge the Lao in Moscow to expedite the capture of the assassin because Phosy was hanging on by a thread and he was more alone than ever.

Sergei the waiter had ordered in a buffet of Russian sweet-meats for his favorite, and invariably only, guests. The salted herring and pickles were the ideal companions for Ochakovo beer.

"All right, let's go through it one more time," said Siri.

"We're eating," said Civilai.

"Some of us can eat and think at the same time," said Siri. "And time's against us. Phosy says the father already knows about his son's killing, which confirms it happened. I'm assuming he didn't learn it from the BBC. We're in the same city as the explosion and we still haven't heard a damned thing about it."

"Which begs the question, how did the father find out?" said Daeng. "As we only mentioned it in code we have to assume he has another informant here with better intelligence than us."

"And if that's true, why's he putting pressure on Phosy to find the killer?" said Dtui.

"Unless," said Siri, adopting his Sherlock Holmes chin grab, "he heard directly from the killer."

"You think the assassin would phone home to Laos and boast to the father about killing his son?" said Civilai.

"Perhaps not the killer himself," said Daeng, "but the individual or group that arranged the hit. This is politics.

Once the perpetrator was certain the killing was successful he could have used it for leverage against the family."

"*The Godfather*," said Siri.

"Exactly," said Civilai.

As usual, Daeng and Dtui were lost.

"Family honor," said Siri.

"You mean something like, 'You mess with my business and I'll blow up your son'?" said Dtui.

"It's not impossible," said Daeng.

"It might help to know who Thonglai's enemies are," said Siri.

"I imagine he has many," said Civilai.

"Well, that's not something we can find out here," said Dtui. "And I'm not going to suggest Phosy starts delving into the old man's business connections. My daughter's father is in enough muck as it is. I know we were speaking in code but I could tell there was a lot he wasn't saying."

"Oh, dear," said Civilai looking beyond the bar. "I think we're about to be arrested."

The others followed his gaze to see Elvis walking toward them. He was dressed to match the Olympic village wallpaper and wore a yellow tie as wide as a kipper.

"Do you think it's about the explosion?" Dtui whispered.

"If it is we know nothing," said Daeng.

Elvis arrived at the table.

"Ah, my little Asian friends," he said. "I see you're sampling our ethnic delicacies."

In Roger's absence, Dtui took on the role of translator.

"When in Rome," said Siri.

"Quite," said Elvis.

The inspector seemed to be in a particularly good mood. He sat in the empty chair. Sergei brought a fresh glass and Dtui poured a beer. Daeng spooned some *hors d'oeuvres* onto a plate for the detective. That was the Lao way, compulsory cordiality.

"Aren't you curious as to how I found you?" asked Elvis.

"Anything to do with the note on our conference room door and the map?" asked Siri.

"Very good, detective doctor," said Elvis. "Then I should ask a more difficult question. Are you also curious as to why I have come to your secret haven to see you?"

"We have one or two theories," said Civilai.

"But you're looking quite pleased with yourself," Siri cut in. "So my guess is that you've come to discuss a closed rather than an open mystery. You've solved the blackmail murder."

"Indeed I have," said Elvis. "Indeed I have."

The Lao cheered and raised their glasses. Elvis nodded modestly.

"If it were not so late I would share a bottle of my favorite vodka with you," he said. "But I have a very powerful wife who would prefer to see me sober every now and then."

"Then tell us about it," said Daeng.

Elvis took a long draft of beer and leaned back in his comfortable armchair.

"Well," he said, "firstly I had to be certain your boxer hadn't returned the following day and killed the blonde. For that I needed to re-examine his alibi more closely. I was able to do that by meeting the North Korean girl he claimed to have been with. After two hours of mild interrogation she conceded that there might have been a nighttime liaison with a Lao boxer but she couldn't be sure due to the fact she had taken some very strong diarrhea medication which affected her memory. We jogged that memory by showing a closed circuit television recording of her disappearing into a bush with Mr. Maen. When asked if she had a tattoo of the glorious leader of the republic on her left buttock she admitted proudly that she did. There was only one way that Mr. Maen could have known such a thing. He'd mentioned it during his initial interview but that fact had regrettably been ignored."

"Here's to the glorious leader," said Siri, raising his beer. The others joined in the toast and Sergei refilled their glasses.

"Next," said Elvis, "I had to find out who was with the blonde on the evening of the murder. Both the downstairs neighbor and the superintendent had seen him leave and had described his appearance as 'Asian,' which in the Soviet Union could encompass many different visages. I assumed he would be a boxer as that appeared to be the target group. A small country easily overwhelmed by the threat of a scandal on the international stage. So I expanded the definition of Asian to include the Indian subcontinent and came up with a list of eight possibilities. Only four of these had boxers. I instructed my men to ask the NOC of each of these countries to account for the whereabouts of their boxers on the night of the murder. We were almost immediately successful."

"Where was he from?" asked Dtui.

"Nepal," said Elvis.

"Asians is Asians," said Daeng.

"Our investigation also uncovered the owner of the non-matching identification tag you passed on to us," said Elvis. "As you correctly stated, he was Vietnamese. He'd had a hell of a time getting back into the village without his I.D.

tag. He said he'd dropped it along the road somewhere, which was a lie. Got the entire Vietnamese NOC out of its beds. The blackmailers had been prolific. They had claimed a victim for each day of the Games, even the Opening Ceremony and the day before it. On the eighteenth was the blond Bahamian, on the nineteenth the Vietnamese, his heart, as he said, snatched from the stadium car park. Then your man Maen and, at last, the Nepali. The latter had the same hairstyle as your boxer and was of a very similar build. He was also a nervous wreck. As soon as we sat him down in our interview room he was only too pleased to get it off his chest."

"He did it?" asked Civilai.

"No," said Elvis. "According to the Nepali boxer he met the blonde in the village and was overwhelmed that she'd find him attractive. She was, as he said, his fantasy woman in spite of her rather heavy makeup, which I assume was to hide the bruises from her previous beatings. He admitted she showed only minimal enthusiasm but he put that down to shyness. At the apartment they began to undress but the woman suddenly burst into tears. She gestured for him to leave but he was too far into the seduction to walk out on such a tasty dish. She became hysterical.

"It was here that the Nepali's version of events became a little farfetched. He said that the large chair in the bedroom suddenly started to move all by itself and it spoke. In retrospect we know that this was caused by the male accomplice leaving his lair. But the boxer was certain he'd offended the spirits and he gathered his belongings and ran out of the apartment. Behind him he could hear voices yelling. He knew it had to be the blonde talking to a ghost as she was the only one there. He sprinted downstairs past the neighbor and the superintendent and into the street, where he found a taxi to bring him back to the village. We found the taxi driver who confirmed that he'd picked up the crazed Asian but that there was no blood on him. Our forensic pathologist assures me it would have been impossible to inflict such wounds to the neck without being sprayed by the blood himself."

"So it was the male accomplice who killed her," said Siri.

"It was indeed. He was inside the secret room taking photographs and filming events and he saw that his moll had lost interest in their plot. This was a disaster given the amount of money they were about to rake in from all the extortion. A fight ensued and he took his knife threats one step too far. When the superintendent came to the room the accomplice retired to his secret room and was probably still in there when the police came to conduct its investigation. When the coast was clear he packed his bag and hit the road."

"You found him?" Daeng asked.

"One of the many advantages of our rather claustrophobic system is that we pride ourselves on knowing where most of our citizens are at any given time. Once we found the original owners of the apartment who sublet to our criminal, we had a name which led us to his criminal record. The NOC of the Bahamas confirmed from a photograph that it was he who had impersonated a police officer and attempted to extort money from them. We traced our perpetrator to a train journey to Novosibirsk where we found him staying at an inn. It is very difficult to be a successful criminal in this country unless you are inside the system yourself."

CHAPTER SEVENTEEN
The Big Bang Theory

Day nine saw the last of the Lao events and they were all on the track. Unless, by some miracle, any of these runners qualified for the finals, this was the last chance for the stadium to hear the Lao Cheer. The first event was at ten but the Lao supporters were there at eight practicing. The final eight days of the Olympics would be devoid of Lao athletes but there was no need to deprive the crowds of their enthusiasm. It was time to choose favorites from amongst the other countries and to put their support behind them. The Thais were boycotting the Games so there wasn't even anyone to boo.

It had been forty hours since the unreported explosion and the men in suits had yet to come knocking on the door of the Lao administrators. The only mystery they had to consider that day was the disappearance not of Siri but of Roger. They'd sent him off forty-eight hours before and seen neither hide nor hair of him since. On this Saturday morning they were enjoying a leisurely breakfast at the Kabul Noodle Bazaar. Daeng, a potential Nobel Prizewinner in noodle preparation, assured everyone they were eating very healthy food. What it lacked in spicy it made up for in savory.

And just after they'd finished making bets on what disaster had befallen their interpreter the small chime over the restaurant door tinkled. And who should walk in but Roger himself? He was sweaty, flushed and out of breath but glowing with excitement and eczema.

"Roger, where have you been?" said Daeng. "We've been worried sick about you." It was Daeng who'd bet ten dollars he'd been shot by the KGB.

"I did it," said Roger.

He sat at the table and ordered a bowl of noodles and a shot of vodka.

"You do know alcohol at breakfast time is the first step toward calamity?" said Civilai.

Roger ignored him. "I went there," he said. "I went to the building. The streets were roped off and even local residents weren't allowed to stay in their homes. But I had my Olympic nametag which says I'm an official interpreter. I told the guards at the barrier that the KGB had contacted me at the village and told me to come."

"To interpret for a dead Lao," said Civilai.

"The police at the barrier didn't know that. I gave them a fake name and number for the officer who'd called me and told them to phone him. Of course they were never going to do that."

"You were very brave," said Daeng.

"I was, wasn't I?"

The noodles and the vodka arrived together but the vodka left first. He ordered another.

"I usually never stand up to people like them," he said. "It's amazing what a bit of confidence can do. A uniformed officer escorted me past another barricade and all the way to the building. You were right, Uncle Siri. The second and third stories on the west side had a huge bite out of them. It was obvious an explosion from below had destroyed most of Manoi's apartment. There was still some danger the rest of the building might collapse. They told me to wait and sat me down under a makeshift tarpaulin on the street opposite. It was a sort of crime investigation center, I suppose you might call it. And while I was there I met an incredible . . ."

To everyone's annoyance he stopped talking and began to eat.

"An incredible what?" said Civilai.

"A fireman," said Roger between slurps. "Or some kind of disaster investigator. I don't know what you call them. I imagine he assumed if I was there I had to be somebody. He'd done his appraisal of the building and was waiting to be debriefed. He'd been up all night. He was the one who told me about the bomb."

Roger forked several more threads of noodle into his busy mouth.

"What about it?" said Daeng.

"PVV-5A plastic, Red Army issue explosive," he said. "Detonator set off by remote control."

"From what distance?" said Siri.

"He said you'd need to be within fifty meters from the building to be sure it went off."

"So if the bomber was that close he was most probably seen by someone," said Daeng.

"Very possible," said Roger.

"And if the bomber was Asian he would have stood out like a nun in a go-go bar," said Civilai.

"Did you get to talk to anyone who witnessed the blast?" Siri asked.

"All the buildings around had been evacuated," said Roger. "There was nobody to ask. But my fireman said the apartment on the second floor was registered in the name of an elderly couple. Their remains were scattered to the four corners of the earth. The bomber had laid the charge directly beneath Manoi's TV room. He believed the murderer must have had inside information to know when the upstairs residents would be together in the same place."

"I'd guess live coverage of the twenty-kilometer walk with a Lao contender would be guarantee enough," said Daeng.

"What else did you learn?" said Civilai.

"Ah, well now, that's the moment that I was arrested," said Roger.

"For what?" asked Siri.

"Just being there, I suppose. I was merely chatting with the fireman when this bull of a guy charges over and asks me who I am and what I'm doing there. I was intimidated by his enormous chest. Nobody really needs a chest that size. I told him I'd received a telephone message that the investigators would need a Lao interpreter. That I'd hurried over and there I was. He swore a little bit and had someone drive me to a room at the back of the Kremlin. It was a good experience. I'd never been inside before. It was a lot less grim than I'd pictured it. There was a sort of interrogation from an unenthusiastic agent who took my statement. I stuck to my story and they threw me into a cell for two nights. I was released and here I am."

"Do you think you might have been followed?" Civilai asked.

"I anticipated that," said Roger. "Back in the sixties it was the least you'd expect. So I went directly to my room at the Village, had a shower, jumped on a free bicycle and took the most convoluted route here: alleyways and staircases and one-way streets. It was all very cloak and dagger but, to tell the truth, I don't think anyone was really that interested in me."

They let Roger finish his noodles and then ordered tea. The vodka and the adrenalin had made him hyperactive and they needed him calm.

"All right, let's go through the suspect list again," said Siri.

"Spectacular," said Roger.

"We're down to two," said Dtui. "Both military. Sompoo was watching the race with his buddies, which rules him out. Sitti the pistol shooter was kind of nondescript and shy but as Civilai says, those might be the perfect characteristics for an assassin. And he'd left the barracks before the marathon."

"He's my favorite," said Civilai. "I finally got access to the military application forms. Sitti spent six months with the unit in Buagaew. That's where my Major Lien was based. They had to know each other. It makes it even more likely that they recognized each other at Wattay airport. You know how I hate coincidence."

"But there's also Colonel Fah Hai," Dtui continued. "None of the team saw him that evening but he could have been watching the race with the Russians."

"But we're sure it's a soldier?" said Roger.

"Not absolutely," said Siri. "The fact that the explosive was Soviet Army issue should steer us toward the shooters but we didn't actually monitor our team at the stadium.

Anyone could have slipped out in the excitement. And it's true that half the boxers were trained during their military service. Some of them have affiliations. Even the runners. Chom the rat catcher spent three years in the infantry. He certainly left the arena before the explosion."

"Maybe he got the scent of vermin," said Daeng.

"So have we officially counted out every disgruntled Soviet State terrorist bomber?" asked Civilai.

"Old Brother," said Siri. "If you're going to make a political point you blow up a police station or an Olympic venue. You don't put a bomb in an old building, especially if it doesn't house a politburo member or a rock star."

"At least we should find out something about the old couple downstairs," said Daeng. "Eliminate them from the reckoning."

"If we must," said Siri. "But, believe me, Manoi was the target of this attack and the man who killed him is right under our noses."

The Olympics continued oblivious to the presence of a murder inquiry. With five days still to go the spectators had already witnessed twenty-eight world records. There had been nine thousand drug tests, all of which were negative. Fortunately for the Lao administrators there were no tests for alcohol dependency. The youngest competitor in Moscow was thirteen, the oldest seventy. A Pole won the pole vault but a box did not win the boxing. That honor was taken by a Cuban heavyweight collecting his third Olympic gold in a row. The coxless pairs in men's rowing saw two sets of identical twins claiming gold and silver. But the fairy story of the Games came in the women's field hockey. Suddenly finding itself without opponents due to the boycott, the Soviet Hockey Association invited Zimbabwe with two months to go before the Games. The Zimbabwe ladies had never played together before and had never seen an artificial surface. Yet they won the tournament undefeated.

"That," said Madam Daeng," is what the Olympics is all about."

CHAPTER EIGHTEEN
A Dozen Marx and Lenin Souvenir Wristwatches

Still, with four days to go to the closing ceremony, the elders had not been able to trace the movements of Sitti, Chom, and Colonel Fah Hai on the evening of the explosion. To keep Dtui's mind off the dangers her husband and daughter faced in Vientiane, Daeng had sent her to the media center on Acemadian Street to see if she could spot Sitti in any of the footage taken on race walk day. The staff members were delighted that somebody might appreciate their efforts enough to look through the hours of film taken at the stadium. Dtui claimed she would like background material to accompany a documentary of Khamon's famous twenty-kilometer walk. The media center was happy to waive copyright and hand over anything Dtui liked.

But in her mind this was a waste of time. Even if Sitti the shooter had gone to the stadium as he said, the chances of him being caught on film in a crowd of seventy thousand were remote. In fact she abandoned the attempt after only an hour as a new idea crawled into her mind. They said he'd bought them all souvenirs. Perhaps that was relevant. If she could find the stall that sold Marx and Lenin wristwatches the seller might recall the little Asian who'd bought a dozen.

She took the metro to Sportivnaya and walked from there to the stadium. It was the way Sitti would have come. She passed a number of souvenir stalls and had the opportunity to practice the phrase, "Do you remember an Asian in a red, white and blue tracksuit buying twelve Marx and Lenin wristwatches on Thursday evening?" Nobody did. By the time she reached the stadium she'd asked twelve times. The crowd inside the arena roared and she considered going inside to watch the events. But on a bench at the feet of the Giant Lenin statue sat a suspicious-looking character in an old suit and sandals with a suitcase at his feet. He called her over.

"You got jeans?" he asked.

"You got jeans?" was the "Hello, how are you?" of the Moscow Olympics.

"No," she said.

He opened his suitcase to display an impressive display of souvenir watches: from Misha, the mascot bear, to an air-brushed Brezhnev, the Olympic Stadium from the air, and a cartoon Stalin. But the majority of his watches were Marx and Lenin staring at each other across a hammer and sickle.

"My brother bought several of these on Thursday evening," said Dtui.

"Well, listen," he said. "Don't blame me if they don't all work. It's the humidity."

"No, they work fine," she said.

He looked relieved.

"I just wasn't sure where he got them," she continued.

"Little fellow in a tracksuit," he said. "Crew cut."

"That's him. How could you remember that?"

"I don't often get to sell twelve of these at any one time," he said. "And, no offense, but Asians are usually stingy bastards. Like to haggle you down to no profit at all. But your brother didn't even bother to wind them up to see if they worked. Didn't argue the cost at all. You want some more? I can give you a better price than any of those licensed rip-off shops."

He looked over her shoulder at an armed trooper patrolling the stadium grounds.

"Might do," said Dtui. "Are you here every day?"

"I . . . er . . . I tend to move around a bit. But yeah, I'll be somewhere between here and the station. Look for the suitcase."

The trooper was approaching them now so the watch man closed his case and headed off.

"But it wasn't Thursday," he said.

Dtui followed him. "What?"

"He didn't buy them on Thursday evening. I wasn't here. Must have been Tuesday morning."

He broke into a jog.

"Are you sure?" Dtui called after him.

"Lady, you don't get to run a successful business like this if you can't keep your sales data in order."

He ran pretty fast for a man in sandals with a full suitcase. The uniformed trooper gave up the chase and returned to his patrol, giving Dtui a dirty look on the way.

Due to some minor disagreements that had caused a diplomatic meltdown, the French embassy in Vientiane had been closed and empty for twenty-four months. It was still

in the care of Monsieur Seksan, a Frenchman of Lao ances-
try who'd been overlooked for ambassadorship numerous
times probably because of the way he looked. He was
Asian. Instead the French government was employing him
as a live-in caretaker of the complex. He'd shown his joy at
the placement by drinking the wine in the ambassador's
cellar, beginning with the oldest, and drawing facial hair
on the oil paintings that hung in the cultural wing. If relations ever returned to normal he would accuse the Pathet
Lao of childish incursions into their diplomatic sanctuary.

More importantly, as far as Phosy was concerned, Monsieur Seksan was a fan of Dr. Siri and had been more than
pleased to do favors for his team. The now-empty wine cellar currently housed a lopsided man who had at last given
up shouting and swearing and was now merely grateful to
be given food and drink. Although his chain had increased
in length he was still tethered, this time to a thick wooden
beam. He had no idea where he was. His captors, non-
speaking and hooded members of Siri's household, had
moved him from site to site in Civilai's old cream Citroën.
He had become disoriented and broken.

Nobody had spoken to him since that night in the
police dormitory washroom. Four days had passed since
then. Phosy walked down the steps to the cellar carrying a
chair. The only light came from behind him. He put down
the chair at a point just beyond the length of the chain and
sat. The messenger said nothing. Phosy crossed his legs
and allowed his foot to bounce up and down in midair.

"You understand, don't you?" said the inspector.

"I . . . no," said the man.

His voice was rusty, unused.

"It's not really that complicated," said Phosy. "You work

for an old man with too much money. I work for people who have no love for capitalism or the hoodlums it buys."

"You're police," said the man.

Phosy laughed. "If we were police you'd have spent a couple of hours in a cell and been released. You'd have been free to go to some other public servant's house and threaten his two-year-old daughter."

"I . . . I . . ."

"Don't bother. The last man who did that died a very slow, very painful death. He got to see his own organs up close before he went."

"I'm sorry. I . . . it was just what we were told to do."

"Following orders. I get it. Anything it takes to make a living in these hard times. It certainly beats selling fruit from a barrow. But I'm very very sensitive about my family."

"Then, why . . . ?"

"Why are you still alive?"

"Yeah."

"Well, to tell the truth, you're not."

The man shook his head.

"I don't understand," he said.

"As soon as we release you from here, you'll be picked up by your employer's other assistants and taken to that sprawling ranch out past the ferry terminal. And they'll find a way to make you talk."

"About what?"

"About what you've told us."

"I haven't . . . I haven't talked to anyone."

"I know. Ironic, isn't it? But all guilty men claim not to have blabbed to the enemy, don't they? We kept you here long enough for the word to spread that you'd been in a luxury seaside resort in Thailand living the life of a king

while you spilled your guts about Thonglai and his operation. All the seedy business deals. All the 'accidents.'"

"Why?"

"Why what?"

"Why would you go to all this trouble?"

"Oh, it's been no trouble, friend. And no expense. A
couple of meals. Water. I'll enjoy watching how it pans
out. You see? When you threaten a man's child you get
what you deserve. And like this, I get revenge on you
and your boss loses one of his messengers. At the very
least you'll be tortured and terminated. You know how that
works. At best, if we're really lucky, the whole operation
might shut down while they assess the damage you've done."

Phosy stood, grabbed his chair and headed for the
staircase.

"Bye," he said. "We'll be dropping you off by the Victory
Monument in an hour. Good luck."

"No, wait!" said the man. "What if—"

"You know you have the right to remain silent," said the
inspector. He'd always wanted to say that.

"We can make a deal," said the messenger.

"You don't have anything we want," said Phosy.

He climbed the stairs slowly.

"I can tell you stuff," said the man.

"Nothing we don't know already. There's a bucket over
there. Get yourself cleaned up."

"I do," said the man. "I know a lot. Stuff you could never
know."

Phosy reached the top landing and stepped through
the open doorway. Once the door was closed there'd be
nothing but blackness down there in the cellar. The dark
can feel like the end of all hope.

"Please," called the messenger. "The killing in Moscow . . ."

The door began to close.

"What about it?" shouted Phosy.

"We organized it. What's that worth?"

CHAPTER NINETEEN
To Catch a Rat

Everyone in the Lao camp was excited about the Closing Ceremony and the farewell party. There had been fears that once the US and her allies dropped out, the Games would flop. But, if anything, the opposite was true. The non-boycotting world had seen 203 events in twenty-one sports. Of course the Soviet Union won the most medals. They'd paid for it, after all. Old world records were beaten and re-beaten ninety-seven times and, to Madame Daeng's delight, the percentage of female participants was higher than for any previous Games. The Olympic spirit had not died. There were still those who believed sport was above politics. And the athletes who'd taken part felt sad for those who had put their hearts into an Olympic preparation only to be told they could not attend. Politics was arbitrary and fickle, but honest sporting achievement derived from acts of chivalry that dated back across the centuries to when ancient battles were decided by an army's greatest warrior.

"Just stick Brezhnev in a ring with the Mujahedeen's head honcho," said Civilai. "See who comes out best after three rounds. That'll save a few billion dollars and a few million lives."

But, of course, nobody ever listened to philosophers.

The Lao had lost every darned event they'd entered but won more hearts than any of the super nations at the top of the medal tables. Their Olympics was over but not their chance for glory. Their warrior, Chom the vermin eradication officer for Savanaketh, was representing his country in probably the most ridiculous competition ever staged on the fringes of the Olympic Games. There were three competitors: Chom, Sammy from Botswana, and Yusov, the official Soviet rat catcher from Moscow's district eight. The rules had been laid out by the administrators of the Moscow Department of Rural Pest Suppression. The event was being sponsored by the *Social Works Newsletter*, which would run the story in its next edition as part of its *In the Wake of the Games* edition. Admittedly, this was no big-budget affair.

The venue for the rat games was a condemned block of two-story terraced houses built mostly of wood and dating back to before the First World War. There were eight in the row. The reporters and judges had walked into each house with the competitors to confirm that there was no advantage to be had. The scent of rat droppings was overpowering. There was no furniture save the mildew mattresses of homeless people gone by. The competitors walked from room to room sniffing, poking at crumbling plaster, stamping on floorboards. There were suggestions that the three men might draw lots to decide which of the eight houses they'd be based in for the night. But there seemed to be no contention. The rat catchers agreed to each have a house with an empty unit on either side. Sammy was in number two, Yusov in five, and Chom in seven. In this way there would be no interference from neighboring eradicators.

The three competitors had been given permission to carry only three items apiece into battle as well as a jar of peanut butter to use as bait. The latter had found its way into Moscow especially for the Games and would probably never be seen again. There was to be no use of electronic devices and no poison. The event was a test of the intrinsic hunting skills of the competitors. Sammy from Botswana requested a fifty-centimeter length of PVC piping, sixty centimeters of rope and a burlap sack. Yusov the Soviet representative requested a twenty-liter plastic bucket, a coat hanger and an old coffee tin with a lid.

Chom seemed undecided at first but settled on a mallet. Through their Lao interpreter the judges tried to explain that he was allowed two more items, but he insisted the mallet would be adequate.

The volunteers, mostly would-be Moscow rat catchers, positioned themselves in front of and behind the selected units to be sure there was no cheating. The competitors were not allowed to leave the building throughout the night and nobody could visit them. At 6 A.M. there would be the official count of rat corpses to decide the winner. The competitors shook hands and entered their respective houses. On his way into house number seven, Chom asked if he might have a light for his cigarette.

"Do we really have to get up at six?" Civilai asked.

"No, we have to get up at five in order to get there at six in time for the award ceremony," said Daeng.

"We're VIPs," he said. "Can't we just send representatives?"

"No," said Dtui.

"Look, doesn't this strike anyone else as being a little . . . I don't know, silly?" said Civilai.

"You're remarkably classist for a socialist, aren't you?" said Siri. "If this were a competition between three Ferrari drivers, first to the Arc de Triomphe in time for cocktails, you'd be there waving your Lao flag in one hand and your olive in the other."

"At least there'd be *petit fours*," said Civilai. "What do you suppose they'll be serving for breakfast at a rat hunt? I dread to think."

"Oh, I love this," said Roger, probably referring to the banter rather than the cocktails they were drinking.

Daeng called to Sergei.

"One more round here."

She'd learned to say it in Russian, "*Yeshe odno butilku,*" or thereabouts. It was a skill she'd have little chance to use back in the People's Democratic Republic. It was also the last night they'd spend with their favorite barman, so they wanted him to feel needed. He'd become a surrogate relative. They missed Laos but after all this free goodness it wasn't going to be easy to return to a land of deprivation in just three days. They understood that none of this was real but it felt so natural.

Madam Daeng told them a story that evening. It was about a small unit of Pathet Lao dug in on the Plain of Jars before the takeover.

"The royalists were advancing and they outnumbered the rebels five to one," she said. "The red commander ordered his men to load up and fire all at once. His men weren't sure they heard him correctly. 'But sir,' said his sergeant, 'we only have the one box of bullets.'

"'They don't know that,' said the commander.

"The rebels fired their final barrage and the royalists turned tail and fled into the jungle."

That was how Siri saw the Moscow Olympics. The Soviets were in Afghanistan burning up their resources like a forest fire. Like Laos, the Soviet Union had become dependent on successful grain crops and Mother Nature wasn't a girl you could bet any money on. The crops had failed once more and nobody was offering to make up the deficit. But here they were with their last pack of bullets staging the greatest show on the planet. Five thousand athletes and five thousand journalists would return to their countries with stories of the organization, the coordination, the razzmatazz and the friendship. Everything had been brilliant: the hospitality, the humanity, the cooperation. But by the time these stories had circulated the government stores would be empty again, the food queues would return and the national pride would continue to erode. That was the opinion of a cynic with fifty years of communist party membership under his belt.

The main reason for coming together at the Nebesa was not merely to drink and pontificate. It was not to make Sergei feel needed. It wasn't even to confirm their certainty that Sitti, the shooter, was at the top of their list of suspected assassins. It was to bemoan their own failings as detectives and celebrate the success of Dtui's husband in Vientiane. The phone conversation with Dtui that afternoon had been two hours long and in regular, non-Arpy Lao. Phosy had been so delighted with events that he even told his wife he missed her and wanted her to hurry home. She wished that were possible.

"But why would the man want to have his own son assassinated?" Roger asked. He'd arrived late.

They had a new round of cocktails and vodka shots in front of them so the time was ripe to sit back on their comfortable armchairs and put together all the pieces of the Vientiane investigation. Dtui was the storyteller.

"Comrade Thonglai, Manoi's father, had started to invest in the communist takeover even back in the sixties," she said. "He came from a well-to-do family that was being drained by the corrupt royalist government in Vientiane. The family was cheated out of land deals and taxed excessively on imports. The generals were queuing up for their handouts. But Comrade Thonglai had a friend from the north. They'd worked together on some shady deals and become friends."

"That was the old man, Pinit Saopeng, who was shot in Vientiane after meeting with Phosy," said Siri.

"Let her tell it," said Daeng.

"Sorry."

"Pinit could see how frustrated his friend was and asked if he'd be interested to meet a Russian who was looking for a broker to smuggle in arms for the rebels in the northeast. A similar network had already been established for the Vietcong in Vietnam. Relations with China were much better then and it was comparatively easy to bring Chinese weapons across the border. But the Soviets wanted to invest in what they saw as the inevitable socialist future of Southeast Asia. They knew the Vietnamese would not tolerate a Chinese-sponsored insurgency and assumed the Lao would follow suit. They'd need support from the big bear. Comrade Thonglai had a similar vision, although his aims were less ideological and more financial. He hadn't lost his love for his country but his dream was a Laos run like a business with a head of state with an organized, logical mind. Someone not beholden to the Vietnamese. Someone more like himself.

"The three allies were very effective. The Russian came often to the region as an exporter of teak furniture to Europe. He eventually established a home and family in Laos. He paid the police and the immigration department and ministry officials and everyone left him alone. Pinit Saopeng was a lieutenant in the Royal Lao army but also an undercover communist agent. He wormed his way into a position at the central command in Vientiane as head of supplies. Thonglai's network operated undetected until '75. The Socialists took over and the three men went their separate ways. A job well done.

"After many years of travel as a gun runner, the Russian returned to Moscow, well respected by the Party for his contribution to the spread of communism. Comrade Thonglai left his family compound and built his own estate out beyond the river ferry port. He too was a hero to the revolutionaries and was handed the plum business deals by his old military comrades. Pinit Saopeng, older than the other two, retired. He'd made enough money to live a comfortable life. But he missed the intrigue. He continued to take on the odd job for his old friend, Comrade Thonglai. He had a good house in the countryside with servants but as a veteran he registered for a room in a retirement block in the city to use as a cover. It was the base of operations for anything from bringing in dollars from Nong Kai to moving people back and forth. And it was the bank. It was where they did their deals and hired and paid their killers."

"Excuse me, Dtui," said Roger. "But how did your husband learn all this?"

"An informant," said Dtui.

"A very talkative informant," said Roger.

"My husband can be very persuasive," she said.

"All right," said Civilai, "this brings us to the son."

"Yes," said Dtui. "When Comrade Thonglai first met the Russian they arranged to send one of his sons to Moscow to finish high school and go on to university. The Russian was the boy's guarantor. It would have looked too suspicious to send all three boys to the Soviet Union so he selected his brightest, the boy who was most like himself. Manoi was the most likely to succeed. Within a year the boy was speaking Russian and reading texts his teachers had considered too difficult for an Asian. He made friends easily. Everything was going to plan.

"But it was then that young Manoi took a step into the gutter. Despite his run-ins with the royalists, his father was still wealthy. He had been sending an extremely generous monthly allowance to his son. Comrade Thonglai believed that a gentleman needed money to pave his own path through life. The boy, sixteen then, in high school in a foreign country, unchaperoned and rich, did what any teenager would do. First it was alcohol, then soft drugs and sex. Then came some of the new designer drugs from the West. He became reckless, almost lost his life on a couple of occasions.

"By the time he graduated, his classmates had begun to fear him. He was a wild man. He'd started to mix with an older, more dangerous crowd. Many were the offspring, legitimate and otherwise, of politburo men, the sons of Red Army generals. To impress them, Manoi became more extreme. He slowly grew to be independent of his father's money as he started to make profits from the drugs and

women he'd sampled in high school. Twice in his fresh-
man year the university threatened to expel him. But a
phone call from somebody's father or great uncle and he
was back.

"It was uncertain when he had his first adversary killed.
There were rumors that even in high school he'd paid
to have rivals beaten up. In his second year at university
he was arrested. A lecturer in Political Science had been
pulled out of the icy sludge of the Moscow River. He'd
been shot. The day before, Manoi had turned up for the
lecturer's class late and drunk. The teacher had humili-
ated him and thrown him out of the room. A hundred
students witnessed the debacle but nobody came forward
as a witness to the murder. And Manoi had an unshake-
able alibi.

"There were other incidents but the father knew nothing of these. The boy wrote to him diligently every month
and told of his normal, hard-working life in Moscow. Once
Laos had been rescued from the tyrants and took its first
baby communist steps, Comrade Thonglai's empire flour-
ished. He was the familiar capitalist face to the outside
world. He imported. He negotiated deals. And the poorer
the country became the more it relied on him. Nothing could go wrong. He'd gold-plated his future and the
future of his son.

"But then the letter arrived from his friend the Russian.
It was in the Soviet diplomatic pouch, twenty-seven pages
long. The Russian had just returned to Moscow and he'd
been asking around about his friend's son, the boy for
whom he'd acted as guarantor.

"'Manoi is out of control,' he wrote. 'He's looking many
years beyond his age from the ravages of excess. He runs

a gang of desperate young men who'd do anything he told them. They see themselves as the disciples of the next president of Laos. That's how he touts himself. "A national leader in waiting." He's lost interest in studies. There are suspicions his undergraduate degree was paid for, as would be his doctorate. And with his unearned degrees in his hand he would go home a national hero.'

"But perhaps the line that frightened Comrade Thonglai most of all was the one that read, 'The Vietnamese have been courting your boy for the past couple of years. I fear that he no longer shares your hatred of Hanoi.'

"Comrade Thonglai blamed most of his country's ills on Vietnamese intrusion into its affairs. He could not allow a son of his to become one of their puppets.

"'I know he's intelligent,' said the Russian at the end of the letter. 'In fact he has qualities that would make him a good leader. But he's been off the rails for too long.'

"Comrade Thonglai wrote back and begged his friend to help. He told him his other two sons had decided not to return to Laos. Manoi was his country's only chance. Manoi was his true heir. He just needed cleaning up. If the Russian could intervene, steer the boy back onto an honest path, one heading away from Vietnam, he would be eternally in his friend's debt. The Russian reluctantly agreed. His first meeting with young Manoi began genially enough. It was lunch in an expensive restaurant. The boy had ordered a bottle of 1954 Pinot Noir and drank most of it himself. Somewhere deep in the boy's eyes there were memories. Recollections of days when he was still innocent. Barbeques in the Russian's garden. Playing football with the Russian's son and swimming naked in their duck pond. They talked of those days and laughed and the Russian had hopes that he might be able to pull the boy out of the mud. He'd written so in his letter to the father. But he made one mistake before the lunch was over. He mentioned Comrade Thonglai's concerns.

"'Your father's worried about you,' he said.

"When the Russian looked up he saw a different person. There were occasions in the final half of their lunch together—some gestures, the odd expression—that caused the Russian to shudder with fear. The young man was rude to the waiter, caused heads to turn when he shouted for another bottle of wine, and was an obnoxious drunk. That's when the Russian realized that Manoi was dangerous. A man shows his true colors when under the influence of alcohol. But the friend would persevere in spite of his fears, as he'd promised his old comrade.

"Four months after their meal together the Russian was hit by a car. It stopped and reversed over him a second time. The number plates were taped over. He died on his way to the hospital.

"Before his death the Russian had sent one last letter. He wrote, 'Your son tells me he has all the support he needs from the Lao Central Committee and Hanoi. He has six months to go on his doctorate although I haven't seen him attend any classes or work on a dissertation. Then he'll be heading back to Vientiane. I imagine he'll be patient but all I can see is that his long-term plan will be to get rid of you and what he calls the stooges you've planted. I shall make one more attempt to talk some sense into him but I think you should take this threat seriously.'"

"Nasty piece of work," said Daeng.

"And he seemed like such a polite chap," said Siri.

"You're lucky you made it out of there in one piece," said Daeng.

"Phosy has the letters from the Russian," said Dtui.

"How on earth did he get hold of those?" asked Civilai.

"The informant had provided a lot of very useful information about Comrade Thonglai's compound," said Dtui. "It included the location of the guards, how the security system worked, when the boss was due to be on his next overseas trip with his bodyguards, etcetera. Phosy put together a group of men he trusted and they raided the ranch. They turned off the alarms and caught the guards by surprise. They knew exactly where to find the incriminating documents. Comrade Thonglai had been overconfident about his status. Most of the cabinets were unlocked.

"There had been a suggestion from the informant that somebody high up in the police department might have been receiving gifts from Comrade Thonglai's company for his cooperation—the type of gifts that left a paper trail. Phosy had been suspicious of his boss for some time. But here was a possibility to collect proof of the man's wrongdoings. Oudomxai, the chief of police, had a cabinet to himself at the ranch with itemized payments for his services.

"Phosy went directly to the minister with his findings and, to cut a long story short, my husband is currently the acting chief of police of Vientiane. Comrade Thonglai is presently out of the country but he'll be arrested as soon as he returns."

They raised their glasses to Phosy.

"Did he find anything on who had the contract for the killing here in Moscow?" Siri asked.

"No," said Dtui. "It seems Comrade Thonglai arranged

it himself. Something personal. Not even the informant knew. He was just responsible for packing the explosive into the team's equipment."

"They shipped it over from there?" said Daeng.

"It makes sense," said Civilai. "The Soviets have been pumping weapons and explosives in for years to shore up our military failings. These things go missing all the time."

"Thonglai's man loaded it in the chest with the boxing equipment the Soviets had donated to us six months earlier," said Dtui. "The explosive was plastic. It wouldn't have taken up much space. The markings on the chest were all in Russian. It seems the customs and immigration at Sheremetyevo had a directive to hurry the athletes through with the minimum of fuss."

"Apart from the illegal import of *lahp*," said Civilai.

"Nobody even looked at our suitcases," said Siri. "We could have walked off the plane with grenade launchers on our shoulders and the Customs officers would have wished us well and asked if we had jeans to sell."

"So, should we be looking for a boxer now?" asked Roger.

"Not necessarily," said Siri. "The military were quick to offload the equipment and carry it to the coaches. We weren't really paying attention. Anyone could have had access to it. But you know what? We could just stop looking now."

"What do you mean?" said Civilai.

"I mean, Phosy's solved everything in Vientiane. We were too late to prevent a killing here. And what if Sitti did sneak off and do away with Manoi? In retrospect, the assassination might not have been such a bad thing."

"You're doing Judge Bao again," said Daeng.

"I am not."

"Yes you are. Arbitrarily dispensing justice. You've

decided you don't much like the victim so it's okay if someone blows up his apartment."

"In that case, yes I am," said Siri. "Who has time to wait
for fate to dispense with its undesirables?"

"So how did the old soldier—the one who got himself
shot in Vientiane—how did he fit into the story?" said
Civilai. "I thought he was on Comrade Thonglai's side."

"And so he was," said Dtui. "The informant had no idea
who killed him or why. He was confident it wasn't connected to the dealings over here. Phosy wondered whether
it might have had something to do with the money."

"What money?" asked Daeng.

"The old man had forty thousand dollars hidden in his
room," said Dtui. "Phosy's commandeered it for his depart-
mental budget. He thinks it might have been intended to pay
off the assassin once it was all over. If someone had learned
he had such a large amount in his possession, that was motive
enough to kill him. But the informant didn't seem to know
about it and the sniper didn't get his hands on it. And if Comrade Thonglai had wanted Pinit killed I doubt he would have
entrusted so much money to him beforehand."

"I still don't see it as a coincidence that he was talking
to Phosy when he was shot," said Siri. "Comrade Thonglai would have learned from the telexes that Phosy was
going to the Good Luck café. He'd have sent his man Pinit
there to see what, if anything, Phosy knew about the plot in
Moscow. It was good news for them that we had the wrong
man. No, the killing had to be something else. Something
unconnected."

"That would mean there was a third party," said Daeng.
"Someone who saw Phosy get together with Pinit and was
afraid of what the old soldier might say."

"I think we should tell Phosy to go back to the Good Luck and look around for another suspect with another motive," said Siri.

"I'll pass that on," said Dtui.

"Why did Comrade Thonglai recruit Phosy and us to search for Manoi's assassin if he already knew who it was?" asked Roger.

"Confirmation that his man had got away with it," said Daeng. "If we didn't know who the killer was, nobody did."

Sergei had put on a cassette tape of jolly Chechnyan folk songs. The Lao were already tapping their feet.

"Oh, and do you think you can handle any more good news?" asked Dtui.

"You can never have too much," said Civilai.

"Phosy said Comrade Noo is out of his coma," she said. "It's looking like he'll pull through. Siri, your friend Dr. Porn is looking in every day and she said the recovery was sudden and dramatic. She said it was as if the old monk had suddenly found a reason to live."

Siri and Daeng performed one of their elaborate high-fives and everyone cheered and toasted their friend back in Vientiane.

"Would you have had something to do with that?" asked Dtui.

Siri had no idea but he hoped his pep talk in business class that day might have had some influence on Noo's condition. He still had little confidence in his own ability as a shaman but it was just possible he'd made contact with Noo's disgruntled spirit and put it back on its flight path. If so, Dr. Siri had earned his wings.

The suburb in which the row of condemned houses stood

was, for obvious reasons, not visible on the illustrated tourist map. It was therefore surprising that such a large crowd could have assembled there in the street even before the first of the three competitors stepped out of his designated unit. The newsletter organizers had set up tables and brought along weighing machines just in case the decision came down to grams.

Despite the early hour, the Lao supporters were all in attendance, still amazed that the sun could ever rise at 4 A.M. The shooters were there. They had been given two nights at the Village rather than the three they'd requested. They wanted to join their compatriots in all the activities that remained. Sitti was one of them, quiet, shadowy, unemotional. Daeng, who knew her fair share of killers, watched him and wondered what thoughts were ticking over in his mind. Did he think he'd got away with it? Was he already planning his next hit?

The runners were there to support their knight of the sewers and the boxers had brought their drums.

"I'm not going to mention this in my final report," said Civilai.

"What if we win?" said Dtui.

"Especially not if we win."

There were announcements in Russian that Dtui did her best to translate for the Lao even though the language was unnecessarily literary. A newsletter official went to the second house in the block and knocked on the door. Sammy emerged with a large burlap sack over his shoulder. The African supporters were not as vociferous as the Lao but they let everybody know they were there. Even at that unearthly hour the women were dressed in bright costumes waving the national flag that looked like one of the Licorice Allsorts. If there was a prize for glamour, the Batswana would have taken first place. Sammy stepped to the front of the judge's table and upended his sack. A pile of dead rats, entwined like figures at the Kama Sutra temple in Madhya Pradesh, formed a pyramid on the stone footpath.

The Batswana screamed their delight and the other supporters offered a polite round of applause. The judges counted the bodies and wrote the figure 27 on their blackboard. They asked the English translator to step forward so that Sammy could describe how he'd been able to trap such an impressive number of rats with just a PVC pipe and a length of rope.

"It's all in the balance," he said. "I knotted the rope around the middle of the pipe and tied it to the edge of the old table in there. Half of the pipe was hanging over the edge. I baited the inside of the pipe with peanut butter just beyond the rope pivot and blocked the overhanging end with old rags. Our friendly rat smells the bait, walks along the pipe, steps beyond the point of no return and the pipe assumes a vertical position. The rat falls to the blocked end and is unable to climb back up the slippery pipe. I undo the rope and empty the rat into this burlap sack. Rats do not do very well in confined, airless spaces so they die of exhaustion and asphyxia."

The audience, growing by the minute, was most impressed with this clever method. Even the Lao allowed the man from Botswana a rally of percussion. They were however saving their Lao Cheer for their champion. A second official went to unit number five, where the front step was crumbling and overgrown with weeds. Yusov the Moscow Area Eight champion burst through the

door. The Soviet supporters clapped and whistled. Many
had turned up merely to complain about the noise but had
become intoxicated by the wonder of it all. Yusov was top-
less and displayed a fine set of abdominal muscles. He
walked to the street dragging an old curtain like a sleigh
behind him. It bore an even more impressive pile of dead
rats. He refused help from the officials and insisted on
lugging the heavy load to the front of the judges' table by
himself. He put down the curtain and posed like a body-
builder for the cameras. As they counted the corpses, the
judges asked Yusov to describe how he'd been able to kill so
many rats in just one night. He ran back into the house and
reemerged carrying a most peculiar device. Roger provided
a translation for the Lao.

"I punch a hole in the top and the bottom of this coffee can with an old nail," said the Russian. "I straighten
the coat hanger and pass it through the holes to make my
axle. Like this."

He held the wire at each end and spun the coffee tin. It
revolved quite happily around the axis.

"I hook each end of the wire around the top of the twenty-
liter bucket," he continued, "which I fill with water. I spread
my bait, in this case, peanut butter, onto the surface of the
coffee can. My rats smell the bait and jump onto the can. The
can spins from their weight and they drop into the water. Of
course rats can swim and one might be able to tread water
through the night. But more than one causes panic and they
end up drowning each other. All I have to do is fish the dead
rat from the bucket and prepare for the next."

The judges in their rubber gloves had finished counting
the bodies. To the crowd's amazement there were exactly
fifty. The officials wrote that number on the blackboard

and the Russian bowed deeply in response to the ovation. Then he turned and crooked his arms in the air to show the crowd what kind of back muscles a man needed in order to catch fifty rats in one night.

The Lao supporters already had their doubts but when the official knocked on door number seven and nobody answered they feared the worst. He knocked again and waited. And waited. And, finally, the door opened a fraction and Chom, half asleep, poked his head through the crack. He clearly couldn't remember where he was and looked embarrassed to see so many people gathered there. The Lao cheered regardless and beat drums and blew kazoos. Those who knew his name shouted "Chom, Chom, Chom." But this seemed to confuse him even more.

Finally, something clicked and he held up his index finger to the newsletter official and went back inside. The crowd remembered that the Russian had returned with a curtain piled with fifty corpses and wondered whether the Lao could better that. But Chom returned with a single, average-sized dead rat hanging by the tail. The crowd was too embarrassed to make any noise at all. The newsletter official offered to carry the one rat to the front of the judges' table and Chom accepted the offer.

"I smell a rat," said Civilai from the heart of the Lao supporters.

"Me too," said Siri.

They pushed Roger forward to interpret for the Lao vermin eradication officer. So as not to seem racist, the judges asked him how he'd been able to kill his one rat.

"I sang," said Chom proudly.

"You sang and the rat came to you?" said the judge, just to clarify.

"That's right," said Chom. There were already some tit-ters from the Soviet section of the crowd.

"And then?" asked the judge.

"Then he dies."

The judges were no longer able to keep straight faces.

"Remarkable," they said.

Roger, wading through the sarcasm, was ready to leave but the rude journalist from the *Social Works Newsletter* wouldn't let the Lao off his hook.

"And may I ask what you did with the peanut butter?" he said.

"Oh, I ate it, sir," said Chom. "It was far too good to waste on a rat, don't you think?"

"Of course. And what type of song did you sing to attract your rat?" asked the journalist.

The Soviet supporters laughed louder. Chom nodded and considered the question.

"It's an ancient Lao folk song," he said. "And it's sung in the traditional language of rodents. It goes immediately to the rats' brains and they are so overcome with emotion that they have no choice but to seek out the source of this magical tune. They die of a broken heart."

After the translation, all but the Lao roared with laugh-ter. Chom smiled with them.

"Perhaps you could give us a sample of this nostalgic rodent song," said the journalist who was now playing directly to the crowd.

"I don't mind," said Chom.

He began to sing the first few lines of the haunting but somewhat squeaky refrain. The laughter was fractionally louder than the Lao Cheer. Chom took a small bow.

"And yet, despite singing this beautiful lilting dirge, it

shocks me that you were only able to capture the one rat," said the journalist, his back to his victim.

"Oh, I didn't catch one rat," said Chom.

"No?" said the journalist. "There's another one?"

Roger was ready to thump the journalist on his puffy red nose.

"Well, sir," said Chom, "I'm not really that good at counting but I think there might be another hundred and sixty or seventy back in the house. I hurt my back in the gym so I didn't want to carry them."

Once they'd heard the translation the officials and volunteers froze for a few seconds before running into the house. They found the rats, almost two hundred of them in a circular formation around an old cushion. It was as if they really had come to listen to their song. The officials brought them out and laid them in front of the judges' table in batches of twenty. The pile reached the table-top. The Lao supporters raised a cheer that would have humbled the previous day's football final crowd. They drummed, they hummed they strummed and they sang. Yusov the Russian stormed off without his shirt. Sammy gave his Lao friend a Botswana hug. The number 187 was written on the blackboard beside Chom's name and he stood proudly on the podium of milk crates and bent forward for the chief judge to hang the gold-colored honey tin lid on string around his neck.

The racket made every street sweeper and armed soldier look up at the village bus when it passed on its way to Lenin Stadium. The Lao had a medal at last and it wasn't a charitable concession or a no-show walkover. It was won with expertise and panache, but not, Siri and Civilai suspected, with total honesty. They sat on either side of Chom, each taking a hand. Daeng and Dtui leaned over from the seat behind.

"Damn fine display," said Siri.

"Thank you, comrade," said Chom.

"It's a coincidence," said Civilai. "My grandmother used that self-same technique to wipe out the cockroach population from her kitchen. She'd sing an old cockroach folk song in fluent cockroach and they'd line up and jump in the wash tub."

"You don't say?" said Chom.

"I swear on her pyre."

"Why do I get the feeling you doubt me?" asked Chom.

"Come on, son," said Siri. "How did you do it? I mean, I have nothing against fairy stories and magic but I sense a more devious sleight of hand."

Chom looked out the window and smiled.

"Promise you won't tell anyone?" he said.

"Promise," they said.

"Well, when we did the tour of the block," he began, "I noticed there were a lot of old mattresses in house number six. They were damp and mildewed but perfect for what I had in mind. I opened the rear window and pretended I couldn't stand the smell. So I requested and was given house number seven. I used my cigarette to keep a small fire burning until I was sure the volunteers were drowsy, then I climbed out my back window and into house number six. I used the stuffing from the mattresses to block all the rat holes on the east side; that was where the Russian was staying. I put a pile of mattresses upstairs and down and set light to 'em. Moldy old mattresses burn real slow and they make a hell of a lot of smoke. The smoke disorients the rats and they come staggering out of their runs. They're looking for any place with no smoke. As they couldn't get into house number five they had no choice but to head for seven. That happened to be my abode. They were blinded and disoriented. I thumped 'em on the head with the mallet and laid 'em out in a circle around some old cushion. That last part was just . . ."

"Showmanship," said Civilai.

"Yeah, that's it. At about four I blocked up the holes and opened all the windows to let the smoke out. I had my peanut butter breakfast and lay myself down for a couple of hours' sleep."

The old boys shook his hand and laughed with him all the way to the stadium. They'd solved another mystery. As the bus entered the Olympic coach park the fire station in Zyablikovo received a call on their emergency line from a concerned citizen. A block of terraced houses had caught fire and was burning like Hades itself.

CHAPTER TWENTY
Closure

It was over too soon. The Kremlin clock chimed 7 P.M. and the trumpeters called in the procession. The national flags led the way, followed by the athletes. In the spirit of the Games the competitors mingled and joked together as they strolled around the track, waving at the crowd. Nations whose governments were not on speaking terms walked hand in hand and heart to heart. Sadly, the Lao had not been allowed to carry their drum. Dtui felt sorry for the terrace of card-holders who had performed their pixilated stunts in both ceremonies. It was they who produced an endless canvas of remarkable pictures and effects by flipping from card to card as per instructions from an unseen conductor who talked to them through earphones. They could see nothing of the spectacle in the stadium, of course, because of the lumps of cardboard constantly in front of their faces. Dtui worried about such things.

In front of a bank of twenty microphones that rendered him invisible, the Olympic Chairman grieved for those not able to participate and proclaimed the 22nd Olympiad closed. The Olympic flag was lowered, someone turned off the gas and the flame died. An armada of doves was released into the night sky to do battle with the fireworks. The athletes joined the spectators in the stands and were entertained by gymnasts with hoops and flags and unfailing smiles and not a gram of body fat among them.

And at the end of it all a giant Misha balloon was escorted into the stadium by enthusiastic and presumably heavy young men and women who held on to his tow-ropes for dear life. Although there was certainly a lot wrong with the Soviet Union, the old bear symbolized all that was right with it. For ten days it had brought together the citizens of fifteen USSR states that didn't particularly like each other and made them feel like family. It had been a perfect show so everyone felt the loss when they let go their ropes and Misha rose majestically into the night sky to the lilting tune of "Goodbye, Moscow." The words of poet Dobronrorov accompanied Misha heavenwards until he was out of sight, probably to play havoc with air lanes and eventually end his days draped over some peasant's hut in Armenia. But, wherever he went, he left not a dry eye in the Lenin Stadium. The magnificent 22nd Olympiad was closed.

There was a mix of emotions in the Village that night. The live bands and performers did their best to cheer everyone up. Athletes who had deprived themselves for four years had a beer or two and began the process of getting out of shape. New lovers walked hand in hand by the fountains and watched the endless firework display. New friends in saris and sarongs, in straw trilbies and fezzes and shemaghs danced together to the ubiquitous sounds of Boney M and for fifty more years when they heard "Ra

Ra Rasputin" on the radio they would probably remember a time when everybody loved everybody else, however temporarily. Civilai was right. The Olympics was a kind of war: a war where the losers don't die and the winners don't gloat, a war where the armies get together afterward for a drink and a cuddle.

It was about three by the time the Lao team returned to their dormitory and collapsed on their shorter-than-most beds and sighed one last pleasurable sigh. Siri and Daeng were the last to retire. They'd just been talking to Phosy on the telephone. They sat now on a fountain wall with their bare feet in the water and a bottle between them.

"It really was something, wasn't it?" said Daeng.

"We'll not see the like of it again," said Siri.

He and Civilai had binged on some twenty movies over the course of the Games but that had not detracted at all from their involvement in a great spectacle.

"What a ceremony," said Daeng.

"It brought a tear to my eye."

"It was all I could do to stop myself wagging the whole night."

"Our team will never forget it."

"I've never seen Dtui happier," said Daeng.

"Every time her man phones it's with better and better news," said Siri. "And how many women learn that their husband is officially nominated to become chief of police?"

"One a year in Laos, I'd say."

"I didn't really need a number."

"Sorry."

"They'll realize their error soon enough," said Siri.

"Phosy won't beg and roll over like his predecessors. He'll stir up all kinds of dung."

"To Phosy," said Daeng taking up the bottle and swigging from it. She handed it to Siri.

"To Phosy," he said.

They didn't really know what it was they were drinking. The label was in Russian and it could have been some type of paint thinner for all they knew. But what a way to go.

"To Phosy," came a gravelly voice from behind them. They turned to see a Russian soldier with an AK-47 trained on them. He was in full dress uniform including the helmet. Everything about the situation told the old couple they should adopt the defensive position and prepare for battle. But they were drunk and couldn't be bothered. And the soldier was even drunker. His boots remained rooted to the spot but he swayed from side to side like a dandelion in a swirling wind. Siri held out the bottle to him. The soldier handed Siri the gun and drank. He then, slowly (and Daeng would confess later, erotically), removed his uniform item by item. When he was completely naked he stepped into the fountain, lay on his stomach and attempted, in thirty centimeters of water, to emulate the great swim of his countryman Salnikov.

Siri and Daeng went to their room delighted that every country has its own Crazy Rajhid and, to Siri's great pleasure, Daeng was still wagging from the sight of the fine-bodied soldier. Once their own Olympic records had been set they fell asleep. Daeng would have slept like a bear if only, twenty minutes later, her husband had not yanked on her arm.

"Daeng, Daeng, are you asleep?" he said.

"I'd like to be," she purred.

"Daeng, I need a map."

It was breakfast time at the Good Luck Café. Phosy arrived late and shook hands with all the coffee drinkers whether he knew them or not.

"Good morning, Chief Inspector," said Oval Man.

"Is there any news that doesn't break first in the Good Luck?" Phosy asked. "I was only appointed yesterday afternoon."

"You can't keep a good spy network down," said Lenin Cap.

Phosy signaled to Mint, the owner, for a coffee and baguette. The Thai embargo was still on so there was no butter.

"Congratulations," said Mint. "But I can think of much more salubrious establishments to celebrate your promotion."

"But none so entertaining," said Phosy.

"Have you solved the murder of your old soldier friend?" Trench Coat asked.

"To be honest, that's why I've come here," said the detective.

"Ah, a killer in our midst," said Flakey.

"I confess, it was me," said Lenin Cap.

"You couldn't hit a tree with a stream of piss," said Trench Coat.

"It's my eyes," said Lenin Cap. "Nothing wrong with my trigger finger. I just can't find the trigger."

The old boys laughed.

"So, tell us, chief," said Trench Coat. "Who'll be spending time behind bars?"

"Have you found a motive?" asked Lenin Cap.

"I'd believed old Pinit had something to tell me about the assassination attempt in Moscow," said Phosy, "and that was why someone silenced him. But I realize now he was just pleased that I was onto the wrong man. When he was sure I suspected the Olympic shooter he was only too willing to lead me off down a cul-de-sac. He was about to spin me a lie or two when he got shot. That's what threw me off."

"And you know who killed him?" asked Mint, the owner.

"I eliminated my first choice," said Phosy. "And that only left me with you gentlemen. Our victim, Pinit, knew I was coming here because he had access to private telexes. But none of you did. So, given the fact that you're all so ancient I wondered what role history might have played in the killing. Pinit had been planted in the Royal Lao Army by the Pathet Lao. So, of course, he knew a lot of soldiers from the old regime. When we took over the country, most of the royalists fled across the river to avoid getting placed in reeducation camps. Others did their best to vanish by changing their identity.

"Pinit didn't need to do any of that because he was one of ours. He was a hero of the revolution. But he was a threat, too. He could recognize old royalist soldiers. He'd never been here to the Good Luck Café before. He only came to listen to me. See what I knew. But what if he turned up that Sunday and recognized one of you? There you are with your new life, safe, new family. And suddenly there's this threat hanging over you. You're not even really certain he remembers you but there's that risk. Do you let him go and take a chance, or do you remove the threat?"

"This is really exciting," said Oval Man.

"I think I should break out a drink of something stronger than coffee," said Mint the owner. "Anyone fancy a drink?"

The clientele cheered as he went into the kitchen for a bottle and glasses.

"There were twenty or thirty of us that morning," said Trench Coat. "Are you going to arrest all of us?"

"I don't think that's necessary," said Phosy. "Once I had my theory together, and I have to thank an old friend for pointing me in the right direction, the answer was logical."

"How many of us come to breakfast with a sniper rifle down our trousers?" said Flakey.

"Absolutely right," said Phosy.

A round of applause for Flakey.

"And the answer is, none," said Lenin Cap. "It has to be someone who could get home and back in time to shoot the old fellow."

"And given our lack of speed that leaves just the one," said Trench Coat.

All eyes turned to the kitchen. Mint was not returning with a bottle.

"Well, I'll be buggered," said Lenin Cap.

"Shouldn't you be chasing him down the road?" asked Flakey.

"And what kind of chief of police would I be if I had to do my own chasing?" said Phosy.

The sound of police whistles sliced through the early morning silence.

He had been as overwhelmed as his countrymen and women by the poignancy of the Closing Ceremony. He had shed tears. He'd joined his teammates that final evening but, unlike most of them, he'd kept his drinking to a minimum. Self-control was his preservation. He'd endeared himself to the other members of the squad and would return to his country with his pride intact, as would they all.

In that other matter, his planning and the execution of that plan had been meticulous. On their first evening in Moscow he'd phoned Manoi and introduced himself by his Lao name but not, of course, by his family connections. He'd merely said he was a member of the Lao Olympic squad and was paying courtesy calls to eminent Lao residing in Moscow. He said he had a gift from the Minister of Sport and asked permission to deliver it in person.

He'd arrived at the apartment building with two beautifully wrapped presents. A gruesome woman at a desk in the reception area spoke into a walkie-talkie and pointed him to the elevator. The bodyguard on the third floor insisted on opening the presents before he'd be allowed inside the apartment. He watched the bodyguard unwrap the first. The box contained two layers of banana rice puddings wrapped in plastic.

"I'm sorry," said the bodyguard, "but I have to taste one of these. You'd better tell me now if there's something poison in here."

The bodyguard survived. The visitor said that the second box was exactly the same as the first and once he'd paid his respects to Comrade Manoi he would be taking it to the Lao Ambassador. He'd rather not disturb the beautiful wrapping or have any of them missing. Perhaps he could leave it with the bodyguard outside the apartment? The man agreed. The whole conversation had been in Russian.

Manoi came to the door to welcome his guest whom he didn't recognize. He accepted the gift and extended his thanks to the Minister of Sport. He opened the box and ate one of the puddings. He asked one or two perfunctory questions about the team's chances, showed him around the apartment, then turfed him out so he could dress for some social event. It had been no more or less than the visitor had expected. He reclaimed the second wrapped present from the bodyguard, said he couldn't be bothered to wait for the elevator and walked down the staircase.

There were two apartments on the second floor. From the street he'd established that there were no lights on in either. He rang the doorbell to the apartment directly beneath that of Manoi and waited. He rang again. Once he was certain there was nobody in, he picked the lock and went inside. He turned on the light in the small hallway. It was a typical, fussy overstuffed apartment of the upper-middle class. There were so many ornaments a team of parlor maids could spend their entire careers there and still not rid the place of dust.

He paced the apartment as he had done in the apartment above and found the area directly beneath Manoi's TV room. There, he unwrapped the ambassador's present. The box contained plastic explosive. He wasn't short of hiding places. Most of the dressers and cabinets had probably not been opened since Napoleon's aborted invasion two hundred years before. He settled on the bottom drawer of a bureau which stuck so obstinately he knew it was never used. He put in the explosive, armed it and connected the remote control. He turned off the light, closed the front door, and left with the empty present box under his arm.

All he had to worry about was the timing. Manoi had to be in front of his TV. He phoned the night before the famous race-walk marathon and told Manoi that, based on times and the current form of the international athletes, there was a very strong chance of a medal. If that happened, the first medal for a Lao athlete in the Olympic Games, there would be unprecedented media interest. They'd want to interview a significant Lao, fluent in Russian, who could explain exactly what this glory meant to a small landlocked country in Indochina.

He put down the phone knowing he'd hooked the bastard. At exactly 6 P.M. the following evening he'd arrived on the street in front of the apartment block. There was a condemned building opposite. The fire escape was gated at the ground floor. The gap beneath it would have been too narrow for the average Russian but a slim Lao could squeeze through with no problem at all. From the third floor balcony he could see clearly across to the room opposite. Manoi was watching the television, the bodyguard was looking over his shoulder. The timing was perfect.

Only one small matter disturbed him. The old couple on the second floor were at home and they too were watching TV. They were everybody's grandparents, fluffy and white and chubby. But perhaps it was their destiny that they'd stayed home that evening. If so, there was no point in feeling guilty. He looked back at Manoi's room. The maid was just arriving with a tray of drinks. Too bad for her, too. He pushed the button of his remote control and it was all over.

That had been eleven days ago. There had been nothing in the news or on TV. He'd scoured them patiently every day. He'd made it a rule to visit the old brain-dead general most days. In the beginning the old man had telexes strewn around the room like confetti. Every day he'd offer to clean up the unread papers. The general missed his batman so he was pleased to have a young fellow look after him. He seemed to have a fondness for strong, good-looking men.

But now it was all over, or it should have been. They'd met with the administrators before lunchtime on the last day. It was supposed to be a quick debriefing in the unused conference room but the general had a speech written so it took him an hour to get through it. They'd all expressed thanks and respect back and forth using the same formal language that killed true emotion in even the smallest of meetings. They promised to keep in touch and Civilai handed out the official souvenir programs. The pouch at the back contained photographs of the competitor whose name was written on the front of the program.

Perhaps it was then, walking back to the dormitory room for the last time, that he allowed himself a brief feeling of confidence. His father had warned him about complacency. He'd always said that when you stopped looking over your shoulder that was when the tiger pounced. And, sure enough, the tiger pounced.

He was back in his room. He'd packed his bag already and was about to fold the souvenir program into the side pocket of his suitcase. He thumbed through it briefly to look at the photos and a single sheet of paper fell out. The message was hand-written in Lao.

I know what you did and I don't have a problem with it. But they know in Vientiane too so

you can't take the flight today. They'll be wait-
ing for you at the airport.
Meet me at the Traktir tavern on Volchansk two
blocks north of Manoi's apartment building, or
what's left of it. I'll have a new ID and travel
documents for you. A friend.

He hadn't heard from Comrade Thonglai for a week so he'd assumed everything was fine. They'd agreed only to contact each other if something went wrong. Now this. His heart sank. In his plan—his miraculous plan—he'd go back to Laos with his head held high. He'd get a wife and they'd produce more children than they could afford to feed and at last he'd be happy. How did they find out? How did anyone back home have the resources to work out what he'd done?

He considered ignoring the message, getting on the plane and facing the music. Comrade Thonglai was still an influential man. The money he'd been promised was there somewhere and it would buy an awful lot of policemen and prosecutors. But then, "*friend*" knew what he'd done. He'd be looking over his shoulder for the rest of his life, waiting for the tiger to go for his neck.

So he decided to meet, go to the bar, and see just how many teeth the tiger had. Then he'd make his decision. He put his suitcase on the shuttle bus, told his room-mates he'd be making his own way to the airport, and took the metro to Park Kultury. The tavern wasn't that hard to find. One question to one local and he was there. The place was almost empty at that time, hungry-looking, as if waiting for the drunks to return from the country-side. It was unusual to find a Russian restaurant without a crowd. There was just one table full and one old woman in a gingham dressing gown sitting by herself. She hissed as he walked past her.

"Sss, foreigner," she said, but didn't look up from her drink. It wasn't so much an accusation, more some sort of traditional greeting.

The barman, a pasty young man, said, "Don't mind her," as he'd probably said every day to every foreigner who'd entered their ratty establishment.

"Do you speak Russian?" said the barman as an afterthought.

"Yes," said the new arrival.

"What can I get you?"

"A beer," he said, even though he had no intention of drinking it.

He took it to a table at the back near the toilets. It was as far from the old woman as he could get. He sat and stared at her. He wondered whether she had some innate ability to recognize foreign blood. His question was answered when a young man with a large briefcase entered.

"Foreigner," hissed the old woman.

"Don't mind her," said the barman. "What can I get you?"

"I'll have a tea," said the new arrival and he went to sit opposite the man at the rear table.

"So you don't only interpret?" he said.

Roger smiled and sipped his tea, which was cold.

"I have a life outside the Olympics," he said.

"And how do I fit into that life?" he asked.

"I establish that you are no risk and I hand over your new identity and the means to get to your new home," said Roger.

He patted the briefcase.

"Just how many people know?" he asked.

"Me," said Roger, "and your sponsor back in Laos."

"Why are you involved?"

"Comrade Thonglai wanted someone to watch over you. Make sure everything worked out. That was a very neat job, by the way. Very professional. Shame about the innocents."

"There are no innocents," he said. "Doing nothing doesn't make a person guiltless. The silent majority can be held responsible for the rise of every tyrant in the world."

"Including Manoi?"

"He would have been the next."

"So you nipped the autocracy in the bud."

"You could put it like that," he said. "History won't remember the little people that got in the way. I mean, look where we are."

"In a tavern," said Roger.

"We're in a public place. There's a barman, a couple of old men and a fat drunk, so you thought this would be a safe place to meet. But you didn't consider for a second that I'd already killed four bystanders just because they were in the wrong place at the wrong time. Why do you think I'd have any hesitation in removing the witnesses after I shoot you?"

"Wh . . . why would you want to shoot me?" Roger asked.

"Because you're an overconfident boy with documents in your suitcase that might or might not be of use to me. But, more importantly, you're the only person in Moscow who knows what I've done. And if you'd thought this through you'd know the most logical scenario would be for me to kill you and take your briefcase. Who would bother to look too deeply into a gangland shooting in a tavern?"

Roger's face color and confidence ebbed rapidly.

"Are you seriously considering this?" he asked.

"Shooting you? No. It would give the tavern keeper time to grab whatever archaic World War Two weapon he has hidden behind his bar. The odds are better with this."

He was up, leaning across the table with the switch-blade in his hand before Roger could take a breath. He was about to slice it across the young man's throat when a hand reached out and grabbed his wrist. He'd been so intent on watching the barman that he hadn't consid-ered someone might come out of the toilets behind him. Madam Daeng had a vice-like grip on the knife hand. From the other side came Dr. Siri with a right and then a left hook to his head that rendered the man incapable of retaliation. He was dazed and confused. He gave up the switchblade without protest.

"You could have prevented that much sooner, you know?" said Roger, still ashen-faced and a little damp in the crotch.

"We wouldn't have let him kill you," said Daeng.

"Goodness me, no," said Siri.

They tied the assassin's hands to the wooden chair behind him. The barman seemed to have no interest at all in what was happening in his tavern. As the attackers and the victim were all Asian he thought he should let them sort it out for themselves. Asians, as they say, is Asians.

When the assassin came around he was still in his seat and Daeng was drinking his beer. Combat always made her thirsty. He smiled.

"How did you know?" he asked.

"We didn't," said Siri.

"But you put the note in my program," he said.

"Not only yours," said Siri. "I put it in the programs of everyone who didn't have an alibi at the time of the race. My favorite was still Colonel Fah Hai. He was never accounted for and I didn't particularly like him. But then last night something occurred to me that made me add your name to my list."

"And what was that?" he asked.

Daeng ordered three more beers and three vodka chasers.

"I looked at the route map of the twenty-kilometer walk," said Siri. "And I thought about the race. There you were, stride for stride with the leaders all the way to the fork in the river. You were looking strong and confident. There wasn't a sudden surge in the pace but even so you dropped back. You dropped back so far and so suddenly that the cameras weren't interested in you anymore. The race passed under Krymsky Bridge, just half a kilometer from Manoi's building. There wasn't much of a crowd around there. No offense, but people aren't that inter-ested in walking. You'd paced the route countless times. You knew there were bushes at the edge of the park. You were wearing a T-shirt. We'd thought that was odd at the time but now we get it. All you had to do was take off your numbered singlet and put it in your waist pack and sud-denly you were just a tourist enjoying the balmy summer evening."

"Brilliant," said Khamon.

"But all that achieved was to tell me that technically you couldn't be discounted as a suspect. No more than that."

"So," said Daeng, "we put notes in the programs of each of our potential assassins. It would have meant nothing at all to anyone who was innocent but would resonate in the mind of the actual killer. And what do you know? Here you are."

"But I'm still baffled," said Siri. "Why did you put in such a performance? Surely it would have made more sense to have just floated along at the back and dropped out unnoticed. You could have walked to the building, blown up your victim and given up on the race completely. But there you were on national television. Half the world was rooting for you. You even had the balls to do the big finish. I don't get it. It seems to me you were challenging fate that evening; mocking it, even."

Khamon the walker looked at his three captors and smiled.

"If I promise not to overpower the three of you, do you think I could get my wrists untied and enjoy a last beer?" he said. "I doubt there'll be a lot of booze where I'm going."

Daeng and Siri had no objection. Once he was untied he downed half the glass in one go.

"To answer that question," he said, "I have to take you to the beginning. Do I have time for that?"

They nodded.

"I told you about my father," he said, "my father the walker. He was what you might call a part-time father. The only reason I joined him on his walks was because I knew he'd be gone again. He brought me books and presents but I wanted a father. When he was away I'd put in hours of practice for the next time he came so I'd be able to keep up with him. I wanted to impress him because I thought that might make him stay. But he always had urgent business somewhere else."

Siri had worked it out.

"He wasn't French, was he?" he said. "He wasn't in the teak export business."

"My grandmother was French," said Khamon. "My father grew up in France but his father was Russian. A devout Trotskyite. There was a push to spread Communism through the third world and people like my father, fluent in French and Russian, were in demand. The French occupation of Laos presented a beautiful battlefield for socialism to take on capitalism. He joined a group whose objective was to empower the poor in Southeast Asia. Through them he befriended a Lao communist who was operating covertly in the ranks of the Royal Lao Army. He, in turn, put my father in contact with Comrade Thonglai, whose family had vast contacts throughout the region. Those three worked together on a number of projects but, especially, to arm the Lao rebels in the northeast. They became as close as was possible in those circumstances. My father established a home and a family that would make him look legitimate as an exporter.

"He taught me Russian instead of French because he insisted the French wouldn't be around for much longer. He told me Russian was the language of the future. Of course I adored him and I would do anything he told me. I met my father's friends and played with their children. They stayed at our house often. I liked all of them except for Manoi. He was a bully even then. As the revolution drew close I saw less and less of my father. He sent us money so we were never wanting. 1975 was the last time I saw him. I walked every day to gain strength in preparation for his return but he never returned. I had no idea where he was or what he was doing.

"Then, five years later, I got a letter from Comrade

Thonglai, the business man. He wrote very coldly that my father was dead. He went into detail about how it had happened and to my surprise he condemned his own son for killing his friend. He told me that Manoi had become a monster and if he were allowed to return to Laos as a leader it would be the end of the republic. But I heard none of this. It wasn't the politics that brought me to Moscow. It was revenge. I'd always expected my father to come home some day. Even after my mother died I had faith that I'd see him again. Then all at once that hope was stolen from me.

"Comrade Thonglai knew about my walking. He asked if I'd be interested in taking a trial for the Olympics. I agreed. It was all fixed, of course. I was technically sound but I could never have made the qualifying times. He arranged it all, bribed the right people, and the next thing I knew I was on a flight here. The rest, you are aware of."

"Except for the answer to my question," said Siri.

"Ah, yes. The race. At the beginning it was imperative I stay with the leaders because I wanted Manoi in front of his TV—glued. So I put everything I had into the first five kilometers. I did my best to look confident but it almost killed me. When I dropped back it wasn't acting. I had nothing left."

"But that doesn't explain why you bothered to finish the race," said Daeng.

"I didn't plan to," he said. "I'd done what I'd come for and all that remained was to return to the stadium. The quickest way back was along the river—the route of the race. Of course there were no onlookers by then. I put my race number back on because my throat was as dry as a bird's nest and I needed a drink. But they'd taken down the refreshments tables and sweepers were cleaning up the used cups and bottles. I set off to the stadium. I race walked because I was still hoping to find a drink as a competitor. I passed a van with an official sitting in the driving seat. He looked surprised. He grabbed his clipboard, looked at my number and compared it to the numbers on the race enrolment. And there I was. I hadn't been disqualified and I hadn't been registered as *dropped out* so, according to the regulations, I was still active.

"I suppose he radioed someone in the stadium because suddenly there was a lot of attention. The van drove along beside me and suddenly there were hurriedly erected drinks tables everywhere. They seemed embarrassed that they'd given up so quickly. I picked up my pace. People were clapping. And, as odd as it may seem, it felt right to be doing it. It was a sort of, I don't know, homage to my father in some way. I could make him proud of me if I got to the stadium. If I didn't give up."

"That's why you finished the race?" said Daeng.

"Unbelievable," said Roger.

"What are y—" Khamon began but Daeng leaned toward him.

"Don't!" she said.

"What?" said Khamon.

"You're looking at the blade in my hand," said Daeng, "and you're weighing up your chances. You're wondering what it would take to wrestle it from me."

"How could you know that?" said Khamon.

Siri laughed. "Much better men than you have misjudged my wife," he said. "She could be seven sheets to the wind and blindfolded and I still wouldn't put money on you winning that battle, son."

CHAPTER TWENTY-ONE
What Really Happened

The Aeroflot pilots seemed to be swerving to avoid clouds. The passengers were being tossed left and right. Two seats in front, Civilai's cheese and onion sandwich threw itself into the aisle.

"Daeng," said Siri, "am I . . . ?"

"No," said Daeng. "This is really happening."

"They do know it's quicker to go in a straight line?"

"Soviet customer service ended the moment we took off from Sheremetyevo," said Daeng. "We're back to earth now."

"Well, it's lucky they turned off the efficiency. If the flight hadn't been delayed by two hours we'd have missed it. And then where would we be?"

"Guests of the KGB, no doubt," said Daeng. "I still feel uncomfortable about leaving Khamon with them."

"We had no choice," said Siri. "He blew up Soviet property and killed Soviet civilians. He brought Soviet justice upon himself."

"It's just . . ."

"I know. He's your type."

"Not physically. Physically I couldn't do any better than you. But . . ."

"But you admire him."

"Not for his lack of respect for the lives of innocent civilians."

"But for his daring."

"You have to give him that," said Daeng. "It was the most audacious crime I've ever encountered."

"It's true. Nobody would have guessed it. He left us suspecting everyone else but him."

"Did Civilai say anything about the other alibis?"

"He used his time at the airport wisely."

"He talked to the other suspects?"

"When they found the handwritten notes in their program everyone stepped up to confess."

"But they didn't do it," said Daeng.

"But still they were guilty of something," said Siri. "Sompoo was keen to come forward to confess that he'd been traveling under a false name. But it hadn't been his decision. The Soviets had said it would be best. You see, Sompoo, alias Nokasad, really was drafted in at the last second. The shooters got the results from their final physicals just two hours before they came to Wattay for the flight. The tests had been organized by the Soviet Department of Tropical Diseases. I assume they didn't want athletes from Third World countries infecting everyone in Russia. Major Lien had a slight irritation in his eyes when he went for the medical and mentioned it to the doctor. She did tests and discovered that Lien had the early onset of River Blindness—Roble's Disease. Even if treated it was likely to have led to blindness. In the short term his eyesight would have deteriorated over the following three weeks to a point where he'd be unable to compete in a shooting event. He wasn't crying when Phosy went to see him. His eyes were watering from the infection. He was going blind and he didn't want his family to know. That's why he didn't tell them the truth."

"Poor thing."

"But the irony is that River Blindness isn't endemic to Laos. The major had been with a military delegation to Ethiopia, one of our socialist allies, and he must have picked it up on a field trip. You'd have to believe the fates were against you when something like that happens."

"So they dragged in Sompoo."

"His problem was that his name wasn't on the long list of thirty the military had submitted to the Olympic Committee two months before. Only names on that list were eligible to take part. Sompoo was a shooter who happened to be at the airport to see off the team. When Lien was pulled at short notice there wasn't time to bring in one of the other twenty-three shooters. They decided to chance Sompoo and see what they could do about his eligibility later. He didn't even have luggage with him. Once they arrived in Moscow it was the Soviet military that suggested he take the name of one of the missing shooters on the list. So in fact he was just helping out."

The announcement came over the intercom that the passengers should fasten their seatbelts as they may be experiencing some turbulence.

"So, what have we been experiencing up till now?" Daeng asked.

"That was basic training turbulence," said Siri. "This is the real thing."

"What about the other two suspects?" said Daeng.

"Ah, now that's a little more delicate," said Siri.

"Meaning what?"

"Meaning Civilai had to swear on his cockroach singing grandmother's grave that he wouldn't tell anyone."

"Yet he told you, which is just like telling everyone."

"I'm hurt."

"You don't keep secrets, Siri."

"For that I won't tell you."

"If you don't I'll break your arm," said Daeng.

"You're such a poet. Very well. You recall that Sitti bought souvenirs for all his teammates?"

"Twelve Marx-Lenin wristwatches, which he claimed to have bought on his way back from the stadium after the walking race."

"Correct. Even though, including himself, there were only seven shooters," said Siri. "But it turns out that Colonel Fah Hai also bought souvenir watches on his way home from the stadium after the road race. He gave them to five of the Soviet officers at the barracks."

"Making a grand total of twelve," said Daeng.

"Except we know from Dtui's astute detection that Sitti actually bought all twelve of them two days earlier."

"So, why would Sitti lie about being at the stadium and buying souvenirs?" asked Daeng.

"Now, to answer that question we have to look back at the early days of the Games. You'll recall that before the Red Guard kidnapped them and forced them to visit palaces and churches, our shooters spent the first three days at the Village."

"Yes."

"The shooters were in three suites with three rooms in each. Sitti and Colonel Fah Hai shared the third suite. The other beds were empty. Sitti and the colonel discovered a common interest."

"Oh, Siri."

"Oh, indeed."

"They . . . ?"

"Absolutely."

"And when they were shifted to the army barracks they were separated so . . ."

"So they couldn't."

"And they set up this elaborate alibi so they could."

"In a tent."

"How adorable."

For an hour or so there was a lull in the turbulence. Siri took the opportunity to visit the bathroom. Daeng nodded off for no more than ten minutes. When she awoke, her husband was not beside her. It wouldn't have been the first time. She hoped nobody had seen him disappear. But in situations like that, particularly when your husband is seventy-six, you tend to go through all the horrible possibilities in your mind. What if he'd been sucked down through the vacuum flush system? What if someone had put a cigarette in the paper tissue refuse box and there was a raging fire in the toilet?

Just to put her mind at ease, she went to the one occupied bathroom and knocked on the door.

"Is anybody in there?" she shouted. "Siri, are you in there?"

The stewardess, a fashion model in a billowy low-cut blouse, stopped to see what the fuss was about. With no common language, Daeng explained in mime that her husband might be dead on the bathroom floor. The stewardess reacted calmly. She knocked loudly, listened, removed the hex key from her side pocket and opened the door. The tap was running but there was nobody inside. The stewardess was confused but Daeng was delighted. Her husband had merely disappeared.

Dr. Siri stepped out of the bathroom and into a bank of snow. But that, as they say, is another story.

Continue reading for a sneak preview from the next
Dr. Siri Paiboun Mystery

Don't Eat Me

CHAPTER ONE
Nineteen Eyes

This whole thing started and finished with her. She was in a crate. A compact coconut wood coffin with narrow slits for air. She'd screamed over and over to no avail. She'd tried to make sense of it. She'd counted the unblinking eyes. Nineteen of them. One eye too many or one too few, but nineteen by every reckoning. And even though there was no light beneath the thick tarpaulin those eyes glowed deep yellow like dying stars.

When she came around that last time she thought she was still in the nightmare and in a way she was. Her knees were tucked up tightly against her chest and there was no more than a shoebox of space at the foot of the crate, but the creatures—the nineteen-eyed creatures—had contracted somehow and packed themselves together so closely there would be no contact with her. Not yet. She could feel their hot breaths against her bare toes. She could hear the wheezing in their throats. But they stared at her, unmoving, waiting for her to lose consciousness again because it was inevitable she would. They would bide their time until she had no more fight in her. Then, and only then, they would devour her.

CHAPTER TWO
The Smugglers

Life sped by in Vientiane like a Volkswagen van on blocks. The streets were crusty with red dust, the uneven sidewalks sprouted half-hearted weeds, and the people neither smiled nor raised their voices for fear of drawing attention to themselves. You could never be sure who was listening. They all knew of someone who'd fled the country and at least one person who'd disappeared. Many had relatives in refugee camps on the Thai side of the border. Many more had ambitions or dreams or plans to join them but lacked the spunk.

This was year five of a socialist experiment that had failed the People's Democratic Republic of Laos in many ways. The Communist vessel was holed and on its way down. The rice collectives program had collapsed. Government workers went unpaid for months. And Thailand had once more closed its Mekhong border due to pissy spats over trespassing and accusations of insurgencies, and, never forget, good old historical animosity. The river guard patrols on both banks had been doubled, but it was a vast river and still the midnight rafts of smuggled Thai goods floated diagonally north on the current, crisscrossing disgruntled Lao heading south on their rubber inner tubes.

So it was a surprise to many on one humid night in August when two elderly Lao gentlemen were spotted paddling their bamboo raft in a northerly direction toward the country everyone wanted to leave. They were dressed in ninja black, but their grumbling and coughing destroyed any pretense of stealth. Between them was a balding cross-eyed hound and a mysterious large object wrapped in a nylon parachute. The latter was roughly the size and shape of a grenade launcher and would certainly have led to the old boys' being shot on sight if they were discovered. Smuggling weapons of war was not a wise pastime for men in their seventies.

"Did they not teach you to row?" asked Dr. Siri, the stockier of the two.

"I was a politician," Comrade Civilai replied. "They only taught us how to bail."

"Then that explains why we're going around in circles," said Siri.

The river ran high and fast at the end of the rains, and the current would have taken them far beyond Vientiane if they didn't lean into it with some enthusiasm. But paddling always appeared easier than it was, especially with a heavy cargo. From somewhere to the north they heard the crack of a river guard's rifle but no accompanying scream. Neither the rifles nor the men who bore them had any accuracy. The old boys were not intimidated by the sound because they knew how little chance there was of being hit.

"And going around in circles would aptly describe the direction of our policies these past five years," said Civilai, mostly to himself.

"Save your breath for a final push," said Siri. "There's our signal. We don't want to overshoot."

From the dense foliage ahead, two lights—one white, one red—flashed intermittently.

"My heart can't take this," said Comrade Civilai.

"Then rest your organs and put your back into it."

All at once they seemed to be surfing the current rather than fighting it. They gathered speed, charging toward the lights. Remarkably, they had timed their trajectory perfectly but not their velocity. Theirs was not a dignified landing. Ugly the dog, sensing danger, abandoned the vessel five meters from the bank and swam home. The corner of the raft snagged in a tree root so the vessel spun around and hit the bank at speed and in reverse. Dr. Siri was thrown to the deck. There was a loud thump when his head hit the bamboo, but his was a hard head. Civilai wasn't so lucky. He was jettisoned head first into the river mud where he sank immediately until only his legs were visible. To his credit he did not kick or wave them pathetically. They merely jutted heavenward like a victory sign. He was rescued by the reception committee. Mr. Geung and Madam Daeng took a leg each and yanked him out of the mire. He emerged with a slurping sound like a large snail being pulled reluctantly from its shell.

"Well that all worked out quite well," said Siri.

The next day, Chief Inspector Phosy arrived at Madam Daeng's noodle shop shortly after the morning rush. There were never enough stools to accommodate all the customers who traveled out of their way to eat the best homemade *feu* noodles in the country. Madam Daeng, never satisfied with shop-bought noodles, had taken to making her own beneath a corrugated tin roof behind the shop. Yet despite all the personal touches and time and effort the woman put into her dishes, and in the face of much criticism from her husband, she refused to increase the prices.

"The poor . . ." she would say, ". . . have as much right to eat food of quality as do the more advantaged."

Even the drivers of the black Zil limousines used by the senior party members had to wait their turn to be served. Their bosses thought they might add a few extra kip as an incentive to jump the queue, but Madam Daeng would have nothing of it. Comrade Civilai often said that hers was the only example of functioning Communism in the republic. She replied that there was nothing political about it. She was just being fair.

"Is he in?" the chief inspector asked.

Madam Daeng saw a familiar scowl on his good-looking face. Since his promotion to chief inspector two months earlier, Phosy had discovered a lot to scowl about. Many members of the central committee considered him too young at forty-six to have been handed such responsibility. But Madam Daeng, twenty years his senior, knew there was nobody more qualified or able to take on the role. She left Mr. Geung to clean the noodle tubs and walked slowly over to the policeman.

"I'm very well, thank you, Chief Inspector," she said. "And you?"

Madam Daeng had been a freedom fighter in the clandestine war against the French imperialists, and she was well aware that she still intimidated even the most confident of men. In fact, her short shock of snow white hair and her piercing hazelnut-colored eyes gave her even more of an advantage. Phosy stood no chance.

"I'm sorry, Daeng," he said. "It just seems that your husband is intent on making my impossible job even more impossible."

"My goodness, what's he done now?" asked Daeng.

She poured the policeman a glass of iced tea and they sat at a table overlooking the river.

He sighed. "You know very well," he said.

"What kind of policeman would assume a wife knew every move her husband made?"

"One who knew she was an accomplice in a criminal act?"

They drank their sweet tea and watched Ugly the dog at the river's edge catching crabs.

"I'm offended," she said.

"You need to work on that inscrutability, Daeng. Not convincing at all."

"And what particular crime am I accused of accomplicing?"

"We'll start with smuggling."

"Oh, Phosy. Smuggling? Really? Twenty years ago that would have been called foraging. Nothing to eat in the village so you head off into the jungle and return with enough game to feed the family. Laos is being slowly starved to death by the Thai embargos, so it's only natural her inhabitants would forage."

"Foraging across a national border is called smuggling," said Phosy. "And if Siri had merely been paddling back from Si Chiang Mai with beans and roast pig I wouldn't be here."

"Then why are you here?"

"We have an eye-witness account of Dr. Siri and Comrade Civilai importing weapons."

She chuckled. "And what witness would that eye belong to?" she asked.

"I'm not at liberty to say."

"Of course you are. Until they get around to finishing the constitution we won't have any laws to speak of. Your liberty to say is arbitrary."

Phosy sipped his tea and followed the progress of a cloud. "A river guard," he said at last.

"A river guard saw Dr. Siri importing weapons?"

"Yes."

"Then why didn't he shoot him?"

"What?"

"Why didn't the river guard shoot Dr. Siri and his accomplices and be done with it?"

"It's delicate."

"Would it be because the river guards have splendid weapons produced in the Soviet Union but that for the past three months, due to some blip in the paperwork, none of them has been issued with ammunition? That in the event of seeing a suspicious craft on the river, our guards have been instructed to set dry bamboo tubes alight because that explosion makes a similar sound to the firing of a rifle and it may just discourage smugglers? The guards do however have marvelous flashlights and permission to shine the beam on suspicious objects. None so far has been silly enough to do such a thing. Thai smugglers are invariably armed and it would be suicidal. Therefore, no river guard on a cloudy night would have the faintest idea what Dr. Siri—if he even were to be on the river—might or might not be smuggling."

Phosy put down his glass. "He recognized all of you," he said. "He even identified the dog. He was in a tree not far from your reception committee. He's a regular customer here."

"Then he should be ashamed of himself," said Daeng. "What's become of loyalty to one's noodle shop?"

"Daeng . . ."

"We often go for a little paddle and a frolic of a night when it's too hot to sleep. Mistaken identity, no doubt. I'll have a word with him. What's his name?"

"Daeng."

"Yes?"

"What was on the raft?"

"There. That's the first thing the old Inspector Phosy would have asked. This new chief inspector's already tangled up in words."

"And if I had asked that question sooner I wouldn't have learned what classified information you have regarding our river guards, would I?"

"Damn, you got me."

"So?"

"So what?"

"So, what was on the raft?"

Other Titles in the Soho Crime Series